DECEPTION

LOVE, LOSS, LEVERAGE, MURDER

A Novel by

C.L. BLUESTEIN

SEDUCTION series • Book 4

DECEPTION
Love, Loss, Leverage, Murder

Seduction Series Book #4

Copyright © 2021 by Carol L. Bluestein,
C.L. Bluestein Books
A Division of Bluestein Publishing
Slingerlands, NY 12159

ISBN Print: 978-0-9966210-8-3
ISBN audio: 978-0-9966210-9-0

2021 Edition V.01

Editors:
Story: Paula Chaffee Scardamalia
Line: Sandra B. Carrk
Copy: Kal VanAvery

SEDUCTION SERIES REVIEWS

"Good read!!! ...I didn't want it to end. Nor did I want to put it down." L.V.

"A good thriller. Story progresses well; plot line clear. Author weaves modern technology into the lives of the characters along with slowly revealing the past. Well done." B.T.

"...great read that incorporates positive ideas on some modern issues." F.A.

"Wild story. Great ending!

"Very enjoyable. Imaginative story line and characters. The ending was great. Couldn't put it down." Gracieon

"A great, fun read. Excellent story line with enough twists to hold your interest, but not so many as to feel contrived." Mozartnyon

"Excellent read! I am an avid fan of Coben, Crais, Parker, Silva, Child, Eisler and now I can add Bluestein to the mix." A.B.

"Loved the series. Can't wait to see it as a TV series or a movie." L.S.

"An intriguing mix of fact and fiction with story lines woven into a surprising conclusion. Couldn't put it down." C.M.

"This book's a page-turner. Couldn't put it down." M.B.

"Politically savvy thriller threads its way through covert politics, those leveraging wealth and power by manipulating the most vulnerable within the dark, chaotic reality of betrayal and greed. DECEPTION, 4th in the Seduction Series, holds your attention. Big screen ready." B.T.

"The series would make the coolest TV mini-series... wonder if any TV writers are looking for brilliant new projects." C.L.

BOOKS BY C.L. BLUESTEIN

Political Thriller
SEDUCTION SERIES

#1 SEDUCTION – Love, Loss, Leverage, Murder
#2 PERCEPTION – Love, Loss, Leverage, Murder
#3 ISOLATION – Love, Loss, Leverage, Murder
#4 DECEPTION – Love, Loss, Leverage, Murder
#5 EXECUTION– **Coming in Summer 2022**

You Want Me To Do What? is available now. Walk in the sandals of our ancestors through this engaging interactive contemporary scripted Story of the Exodus/Passover for Jewish and Interfaith Families. Targeted but not limited to tweens.

REVIEW: "You Want Me To Do What" is the most innovative addition to the Passover literature I've seen. This is not just another pretty Haggadah....these interactive mini-dramas will make ANY Seder using any Haggadah come alive for all ages."   Cantor Charles Bergman, Los Angeles, CA

Free download at http://carolbluestein.com/

DEDICATION

With my love and gratitude to and for
my late husband, Michael R. Bluestein,
our children Sandra, Mark, and Lisa,
and their families

They are my inspiration.

ACKNOWLEDGEMENTS

First and foremost, I'd like to thank my family for their unwavering support.

Also, I want to note those who have passed but, in their own way, made my journey possible: Michael Bluestein, Roslyn and Noah Levine, Alynne Levine Sharp, Jack D. Main, Abraham and Selma Bluestein, Daniel Bluestein, and Ilse Bluestein Vanderpot.

Special mention for my friend and editor, the late Anne Frazier Walradt. Her spirit sat with me, her words echoed, and her unfailing encouragement accompanied the entire writing of this book.

As I worked on each chapter and phase of the book, I shared my words with my monthly writing group, Women Who Write. They listened and critiqued chapters with open hearts, frank critiques, and generous suggestions that contributed to the overall process and book.

In particular, editors Paula Chaffee Scardamalia for story, Sandra B. Carrk for line/copy edits, Kal VanAvery for copy/language edits, and my friend and neighbor, forensic accountant Joanne Floser.

My beta readers: Carol Marchewka, who keyed into the emotional connection; Barbara Traynor, who caught the non-essential passages and pacing; and Margaret Brennan, who loves a good thriller.

Thank you to my teachers and friends at The International Women's Writing Guild (IWWG) who continue to replenish my soul and offer insights into to the wonderful world of expression. It takes a village to support an author and the IWWG is all about encouraging writers and sharing stories.

Finally, the patience awards go to Cooper and Kelly, my rescued schnoodles. They fill the exalted positions of snugglers, walkers, jesters, kissers, listeners, and protectors.

Contents DECEPTION

DECEPTION

Chapter 01 ▶ Harrison, New York

Friday, 25 May, 9 a.m.

Special Agent Eric Jerrod answered his phone as he walked to his car. "What's up?"

"My partner and I just arrived at Kilmer's Harrison house. We can find no evidence subject is on premises. She didn't answer the door and offer us coffee like she usually does."

Eric slid into the driver's seat, strapped in, and engaged the motor. He hooked up the flashing red light and attached it to the roof of his car.

"No ankle-monitor pinging."

"Right. No monitor heartbeat either."

Eric said, "I'm on my way. Wait for me. Stay in touch by phone."

"Will do. Line is open."

Eric pulled into traffic, exited to the highway, and sped northward to Westchester, leaving New York City behind. He heard the agent's monitor crackle.

"We got something. She's alive. Going in."

Eric heard car doors open and shut, and footsteps pounding on concrete. Three thuds and a crash. The front door gave in. He said into his phone, "Your shoulder okay?"

The agent said, "It will be."

Eric smiled. He'd busted more than a few doors in his time. It hurt like a son-of-a-bitch.

"Not in the house. Around back. We're going down the side path. Through the back gate. I see her. She's in the pool."

Eric said, "Get her out. Call the EMTs. Be there in ten."

He wove in and out of light traffic, making good time. He and Lucy Kilmer were not strangers. He had tried, in vain, to muster enough evidence to convict her for the Meyerson family California murder. Five missing people. All he had was circumstantial evidence and a photo from a dead man's phone. All she got was a year of FBI-monitored probation. Under his breath, he said, "I've finally got her. Breaking probation isn't a lot but it's something."

By the time Eric arrived, the EMTs were working on Lucy. Her fully clothed body lay on the ground, face up, as one EMT pumped fluids into her body and the other cut away her wet clothes, replacing them with blankets. An agent held a plastic evidence bag containing a bullet-proof vest with a massive dent in the chest area.

Eric approached the medics. "Is she bleeding anywhere?"

One EMT looked up. "No. She took a serious blow to her rib cage, which appears to have impacted her heart."

The other said, "I'll call Base." He looked at Eric. "We're taking her to White Plains Hospital."

Lucy's eyelids fluttered.

"She's gaining consciousness."

She moaned, shivered, coughed, and opened her eyes as the EMTs transferred her to a stretcher.

Eric said to Lucy, "I'm going with you." To the EMTs, he said, "She does not leave my sight."

<~<~|~>~>

When she opened her eyes, she had to squint. The golden light streamed through the window on her right. IV infusion bags hung on a stand, wires hooked into a machine and tubes sending life-saving fluids through the needle taped to the back of her hand. A male voice said, "Miss Kilmer, you want to tell me what happened?"

She turned her head toward her visitor and smiled. "Special Agent Eric Jerrod."

Eric said, "I'm not here on a social call. You violated your parole and I want you to tell me what happened."

"I have no idea." She licked her lips. "Water."

Eric handed her a paper cup with a bent straw. "Here you go."

Lucy filled her mouth with water before swallowing. Handing the cup back to Eric, she said, "You tell me."

"Miss Kilmer, we've been monitoring your every move. Last night, you went to bed early. This morning we lost your infrared image and turned on our sound. We found you in the pool, in shock, wearing a damaged bullet-proof vest."

"I don't, can't, remember." She shivered, pulled up the blanket, and tucked in her chin. "I'm cold and my chest hurts."

Eric said, "You get a pass for now. There'll be men stationed outside your door. I'll be back later to hear the whole story."

He left and a nurse appeared. She fussed with the blankets, offered water, and fiddled with the infusion. "A little something to help you sleep." She lowered the window shade and turned off the lights as she left the room.

Lucy drifted into a dream state. Her phone buzzing. Not her phone. Still, buzzing until it stopped. She was moving. Fast. Silence interrupted by more buzzing. Nausea from unfocused undulating landscapes. Swaying and weaving. Pain. Something, someone poking her. She pushed it away, again and again. Annoyed, she grabbed it.

"That's my finger. May I have it back?"

Her eyes popped open. A doctor stood by her side.

"You've suffered quite a chest bruise. The good news is, no bones are broken. The bad news is it will hurt every time you move for two to three weeks. Questions?"

Lucy shook her head.

"Good. I'll check on you tomorrow and see when we can send you home."

After he left, the nurse came in. "Are you alright?"

Lucy said, "I'm fine," closed her eyes, dozed off, and entered a dream state.

It was twilight. After dinner. One of her unregistered phones buzzed. She answered. A voice she didn't recognize outlined her next contract. It told her who, where, when, and how much had been wired to her account.

She slipped into a thermal suit to hide from the infrared scanner outside and clicked on the heating pad arrangement under her covers to mimic her body temp. She overrode the door sensors, slipped out of her suburban house into her SUV, and sped down the highway. Every second counted because she had to be back by morning.

Within hours, she sat facing her victim. When he left the room, she got up, prepared his phone with a lethal contact poison, and returned to her seat by the time he returned. Without looking at him, she knew something had changed. His breathing came faster. His step more confident. His stride more commanding. He even smelled excited. He passed her and sat in his executive chair behind his desk and across from her. He leaned forward, placed his left elbow on the desk, paused, and gave her a "fuck you" smile. Blackness.

The nurse said, "Wake up. We have to take vitals, blood, and your lunch is here."

She administered the tests, left, and returned with a tray. "How's your chest feeling? Are you having any pain when you breathe?"

Lucy put her hand to her chest. "Not too much. I guess I'm feeling okay."

"It's the medication. It also makes you unsteady. Miss Kilmer, don't get out of bed without help. Use the call button. Although you should be all set since your catheter will expel liquids while you hydrate. The doctor will remove it tomorrow."

"My phone?"

"Tomorrow. Today you rest."

Lucy nodded. "Okay, you're the boss."

The nurse smiled. "You have a visitor."

Eric walked in. "It's been several hours. I thought you might like to tell me where the ice crystals in your blood came from."

Her eyes widened. "Ice crystals?"

"Our pathologists seem to think you might have been frozen."

"Frozen?"

"Like you fell through the ice."

"Flash frozen?"

"From what I understand. Anything you want to tell me?"

"No. I'm as confused as you are."

Eric gave her a wry smile. "I doubt that." He walked to the doorway, paused, and turned to look over his shoulder. "However, I will find out. With or without your help."

Two days later, Lucy Kilmer sat in her living room, listened to soft rock, and sipped her tea. Better and quieter to be home than in the hospital. She held the hot mug chest high and stared out the windows. Her memory had returned.

James Vanderhagen, spokesman for a global cartel, commissioned her to plan, organize, and carry out the mass genocide of thousands of African war refugees living outside Damir, Tawanda's capital city.

Despite her success, the Tawandian government's insatiable greed undermined their momentary advantage and caused its collapse. Their error had cost the cartel

billions of dollars. In retaliation,
the cartel hired her to execute
James Vanderhagen, which she did
with a fast-acting army grade
contact poison.

She shook her head. Dwelling on the past would only hamper her intention to go forward. Clients, including Tavius Global, waited for her unique set of skills and trained teams to deal with their high-status targets. Lucy loved the work she excelled in. Her fees were high. Her work impeccable. She lived as others could only dream of.

Lucy looked down at her new ankle-bracelet, courtesy of the FBI. It hindered but did not stop her. Her professional life lay in technology hidden beyond the back wall of her clothes closet and in the hollowed-out attic beams. She had threaded her internet connections through a web of servers located all over the world.

Still, there were ice crystals. Only the ninja housekeeper could shed light on this anomaly. Lucy made the call. "You froze me?"

In even tones, the housekeeper said, "Cartel orders. Remove you and trace evidence before police arrived."

"So, you *froze* me."

"No, 'chilled.' Used a meat freezer."

A knock on the door forced Lucy to end the call.

A muscled young man in gym clothes entered. "Are you ready?"

She shook her head. "Ultan, I can't do a massage today. I've been in the hospital. Bruised ribs."

"Hospital. I thought you were on a job. What happened?"

Lucy explained, ending with, "So, you see, I need a few days."

Ultan said, "I understand. Perhaps Thursday."

"By the way, did we have any contracts this weekend?"

"One. In Phoenix. The team eliminated the target three hours after the alert. We used the Emergency Meeting Protocol with no outside contact. He packed his bags for a two week stay and said good-bye to his family. In the SUV, the team applied standard practice—anesthetic, gas, and woodchipper. As of today, he is lizard food. As far we know, no inquiries have been made as to his whereabouts, but it's only been a week."

Lucy smiled. "Did you monitor the operation from here?"

"Of course. You taught me well."

Chapter 02 ▶ Tavius Global, Chicago, Il

Nine months later, Monday, 4 February, 1 p.m.
Winnifred Bradford Santiago and her two children walked into one of several Tavius Global Welcome Suites in the Chicago, Illinois compound. A far cry from the soulless public shelters, she felt human again. The deep-piled throw rugs on marble floors, the pillowed chaise lounge, and the mirrored dressing table took her breath away. She thought she'd lost this luxury forever.

Eight-year-old Eva said, "Mommy, is this really for us?"

Twelve-year-old Bobby said, "This looks like a girls' room. Do they have one for guys?"

Winnie said, "No. We're sharing, and we don't have to worry about being harassed." She walked across the room. "Look. We have our own sets of clothing and an array of toiletries to choose from."

Eva said, "Toilets? How many?"

Winnie laughed. "I meant toothbrushes, toothpaste, combs, brushes, shampoos, and stuff like that."

Bobby said, "Looks like they're bribing us."

Winnie said, "Don't be negative. Tavius Global is offering us a refuge. We won't have to worry about food or safety again."

"If you say so."

Winnie said, "I do." She pointed. "On the right is a shower, and on the left is a bathroom."

Bobby grabbed a towel. "I'll shower first."

<~<~|~>~>

The Human Resources director looked up when the guide entered the office and said, "Where are they?"

The guide said, "Showering and dressing. Here's their information." A few taps on the guide's e-pad screen and the information projected onto the wall.

The director said, "This is the family the chairman approved over my veto?"

"I'm surprised you don't like them. They seem nice."

"Like is not the issue. They won't be happy here. They are each, in their own way, too smart for our program."

The guide said, "I'm sure it'll work out. I'll help any way I can."

"Thank you. You can go."

The director sat and stared at the information. Santiago's husband had a gambling addiction. Tavius Global agents goaded him into betting the ranch, as it were. The man lost everything and took his own life. His wife and kids were left without a home, car, cash, or resources. They were literally dumped at a family shelter with the clothes on their back. The director walked over to the window and stared at the horsetail clouds. The chairman wanted the wife's extraordinary analytical skills to ramp up his information systems. It had taken him less than a year to make it happen.

The director closed the digital file. Winnie Santiago, desperate to save her family, had no other viable choice except Tavius Global. His plan worked. It always worked.

<~<~|~>~>

After the family showered and changed, the guide appeared. "You look like you feel better. Did you pack your new suitcases and backpacks?" Everyone nodded. "Good. Now, put on your winter coats. It's cold and windy outside."

Winnie and her children complied.

"Ready? Follow me to our transportation center at the Tavius Global Mall entrance."

When they arrived, an electric golf-cart festooned with banners pulled up. "Bobby and Eva, it's time to say good-bye to your mom and register at our boarding school."

Winnie said, "Wait. I want to go with them."

"That's not our protocol. All the preliminary work is done, and the children's grades have been transferred from their previous school." The guide produced two Tavius Global boarding school badges. "Here." Bobby and Eva accepted the IDs and put them on. Moments later, the school bus arrived. The driver loaded the children's belongings.

The guide said, "Everything's ready. Say your good-byes."

Winnie hugged the children. Bobby resisted. Eva clung.

Winnie said, "It's going to be okay. I'll see you soon." She kissed them both goodbye and waved them off with a big smile on her face. Seconds later, the smile disappeared. "I want to see the school. Meet the principal and teachers. Take a look at the rooms and the books they'll be using, and their dormitories. I also want to see the student guidebook, make sure there are protocols in place to prevent, and, if necessary, deal with abusive behavior by other students and teachers."

The guide said, "The children will be well taken care of. Now, it's just us and we're going shopping."

"I'd rather see the school and make sure Bobby and Eva are settling in."

"It'll be easier for them if you allow them to navigate the process themselves. I know you are worried, as other parents have been, about their adjustment to a whole new independent learning-living environment."

"I have to be sure they're safe."

The guide said, "I assure you they are. Now, we need to address your new life and start by going to the mall."

Winnie followed the guide. The last time she'd been to a mall was for the sole purpose of shielding her family from a brutal snowstorm with single digit temperatures. This felt normal, like the old days, before her world had collapsed. She felt a surge of normalcy. Her stride lengthened and her smile returned. Stores, filled with familiar products and restaurants featuring fast food to elegant dining, stretched along the central promenade. She heard sounds of movement, conversation, and elevator music. "This is nice."

The guide said, "You can come here whenever you have the time. Here's your ID. Use it to pay for whatever you buy. It's a like a credit card except you don't get billed."

Winnie stopped. "Clothes, food, and supplies are all free?"

"Yes and no. It is underwritten by your salary. Because everyone is entitled to everything, shopping is no big deal. Most people get what they need and spend their time doing other things. As of today, no one has ever out-spent their limit."

Winnie hung the ID around her neck and turned to face the guide. "While nice, when do I get to see my children?"

The guide produced a packet. "Everything you need to know is in here. Visiting hours are set, although you may request to see them any other time, and they can do the same. There is a Face2Face app on your Tavius Global phone. You can talk to them when they are not in class. Most important, they'll be home weekends."

"Home? I have a home?"

"You have. Would you like to see it?"

Winnie followed the guide for a short walk to the housing complex and an elevator ride to the fifth floor. A long walk down a tiled hall ended when the guide stopped and opened the door to apartment 5139.

Winnie walked into an open area. To the left, a kitchen with an island counter and two stools. In front of her, a dining table with four chairs, and to the right, a living room with two doors. One led to a bedroom and the other to a bathroom.

In the bedroom, she saw a two-person dorm set up. "For my kids?"

"Yes. The desk in the living room folds and a large queen-size murphy bed pulls down."

Winnie turned to the guide. "The ambiance reminds me of a bare-bones college dorm."

The guide walked over to the kitchen and opened a drawer, pulled out a packet of swatches, and put them on the counter. "Here are the available fabric choices at our decorator center in the mall. You can call or go check it out. Up to you. Tavius Global wants you to be happy, healthy, and productive."

"Looks like you've covered all of Maslow's list of basic needs."

"You'll find it's more than enough because you won't be spending much time here. Look out the window."

Winnie walked over to the large picture window and raised the privacy shade. People dotted the walkways, the outdoor sports complex, library veranda, and the park.

The guide said, "All you see and more is available to you and your family free of charge. Just use your ID."

Winnie opened the refrigerator. It was clean and filled with a stack of four 12x12x2 inch cardboard boxes.

"Those are the take-out and delivery meals. I thought you might like to try them. As soon as you're ready, you can shop at the mall for food or make life easy by eating there." The guide opened a drawer and pulled out the menus, laying them on the swatches. These are all your choices."

"Clothes?"

"At the mall. You can literally 'shop 'til you drop.' Your two children have already received their school outfits, workout clothes, and casual attire. You can buy them more things when they come for the weekend.

"Laundry?"

"There is a small washer/dryer combo in the bathroom. For larger loads, you'll see a large laundry bag with your apartment number stenciled on it. Fill it and leave it outside your door at night. Our service will collect it and return it in 24 hours. If you need something sooner, just go buy it at the mall."

"What about computers, phones, and TV?"

"I'm glad you reminded me." The guide produced a phone and handed it to Winnie. "This is yours. Your children's numbers are already in there as are key numbers for our various facilities and departments, as well as apps to make your life here effortless."

Winnie took the phone. "Computer?"

"In the desk drawer and already synced to the Tavius Global server. If you go to your TV app on your phone, when you press the access button, the camouflage disappears to reveal the wall. Here, let me show you." The guide took the phone, activated the app, and tapped the link.

Winnie's eyes widened as a wall section became transparent to reveal a giant screen glowing with the Tavius Global icon.

The guide laughed. "Impressive. I know." Putting the phone on the counter, the guide said, "One more thing. Here is a special badge to wear the first few times you go anywhere. It identifies you as a new employee and our roaming ambassadors will help acclimate you."

Winnie said, "Thank you. I guess I'm set for now, except I want to see my children."

"As I have explained, and as it is presented in the written materials, your children are accessible through approved channels and appointments. They will be home weekends after they've completed their month-long total immersion acclimation course. Please don't worry. They're fine and totally taken care of." The guide turned to leave.

Winnie grabbed the guide's arm. "Did you just say a month? I though you said I could see them anytime."

The guide removed Winnie's hand. "Any time after a month."

"Two weeks."

"What?"

"I intend to talk to my children tomorrow and in two weeks. Tell whoever's in charge to make that happen."

Without answering, the guide went to the door, paused, and did a half turn. "Tomorrow morning at nine, wait for a work team member to pick you up. They will have your schedule and make your adjustment go smoothly."

Alone, Winnie had time to reflect. By the time she closed her eyes, she had no idea what she'd gotten her family into.

Chapter 03 ▶ Tavius Global, Chicago, Il

Thursday, 14 February, 4:30 p.m.

Winnie finished her shift and changed into her workout clothes. As she walked from her apartment to the Physical Fitness Center, Petra Volk, a co-worker, fell in step beside her. "How are you doing?"

Winnie smiled. "I'm doing. Despite the rigid schedule, I'm grateful."

"That's normal," Petra said. "You'll find it's nice not to have to think about where to be or what to do next."

"The perfect balanced life courtesy of Tavius Global."

"Are you being sarcastic?"

Winnie caught herself. She didn't really know Petra as more than a co-worker. She kept her thoughts to herself. "No. I'm appreciative."

"Me too." Petra lowered her voice. "I'll let you in on a little secret. Just when you think you can't take one more day of it, they change it up, making it feel new again."

Winnie looked at Petra. "How long have you been here?"

"Almost two years. I was one of our team's first members."

Winnie stopped when they reached the building. "This is me."

Petra waved, said, "See you tomorrow," and disappeared into the walkers.

Winnie looked at the time and smiled. She'd made an appointment to talk to Bobby.

"Good evening, Mrs. Santiago. How can I help you?"

"I'm calling to speak to my son. I have an appointment."

"Bobby and Eva are both at an orientation session. I'm sure we sent you their revised schedule."

"I've gotten at least three revised schedules in less than a week, which do not mention parent visitations."

"They have been very busy. I'm sure you'll find time to see them."

"When?"

"When what?"

"When, exactly, will I see them?"

"Mrs. Santiago, please check the schedule."

The call ended.

Winnie vowed to see them by the end of next week, if not sooner. She would not give up.

Two days later, during lunch, Winnie saw Petra sitting alone. She walked over and sat down next to her.

Petra smiled. "Hi. Have to go."

"Wait," Winnie said. "I've seen you upstairs but never at a good time to talk."

"I know. Short breaks discourage socializing. The company believes it cuts into productivity."

Winnie picked up her sandwich and said, "Actually, that theory…" She didn't finish. Petra was gone. "Odd," she said to her herself and returned to her lunch. Before she could take a bite, somebody sat down next to her.

"Hi," said a man, who now sat in the seat vacated by Petra. He looked to be in his mid-thirties, wore rimless glasses, and had two pens and a pencil in his shirt pocket.

Winnie said, "Hi."

The man placed his drink and a napkin on the table. "You're new here, right? An analyst and designer. Right?"

"'Yes' to both questions. You are?"

"Ken. Are you Management?"

"No. Technical."

"This culture is a learning process."

Winnie turned to face the man. "Who are you?"

Ken smiled. "The unofficial worker welcome guy."

"I've been here a week. How come you're welcoming me now?"

"We only welcome those showing dissatisfaction with the status quo—like you. I'm right, right?"

"How do you know?"

"I can see you're trying to connect. Your eyes take in everything, and your body is never relaxed. Right? Plus, you're ready to check in with human resources. Right?"

Winnie didn't respond.

Ken said, "Good answer. Mavericks disappear. Their workload gets distributed to remaining team members."

He finished his drink and put the glass on her tray. He wiped his mouth with the napkin, scrunched it up, and tossed it next to the glass. "We'll talk again." He got up, shot a look at the napkin, and left.

Alone again, Winnie finished her meal, lingered over her coffee, and picked at the yogurt-fruit parfait, ignoring Ken's garbage. However, at the tray return, she threw away her paper trash and pocketed his napkin.

On the way back to her desk, she stopped in the restroom, went into a stall, and locked the door. Winnie flattened the napkin and read Ken's message— "Activity Center, seven o'clock. Add this stop to your daily activity."

She shook her head. *Somehow, I've wandered into a spy movie.* She played along by ripping up the napkin and flushing the bits into oblivion.

Her shift ended. The time had flown by. Winnie, excited and intrigued by the meeting this evening, felt her world was about to change.

The pavilion pulsed with activity, much like a train station at rush hour. People drifting, walking, trotting in and out of alcoves, rooms, and the lounge. Group activities buzzed with interactions and occasional laughter.

Winnie looked for Ken.

"Can I help you?" said a voice next to her. "I'm the coordinator."

Winnie took a step sideways so she could face the speaker. "It's my first time here. I wanted to get my bearings before deciding what to do or where to be."

"I thought as much." The coordinator handed Winnie a piece of paper. "Here is this month's schedule. In the future, go to your phone and click on any building on the interactive map to see one or more schedules."

Winnie took the hard copy.

The coordinator said, "Feel free to take a seat in the lounge or check out anything you find interesting. If I can help, my station is to your right."

Winnie said, "Thank you," and wandered over to the first seating area.

She didn't have to wait long before a woman sat down next to her and said, in a soft voice, "Winnie?

Winnie nodded.

"I'm Mary. You're in the right place. Plan on being a regular so people and staff get used to seeing you, until they don't."

Winnie nodded again.

"Look at the schedule. Fourth from the top."

Winnie did and said, "Checkers?"

Mary said, "For you, it's always fourth from the top regardless, no matter what the activity is. You'll start to meet people who you can trust. Most workers follow protocol and keep to themselves. Management does not encourage relationships. They're distracting. Here, it's not about sharing. It's about getting your work done and staying healthy so you can get your work done."

"Relationships are part of being balanced."

"Nevertheless, don't make waves," Mary said. "If you need to talk, sit here. Someone will stop by and greet you as I did."

Mary stood up and smiled at Winnie, who said, "Tonight, checkers it is."

Chapter 04 ▶ Tavius Global, Chicago, Il

Monday, 18 February, 8:30 a.m.
Winnie had not seen her children for two weeks since their arrival at Tavius Global Enterprises. She had adhered to the rules and followed all protocols except for the month-long isolation period. The boarding school thwarted her every attempt. Calm voices explained policies, schedule changes, extended classes, or transportation breakdowns.

This morning, sitting at her work desk, she drew her line in the sand and called Bobby.

"Good morning, Mrs. Santiago. Bobby is in class."

"I am his mother and it's two weeks since I've seen Bobby and Eva. I want to spend time with them after class and take them out to dinner."

"Mrs. Santiago, we have talked about this before. Policies are enforced for a reason."

"I have studied and followed every directive I've received. Every action I take is refused for one reason or another."

"Mrs. Santiago, I can hear the frustration in your voice. You must know childcare guardians must be flexible and encourage independence."

"I want to see my children after school today. Spend time with them and take them out to dinner. Afterwards, I will bring them back. Next week, I'd like them to spend Saturday and Sunday with me."

"Mrs. Santiago, I am doing my best to accommodate your requests. If you feel there is something amiss, I encourage you to talk to Human Resources."

Winnie ended the call, folded her arms across her chest, and stared at the Tavius Global Enterprise logo on her monitor.

Her manager appeared fifteen minutes later. "Mrs. Santiago, Winnie, you've not logged in today. Is something wrong with your equipment?"

Winnie didn't move. "No. I'm not working until I have a firm, guaranteed, ironclad agreement allowing me to see my children this afternoon."

Her manager said, "Children have nothing to do with your job. Please log in and join the rest of your team. We need your leadership."

"My work affects Tavius Global Enterprises, and my children affect me. If they can keep my children from me, I can keep my work from the company."

"Winnie, you're defying corporate policy. It's out of my hands and above my manager status."

"Do I see my children today? Or do I become the weak link and sabotage company goals?"

The manager stroked his chin. "How about you start work and I'll see what I can do?"

Winnie said, "I prefer you do your part first before I do mine."

The manager sighed. "This will not end well," and walked away.

Winnie's gaze shifted to the large industrial clock on the wall. *I bet I get the okay to see my kids in ten minutes, twenty on the outside.*

She got the call in six.

"Mrs. Santiago, I've arranged for you to come and pick up your children at the end of your shift. Please have them back at school by 8 o'clock this evening."

Winnie could have jumped for joy. Instead, she joined her team and the project in progress. Before she knew it, it was time to leave. She ran to the school, as her children emerged from the building's inner hallway to the large foyer, she opened her arms for a group hug. Bobby and Eva rejected her enthusiasm. They offered restrained smiles and allowed her to hug them.

Bobby said, "I'm missing last period."

Eva said, "Why did you take me out of free play?"

Winnie had dealt with these "why do I have to do what you want me to do when I'd much rather do what I want to do" behaviors before. She said, "Because I'm your mother, I love you, and I haven't seen you for ages."

She took Eva's hand in her right hand and Bobby's hand in her left and led them out into the sunshine. "Come on, guys. Isn't it good to be outside and together again?"

Bobby said, "What are we going to do?"

"Are you hungry?"

The children shook their heads.

"Okay. How about we go to the park? You can tell me everything about your new school."

Bobby and Eva walked without speaking.

Winnie said, "I see I'm going to have to interrogate." She guided them to a round picnic table.

The kids sat, backs straight like West Point cadets. Winnie put her elbows on the table and leaned in. "Tell me all about your new life." She looked from one to the other. They had changed. Thinner maybe. Not so soft. Independent.

Bobby said, "What do you want to know?"

"Do you like being here? How's your room? School? Did you make new friends?"

Eva said, "It's much better than the shelter and not as good as home before Daddy died."

Bobby said, "It's clean and nobody steals."

"Do you like your room?"

"It's okay. Nothing special. I've got seven roommates. We sleep on bunk beds."

"How's that working out?"

"We don't spend much time there. Mostly, it's just the room where we sleep."

Eva said, "I sleep on a top bunk. I don't like it."

"Did you ask to be changed?"

Eva said, "Nobody complains."

"What do..."

Bobby cut her off. "Mom, the rules say no questions and no complaints."

Winnie bit her lip. She'd hoped their initial coolness was transitory. But, no. Defiant Bobby and wild-child Eva had changed. Domesticated. No. Wrong word. Dominated. No. Subservient. The light had gone from their eyes.

She energized herself. "Come on, guys. We've got some time. Do you want to play a game? Go to a movie? Walk around the lake? Or maybe we could do an art project. What do you think?"

The kids shrugged their shoulders. Eva looked to Bobby.

Bobby said, "Let's eat."

Winnie smiled. Making headway. "Which restaurant?"

Bobby looked at his mother. In a flat voice, he said, "It doesn't matter. It's all the same food anyway. Same food, same clothes, same everything."

Winnie's eyebrows shot up. "What?"

Bobby looked at her. "You mean you haven't noticed?"

Winnie didn't know what to say.

"Mom?"

"I've been so worried about you I haven't had time to think about it."

"Yeah, well, now's a good time." Bobby said. "Our meals are part of a twenty-four-seven fast food chain."

Before Winnie could respond, Eva perked up. "After we eat, can we go shopping? You know, like we used to."

Winnie hit the table with both hands. "Absolutely. Great idea." She stood up, reached for Eva's hand, and put her arm around Bobby's shoulder. "Let's go."

Over the course of their time together, Bobby and Eva started to warm up and respond to her. At the eight o'clock bewitching hour, Winnie had them back to school. She kissed them good-bye and watched as they walked away, down the hall, out of sight. They never turned around, threw her a kiss, or even waved.

Their actions made her feel invisible and it broke her heart. She wandered aimlessly around the Tavius Global Complex. Dusk to dawn motion activated lights lit her way. She stopped at a pond and dropped, cross-legged, onto the grassy edge. She felt the cool blades and combed her fingers through the turf. No weeds. No crabgrass. No clover. Manicured, perfect grass.

Bobby's words echoed in her head—*it's all the same.*

Bzzz. A text message. She read it. "Human Resources has recorded your children's loss of educational time, and your missed team practice. Deviation is not encouraged. Be prepared for disciplinary action if any further unscheduled or deleted activities interfere with the Tavius Global worker maintenance protocol."

"What the fuck?" Winnie jumped to her feet and marched over to the administration building. Her guide from the first day welcomed her into a private office. "Mrs. Santiago, good to see you again. What can I help you with?"

Winnie pulled out her phone and displayed the message. "What's this?"

"Isn't it self-explanatory?"

"Seeing my children is cause for disciplinary action?"

"Only if you insist on seeing them outside of our stated restrictions."

"They were never able to make the assigned meetings."

"It's only been two weeks. No communications were to take place for a month."

The guide stared at her for a moment before producing an e-pad and activating the information screen on the wall. "Here are the notes from the school. You can see your children took a little longer than average to adjust to their educational program. Since they accepted the boundaries and schedules, they are regularly in the top percentage of their class."

Winnie shook her head. "I'm not surprised. What I find objectionable is the lack of our time together."

The guide manifested a thin smile. "You have your schedule too. We encourage all our employees to be fit in mind and body. Tavius Global recognizes it takes time to internalize our expectations. We are committed to investing in you. In return, we ask you respect our policies regarding your children."

"Are you asking me, us, to give up our parent-child relationships?"

"No, of course not. We want you and your children to thrive."

"What if I want more time with my children?"

"Mrs. Santiago, please trust us. We have been working with people and families for years. You have entered a new phase of your life here. We understand it is different. However, if you look around at your work group, exercise partners, sports team members, and social mealtime companions, you will see happy productive people. We want you to be happy and productive as well."

Winnie clenched her teeth and narrowed her eyes. A second later, she decided this was not the time for anger. Softening her face, she stood up and smiled. "Thank you." Outside, she took deep breaths. People were out and about. She walked to a bench, sat down, and watched, remembering what Bobby had said—it's all the same.

She looked around. Nothing looked out of place. No one looked troubled. Or in love. Or pregnant. Everyone looked happy, fit, and focused. *Why not? They have nothing to worry about and neither do I. Why am I even thinking about it?*

A voice said, "You've been sitting here for a while. Can I help you? Is something wrong?"

She looked up. Security. "No, I'm good."

"Don't you have someplace to be?" Winnie looked at her watch. "Home."

Security smiled. "Problem solved."

She stood. "No problem. I'm going." Winnie walked into the crowd. When she glanced back, Security still had eyes on her.

The next evening, Winnie entered the Activity Center at seven. The fourth scheduled activity was Poetry. She made her way to the meeting area populated by a small gathering of people she knew, including Ken and Mary.

Sitting in the small circle, Winnie said, "I have some very personal poetry to share. Is there somewhere a little more private?"

Ken stood. "I know, by the fountain out in front. Let's go."

They reconvened by the sound of loud splashing water. Ken put a white noise filter in the center of their small circle and, as if by magic, when they leaned in, they could hear each other.

Ken said, "Cover your mouth when you talk, if you can. People watching can lip read."

Winnie nodded and got right to the point. "Human Resources reprimanded me for seeing my children. Is this standard?"

Mary said, "Emotions and close relationships are messy and reduce focus."

Winnie said, "They are also stress relievers."

Ken said, "If you stick to the regimen, which is designed to keep you working at your optimum alertness and eliminate stress, the company expects everything to run smoothly."

Another group member said, "Tavius Global does not want to deal with people problems. It's expensive in terms of time, it's disruptive in terms of scheduling, and it's distracting to everyone involved. In short, not productive."

Winnie said, "I see. I'm to be grateful for being safe, for my children being safe, and the quid pro quo is to not make waves."

Mary said, "If you persist, and become a problem, you will be transferred."

Ken said, "No good-byes. Just gone. No one here will ever see or hear from you again. Ever."

Winnie said, "Dead?"

Ken said, "Don't know."

Winnie said, "Has anybody tried to negotiate a change to the company protocols?"

Heads shook around the circle.

Mary said, "Nobody's had the gumption to speak and become the target."

Winnie said, "Can you get fired?"

Her question hung, unanswered, in the air.

Chapter 05 ▶ Tavius Global, Chicago, Il

Monday, 1 April, 9:00 a.m.
Mr. Octavius, Octavius to his friends, sat on leather seats in his chauffeured limousine, destination Tavius Global Industries, Chicago.

The complex sat on the former Acme Coke Plant site located on the shores of Lake Michigan. He had bought the toxic land and the old buildings for a song. He used another Tavius company to flatten the useless structures and gut the contaminated soil. After passing the minimal government safety standards, he built the first all-encompassing manufacturing center, intending it to be the model for all future industrial ventures.

Taking a page from the standard late 1800's coal companies handbook, he built a small village to serve the media industry. His motivation had been to offset all the bad press corporate giants received on a regular basis: job insecurity, layoffs, low wages, overtime, non-job-related costs like commuting, company dress requirements, healthcare, disability concessions, poor housing, and no investment in education.

Today, six years after opening day, the complex had grown to include manufacturing of active and leisure wear for giant name brands. Since his effort had been more than worth it, he'd build another complex in Kansas, and was in negotiations for the next one.

As the Chicago center filled the horizon, Octavius smiled. The architect had used the prefab components in an unusual way to reduce mass and emphasize the artistic elements of line, color, form, and movement. The design won the Industrial Architectural Award.

The large iron gates' sensor read the license plate and the limo sailed through the arch to the Welcome Center. He exited the limo and walked to the left, through the Tavius Executive Tower sliding glass doors, past the reception area, and into the elevator. He rode to the top floor presidential suite.

His secretary met him as he stepped onto the marble floor. "You have people waiting for you."

Octavius glared at her. "I don't meet with people. My people meet with people."

"Sir, this demands your attention."

He walked past her into his office. His manager stood at attention and said, "Sir, we have a small problem which needs to be shut down fast."

"How small?"

"A group of workers wants to meet with you. They want to leave the compound and take their families on day trips."

"Why? We have recreation facilities on site."

"Alone, sir. They want to be alone with their family. Away from here."

"They can get away on their vacations to Tavius Island in the Caribbean."

"Sir, they want to have time away from Tavius."

"How many are in this group?"

"Three, and a petition signed by fifty."

"Let them go."

"Sir?"

"They can go, but they can't come back as per our agreement. I'll even provide transportation."

"Mr. Octavius, they don't want to lose their jobs. They want to meet with you to discuss amendments to the standard agreement."

"Did you tell them I abhor amendments?"

"Sir, they're in the conference room."

Octavius sighed, narrowed his eyes, and said, "This is unacceptable."

"I know, sir. It's incomprehensible because workers have everything they need. Still, we had to transfer one worker two weeks ago and considered the matter closed. Now this. We can't afford ongoing internal disruption with company contracts on deadline."

"I see," Octavius said. "Give me their names."

The manager gave him the petition. "Their names are starred."

Octavius took the information without looking and said, "I'll meet with them this time. You draft a company-wide policy regarding negotiations, and by that, I mean it gets handled by division heads. This company does not have an 'open door' policy."

In the conference room, Octavius took the seat opposite the three representatives and slapped the petition on the table. "I understand you want to talk with me."

The woman directly in front of him said, "My name is Winnie Santiago. We are here to negotiate time away from all that is Tavius."

Octavius examined his cuticles. "To spend time with the poor, needy, and oppressed?"

"No, sir. To experience freedom without regimentation and monitorization."

"I'm afraid I don't understand. You are free to do whatever you like."

She spoke again. "Within the compound."

"The hundred-acre compound and Caribbean island resort."

A man on his left said, "As an example, you provided free clothing—a savings for sure. However, since it all comes from the same retailer, we all look alike."

Octavius said, "You are clothed, fed, and clean. You have a place to live, free healthcare, free education, free library, free activity center, and a free sports complex. In return, I expect a commitment to your work, without distraction." He looked around the table. "This meeting is a distraction."

Winnie said, "We feel dehumanized, unstimulated, and uninspired. We need more time with our children and the opportunity to form meaningful relationships."

Octavius looked her. "You're new here?"

"A month."

"Do you not feel it is too soon to form such negative reactions?"

Winnie looked him straight in the eye. "You mean before I've accepted your control as my new normal."

"I see." Octavius stared at her. "You were meant to be a major player in our global initiative."

Octavius stood, pointed to Winnie, and said to the manager, "Transfer this worker."

Chapter 06▶Gramercy Avenue, New York City

Tuesday, 9 April, 2 p.m.
Rachel stood by the triplex apartment door while her service dog, Zeus, a caramel and white pit bull-American bulldog mix, waited by her side. She turned the knob. At the crack of light, the dog bounded through the opening and into the triplex, to get his usual effusive greeting from his second most favorite human.

Chris, Rachel's husband, laughed as he petted Zeus's undulating body, being careful to avoid the whipping tail and wet pink tongue. "How did your walk go, Mrs. Gregory?"

Rachel grinned. She held up her wedding ring finger and wiggled it. "I never get tired of hearing you say that." She hung up her coat, unleashed Zeus, and removed his "service dog" harness. Turning to Chris, she did her best Marilyn Monroe walk to his side and dropped her body into his lap.

After a long lingering kiss, she said, "I can't believe we've been married 6 months."

"I can," Chris said. "I waited a very long time for the Allen-Gregory union and I'm enjoying every minute."

"I still find it hard to believe you, an insufferable twenty-something computer geek, fell in love with the seventeen-year-old me twelve years ago."

"How could I not? You were a stunning, brilliant, smart-ass intern volunteering on the Clinton campaign."

"Why didn't you say something instead of disappearing from my life?"

"It's called statutory rape and a damned good reason to back off."

"My hero. You saved me from myself."

"I knew if I waited long enough, you'd come back into my life and, Mrs. Gregory, here you are."

"Karma is an agonizing journey." She kissed him. "Remember when you left, you took the fireworks app you programmed into my computer start-up?"

He nodded.

"I missed it. Every day."

He kissed her. "Enough reminiscing. You need to go do whatever it is you do, and I have to finish up my extremely important work as head of an international computer security conglomerate, so we can afford to eat dinner at a reasonable hour."

Rachel laughed and kissed him again. "Congrats. To date, that's your most oblique yet transparent applause to my book in process, which keeps getting interrupted by conference calls with the President of the United States."

Chris lowered his voice, "I love it when you talk dirty."

Rachel chuckled and stood. She put her arms around his head, fingers sliding through his hair, and hugged his head to her abdomen. Moments later she released him and bent over to kiss him.

Chris accepted the kiss. "Okay. Okay. There are no slackers in this room, except our sleeping dog, which we'll let lie."

She checked the wall clock. "It's two. I'm going upstairs to work. How about dinner at six? It's my turn to cook, so pick your restaurant or we can eat leftovers."

He shook his head. "Sorry, the leftovers were my lunch. However, I relieve you of your dinner obligation as I've already made plans."

Rachel paused on the second riser. "Plans?"

"Go work. All will be revealed at 6:30."

She opened her mouth to speak, and Chris said, "No questions. Go work."

Rachel reached the top step when Chris called out, "I forgot. Dani called."

She put her hand in her pocket expecting her phone to be there. It wasn't. In a rising panic, she checked every pocket. Her phone held her life in its digital drives. Even though Chris had assured her more than once that her data resided somewhere in the cloud, it didn't mean as much as the actual phone in her hand.

Beads of perspiration formed at her hairline. Her pulse raced. She heard her heartbeat pounding in her ears. She felt lightheaded and dropped to her knees. *This shouldn't be happening. I've come too far to...*

Rachel's mind shot back to her college days. In the twilight, she took a shortcut through buildings where the motion sensor didn't work. There, in the dark, a male foreign exchange jumped her, dragged her in the bushes, raped her, and tried to beat her to death.

She found out later that Philanthropist and vigilante Ted Donovan saved her.

After years of therapy for depression and PTSD, she took the big step of moving to New York City, into one of Chris's apartments. With his help and Zeus's, she overcame her agoraphobia, but not the occasional panic attacks, like now.

As she gasped for breath, Zeus bounded to her side. The dog pressed his body against her, knocking her to the floor. He licked her face and nuzzled her neck and hands. "Good boy," Rachel said, hugging him, patting his head, and scratching under his chin and behind his ears. "I'm okay, Zeus. Good boy. Just looking for my..."

Her phone buzzed and vibrated on her desk. She got up, ran over, picked it up, and sat down in one fluid motion. "Hi Mom."

"I thought you'd forgotten us," Helene Allen said. "One wedding and now you're Missus Independent."

Rachel laughed. "You know it's not true. You and dad gave us one beautiful wedding. You did a great job."

"Thank you. I love to hear it," Helene said. "I also called to wish you a happy six-month anniversary. Are you doing anything to celebrate?"

"Chris has something special planned for tonight and wants it to be a surprise."

"He's a keeper. I knew from the minute I met him."

"Really? You gave him a hard time."

"It was a test. I wanted you to be in safe hands."

"Mom, he was renting me an apartment and you asked, no, told him to gut the place."

Helene laughed. "I did, didn't I. I couldn't help myself. He played up to me, being as charming as he could be. I loved every minute of it."

"Maybe you were his first love."

"More important," Helene said, "He did it, stuck it out, and took the whole package. I'm very happy for you both."

"Thanks, Mom. We're happy too."

"And..."

"And what?"

"You know."

"Mom, I'm not having the baby discussion with you every time we talk."

"You're not getting any younger."

"Mom, I've got to go. Talk to you later. Love you."

"Love you too."

Rachel punched the END button. She didn't want to talk about babies. In fact, she thought she'd be pregnant at her wedding. She wasn't. She tried to hide her disappointment behind her work.

She, Rachel Allen, author and recognized authority on human rights, didn't have time for babies. Her books always made the New York Times Best Seller list, as well as required reading in college courses.

Although she was in the middle of writing her new book about American worker rights, she wanted time to enjoy her newlywed status. A baby would divert her time and energy.

Even she didn't believe what she tried to tell herself. Her free hand dropped to her belly as a tear rolled down her cheek. *I'm just being silly.* She shook her head, her dark-brown curls bounced into her eyes. She finger-combed them back in place, cleared her throat, and picked up her phone. Time to get back to work.

Rachel found Dani's call in her messages. Rachel pressed "Dani" and put her phone on the desk with the speaker on.

Chapter 07 ▶ White House, Washington D.C.

Tuesday, 9 April, 11 a.m.

President Dani Mitchell saw the ID on her private phone and answered. "Rachel, thank you for getting back to me. You're the only sane person I know."

Rachel said, "Politics can be rough."

"Now, understand I'm not complaining when I say I've been President for over a year and have at least five new gray hairs for each month."

Rachel laughed. "No one said it'd be easy. You've had to deal with a lot of clean-up. You should be proud. Your Tawandian immigration program is a success."

"Yes," Dani said. "However, problems always ride the coattails of success."

"What is it this time?"

"Jobs, workers, and climate."

"I'm working on book about workers' human rights," Rachel said. "Can I help?"

"You absolutely can." Dani sat straight up. "I'm getting a lot of pushback on my Mixed Economy Initiative. Corporations don't want to give up their profits to benefit workers. I need to find their underbelly to make sure they'll negotiate in good faith."

"What I've found out may not be what you expect or want to hear."

"I need to see your take on how this country must move forward."

"Of course," Rachel said. "I'll send you a copy of my first draft as soon as it's ready."

Dani ended the call, turned to look through the windows at the tranquil garden beyond, and thought about her game plan. She used her private phone and called her cousin, Peter Powell. When he answered, she said, "Hi Cuz, how's it going?"

"Great," he said with a flat voice. "I love being cooped up in this mausoleum with the Ninja, our monosyllabic androgynous housekeeper."

She laughed. "Ninja is the perfect description. I can't remember the housekeeper, er, Ninja, uttering a sentence with more than five words, seven at the most."

"You're not helping."

Dani smiled. "Oh, come on, it can't be tough living in the lap of luxury."

"It's a solitary life, sitting in my office, making calls, adjusting investments, and carrying out cartel instructions." he said. "I have to get out of here. After all the excitement freeing the Tawandian refugees, I'm no longer suited for a desk job."

Dani said, "You're handling the family's finances and sitting on a multinational board. We're counting on you."

"I'm going to New York."

"What?"

"I'm leaving Philadelphia."

"Peter."

"Stop, Dani. I can make phone calls and take digital meetings from anywhere. I want to get back to Mom, she's still not over losing her wife, and resume my ombudsman role for the PRAISE Foundation."

"The Vanderhagen house has been the hub of our business operations for years."

"It's yours, Dani. I'm going in a different direction."

"Take the Ninja with you."

"Can't. No room."

Dani tapped the desktop. "I'll keep the Philadelphia house and the Ninja. You may need them now and again."

"Fine. It keeps my options open," Peter said. "I'll call you when I'm settled in New York."

"Wait. Tell me, how's the new investment going? We're not traceable, right?"

Peter said, "Our interests are hidden under multiple holding companies and acquisitions."

"Excellent," Dani said. "How did the meeting go?"

"That's tomorrow. If any stats change, I'll let you know," he said. "Anything else?"

"Hmm." Dani leaned back in her chair. "Since you're so bored, would you be interested in an on-site evaluation on the Alaskan permafrost situation?"

"What about your Environmental Protection Agency? Isn't it their job?"

"I get their reports," Dani said. "You're my trusted eyes on the ground. I'll let the State Department know. They'll give you access. While you're observing, scope out any investment opportunities. Melting permafrost can't be all bad news."

"Under the radar?"

"Please."

Dani's intercom buzzed. "Chief of Security needs to speak to you."

"Send him in."

Wesley Warren marched in and faced the president. "Ma'am, we have an issue at the front gate. A man named 'Taxi' demands to talk with you. He asked me to give you this."

Dani took the envelope, opened it, and read the brief message. "Wes, bring him in." He left. She texted Isabel. "*Push my next meeting to this afternoon. When done, come into the Oval Office.*"

Chief of Staff Isabel Upton said, "Good morning, Madam President."

Dani returned the greeting and said, "Isabel, my friend Taxi, the Tawandian rescue mission hero and refugee organizer, is coming up to talk to me about some serious allegations. I want you here as a witness, and I expect your support on any actions to be taken."

A knock on the door suspended the conversation. Wes opened the door for Taxi and closed it without entering the room. The tall, well-built African strode into the room and said, "Madam President."

After shaking hands and introducing Isabel, Dani took a seat and said, "Sit down and tell me what's so urgent."

Taxi said, "The resettlement projects are encountering pushback from the communities."

"I'm surprised. The reports I get are glowing."

"Your reports are doctored."

Dani turned her head to glare at Isabel. "If this is true, I want to know who and why, as soon as this meeting is over."

Isabel scribbled on her ever-present steno-pad. "Yes, ma'am. Right away."

Dani looked at Taxi. "Are you sure your information is accurate?"

Taxi said, "I would not be here otherwise. Helping to lead my people to freedom has made me responsible for their well-being." He opened the flap of his courier bag and produced a well-worn composition book journal. "The young man, a former government clerk who wrote this. His family sent it to me after his funeral. They want me to use it to get justice for the refugees." He handed it to Dani.

She opened it, flipped through the pages, and said, "It's in Tawandian."

Taxi nodded. "I wanted you to see it is genuine." He took the original back and pulled out a manuscript and handed it to the President. "Here it is in English."

Dani said, "Good. This is far more helpful, and I'd like to read it now. Let's adjourn until eleven, go over this material, and have lunch afterwards."

She turned to Isabel. "Take Taxi to my private waiting room, go do the research on the reports, and hold my calls."

Once the room emptied, Dani retrieved a highlighter and pen from her desk, poured herself a cup of coffee, placed it on the table next to the easy chair, and sat down. She took a deep breath. Since the young man who penned the journal had died, she knew this wouldn't be an easy read.

The journal engaged her from the first page. She highlighted several sections as a convenient summary.

Mamadou's Journal #5

27 May. Last day in Tawanda

I am an outcast and a cast-away. The Tawandian war with the Democratic Republic of the Congo cast me out of my home and village. The refugee camp where I lived, outside Damir, held all the war refugees and outcasts. When the sinkholes swallowed over half the camp, I went into a holding area and then into the mine encampment.

Until this time, I was not in charge of my life and never given a choice—a piece of sand blown here and there by forces far greater than me.

In the mine, during the night whispers, someone asked me if I wanted to go to America. I asked, "Will it be better than this?"

"Yes," the man said. "It will be better, and you will be free."

"Free?"

"As you once were. Free to make your own choices."

My heartbeat faster than a racing Bohor reedbuck. "I want to go."

I didn't sleep that night.

2 June. First Day in America

The air smells different. I notice it as I wait on the endless lines for doctors, for clothing, for something called a "subcutaneous tag," for living assignments, for food, and for orientation. The people are nice, their faces are kind, and their hands are soft. Tomorrow we start classes to learn American English. This is a good place. For the first time since I can remember, I have no fear. I am feeling calm and well cared for.

6 June. Flight to Springfield, Missouri

We have been told Springfield is in the top ten safest cities in America. Two hundred refugees are going to the middle of America. Our mission, they say, is to revitalize communities suffering from job losses. They say children do not stay when they grow up and do not move back. We are their hope.

I look around the airplane. I see my parents, families, and the rest are mostly single men. Single women are in the minority. I cannot tell the ages as the refugee camp made us all look ancient.

I am fortunate to have a seat by a small window. I feel like I can touch the clouds. When the clouds disappear, I see patterns on the earth. I cannot take my eyes away. When more clouds come, I will draw the patterns as a reminder.

6 June. Trip to Kryller, Missouri

I am riding in the last of four buses. Behind the bus are trucks and vans. We are going to a village outside of Springfield to build a healthy food farm. Each of us has been given a paper about our government sponsored initiative in case anyone asks.

This paper says, by accepting and integrating the resettlement compound, the village will have more trade, more food, a new medical clinic, new roads, more teachers, and an expanded social network.

I have seen government promises before.

13 June. First week in Compound

The village is 98% white with a population of 300. I know this because it was part of our orientation.

On Sunday, the pastor invited the compound people to church. When we walked in, the villagers sat on the right, reserving the left side for us. While much of what went on is familiar, I had difficulty understanding the language.

We received smiles and head nods before, during, and after the service with little actual engagement. I can tell the villagers see us as black foreigners, as different culturally as could be imagined, speaking a language they've never heard as well as very poor English.

20 June. Two weeks in Compound

My first job is putting together things called "modules" which, when assembled, create instant buildings of apartments for our compound which are set in a half-circle facing the fields. I am sharing a two-bedroom module with my parents.

Other jobs, supervised by the Americans, are marking out and creating gardens, putting down roads, and erecting a barn, equipment storage, and produce storage.

I have gone into Kryller three times. I am not greeted with kind faces. Smiles are forced. Eyes watch me. I would like to engage the townspeople in talk to learn more about living in America. I try to speak about this wonderful country. People are polite. A few words. I do not feel welcomed as our rescuers promised. I am free and still an outcast.

13 July. 6 weeks in Compound

Our crops are growing. Our community is hard working and determined to make this healthy food for ourselves, the townspeople, and Springfield. No one from the town ventures near us. Almost everyone watches from their front porches when they are not in line for the fully staffed new medical clinic. It is here most interactions between the townspeople and the compound people occur. It is polite. Sometimes there is inquisitive conversation about the garden or the "modules." In all cases, it is short.

3 August. 9 weeks in Compound

The government resettlement team has talked with Kryller's mayor and set up a picnic for tonight. The main street in town will be closed to traffic at five o'clock in the afternoon. The church will set up tables and chairs. The townspeople will make their favorite foods and the Tawandians will make theirs. I am looking forward to this merging of cultures. It is time.

When Dani reached the diary's last page, she found this newspaper clipping, taped to the page.

DEPUTY THREATENED
3 DEATHS RESULT
Dateline: August 3
Mike Jones, Kryller Sentinel,
First Person Account
    Page 8 exclusive

When I arrived, the potluck dinner was spread out over four tables and combined the mid-west culture with the west African culture. The music of Banjos and guitars blended in with drums and flutes.

At six-thirty, the mayor reached into his pocket for his father's well-known heirloom watch. It was gone. After searching frantically, he stood on a chair and ordered everyone to check around their area.

The jostling of chairs and people led to altercations which elevated to fistfights. The sheriff and his deputy were unable to control the crowd.

In the scuffle, the deputy took a punch and fell to the ground. Furious, he pulled his gun. As he stood, the gun went off and his bullet killed Alain Jakande, 34.

Cardin Ohakim, 31, elbowed his way through the crowd to his friend's side, and received a knife wound to the stomach. He staggered to Jakande's side, fell over, and died.

The deputy, still holding his gun, looked pale and confused. His eyes searched the crowd as if looking for someone who could explain why two dead men lay on the ground in front of him.

Instead, a wild screaming Mamadou Effiong, 25, raced towards him.

I saw the deputy falter. He took a step back, hands raised, as if to show he meant no harm. It didn't stop Effiong, who kept coming.

Next, I heard, "Shoot!" I whipped my head around toward the crowd to see and silence the person who shouted. To no avail because other people called out, "Shoot!"

I turned toward the deputy. His gun hand shook so much he had to hold it with both hands. When Effiong burst through the crowd and saw his fallen friends, he let out an ear-splitting wail directed first to the heavens and then to

the deputy, who shot Effiong point
blank.

Later the same evening, the mayor
found his watch on his dresser. The
sheriff declared the entire incident as an
unfortunate error in judgement. No
charges were filed.

Dani put the diary down and summoned Isabel and
Taxi to join her. They sat down and she said, "Thank
you for sharing Mamadou's story. I'm saddened this
happened and is still happening in other settlements.
Taxi, this is not what I envisioned."

Taxi said, "Sometimes it is hard to get people to
understand we are much stronger together."

Dani said, "Clearly."

Taxi produced a piece of paper. "I just got this
email and Isabel printed it for me. May I read it?"

Dani nodded.

Taxi said, "The Tawandians organized the
service for the three dead on the compound meadow.
When the villagers observed the gathering, they came
to join the mourners. Many carried food or flowers."

"Was it a cultural breakthrough?"

"Yes. The sadness and celebration of these lost
lives surpassed the language barrier and created a
human bond."

Isabel said, "I also have updates." She produced
a file.

Dani looked at her Chief of Staff. "Isabel, I
didn't have time to read the updated reports. Please
summarize them."

"Of course," Isabel said. "As you know, previous
reports were all positive. They covered assimilation,

farming progress, housing, and access to food, clothing, and transportation.

Digging deeper, I found out there are problems at every refugee relocation. They've been harassed by locals and law enforcement.

Where the organic farms are successful, instead of strengthening the markets, other farmers see them as competition. Our inquiry identified several instances where frustration and anger surfaced and resulted in altercations and damages to refugee farms."

Taxi said, "My people work hard to be successful. However, in the areas of extreme prejudice, they are disheartened."

Dani stood. "I'm not going to stand by and watch this initiative fail. Isabel, I want teams of four to go to each settlement and create the environment for peaceful co-existence."

"Madam President," Isabel said. "We…"

Dani held her hand up. "Stop, I don't want to hear it. This is supposed to be a model for resettlement. We must figure out how to handle the issues because our research predicts more than 200 million climate refugees over the next two decades and we will have to up our local food production. There must be a workable plan in place."

"I understand." Isabel stood, collected the folders, and said, "I'm on it."

Dani watched her leave and looked at Taxi. "Let's go. Dinner is on me."

Taxi raised his palm and he looked at his phone. "Wait, there's a problem." He looked up at the President. "Who are the AKAW?"

"Why?"

"They're staging a rally in Kryller this weekend."

"Americans Keeping America White. They are a terrorist white nationalist group."

Taxi stood. "I'll take a raincheck on dinner. I've got to go."

Dani watched him leave. She'd found the loophole allowing the U.S. to accept the Tawandian refuges and developed the resettlement program. Nothing was going to tarnish this project because her name and reputation were all over it.

Dani called the FBI Director. "The AKAW supporters are marching in Kryller. They must be stopped. I don't want anything, and I mean anything, to jeopardize this initiative."

Chapter 08 ▶ Federal Building, NYC

Tuesday, 9 April, 4 p.m.

"Help. They are going to kill us.
Tavius Global Industries is transferring
my family and me from Tavius Chicago
to Tavius Kansas today. Transferees
never make it. They disappear. We will
disappear. You may find a Winnie
Santiago and her two children in
Kansas, but it won't be us.
<attachment>"

Special Agent Elizabeth Neilson, the FBI's Missing Person's Division head, looked up from the note Special Agent Eric Jerrod had handed her. "What is this?"

"It is, apparently, the last words of a missing woman and her two children. We received it two days ago. It describes her experience at Tavius Global."

Beth said, "Eric, has this been checked out?"

"Of course. I wanted to be sure we weren't being played before I got you involved."

Beth said, "Cute kids. Did you find them?"

"There's a Santiago family in Kansas, but not matching the picture."

Beth stood up. "This is not good."

"Worse," Eric said. "I sent people to interview other employees in Chicago to find out who saw the family last. Want to guess what they found?"

"Tell me."

"The last person who saw the family watched them load their suitcases and themselves into a black SUV." Eric paused. "Anything sounding familiar?"

Beth walked over to the window, paused, and turned to Eric. "The missing Imanuela Myerson family?"

He nodded. "Exactly."

She said, "We know Lucy Kilmer seduced the Myersons with an all-expense paid trip around the world and killed them somewhere between the house and the plane."

Eric's laugh was hollow. "It kills me we don't have enough evidence to lock her up."

"Still," Beth said, "it appears to be the same operation. Do you think she did it or trained someone?"

"How? When? She's been under surveillance since she walked out of here almost a year ago."

Beth said, "True. Hmm. Wonder how she did it?"

"If she did it." Eric shook his head. "I'd also like to know how she wound up freezing and floating in her pool."

"What?"

"I just got back from the Kilmer house and the hospital. Lucy will live and I will find out what happened. From there, I'll figure out how she could be working for Tavius Industries without leaving her house."

"Excellent. I love a good mystery," Beth said.

"Before I go, read this. It's the attachment and it details Santiago's experience."

Beth read the document and looked at Eric. "I can't believe she knew what she was up against and still tried to make things better."

"It seems Tavius Global doesn't like squeaky wheels."

"Clearly. However, if the whole complex is on a private and controlled server, how did she get this document past the censors?"

Eric said, "I'm guessing," and leaned back in his chair, shifting gaze from Beth to the ceiling, "she had access to an offline computer which ran the letter through an encryption program. Afterwards, she put it on a thumb drive and begged a supplier's driver to use their on-board computer."

She smiled. "That's one hell of a guess. I know you're good, but not that good."

He sat up and laughed. "You're right. I had an agent track down the computer and interrogate its owner."

"The driver?"

"Yep. He confirms she ran up to him and pleaded with him to use his computer. He refused. She got between him and his truck and became, in his words, ferocious. She spoke in a low voice, grabbed his shirt, and threatened to scream 'rape' if he didn't give her two minutes. She finished her download in one, gave him a kiss on his cheek, and disappeared."

Beth said, "We'll never get a warrant based on a woman's letter stating she's been murdered."

"True, but maybe it is enough to open an investigation. Hiring desperate people from shelters is either philanthropic or nefarious."

Beth paced the office. "Not permitting access to the outside world can't be a good thing."

Eric leaned forward, elbows on his desktop. "Agreed. Plus, Santiago never mentioned an actual salary. We may be looking at corporate human trafficking."

Beth stopped and faced him. "Let's start with the shelter. Find out if there's a connection with Tavius."

He nodded. "I could send an agent. However, if it's okay with you, I'd like to go myself and not tip off the shelter staff or Tavius Global about FBI interest."

"Good idea. You can leave now."

Eric smiled. "I'll go first thing tomorrow. We have plans tonight."

Chapter 09 ▶ Gramercy Avenue, NYC

Tuesday, 9 April, 6:30 p.m.
Rachel, deep into her research—reading and typing, didn't hear Chris, but Zeus did. The dog's ears pricked up, his tail started thumping, and he raised his head to gaze at his owner. When she didn't respond with her familiar scratching behind his ears, he whined. Nothing. He sat and put his paws on her lap, stretched to a stand, and plopped his nose on top of her hands.

"Oh, look what you've done," Rachel said. "I'll have to..."

Chris called out, "Rachel. Dinner."

She smiled and took Zeus's face in her hands. "Okay. I forgive you." Zeus answered with a big sloppy kiss. Rachel stood, called out, "Coming," and looked at the dog. "Ready for dinner?" Zeus barked and ran toward the top step. They went down the stairs together.

Zeus left her side and ran to Chris, working in the kitchen.

Rachel said, "What's for dinner?"

"Don't rush me. It'll be ready in a minute."

The doorbell rang.

Rachel looked at Chris. He shrugged his shoulders. She followed Zeus to the door.

Chris called out, "It's okay. Let them in."

She flung open the door, saw a huge balloon bouquet and heard, "Surprise! Happy Anniversary," from her two favorite people, Beth Neilson and Eric Jerrod.

I loved the baked salmon," Rachel said after eating the last bite on her plate. "I can't believe you did all this."

Chris smiled. "Not too hard. I called the chef and he agreed to reproduce our wedding dinner for tonight."

"How did you manage to get our bridesmaid and best man here?" Rachel smiled at her friends.

Chris said, "A lot of planning and convincing."

Beth laughed. "We've had it on our calendar for weeks."

Eric said, "Speaking of calendars, you need to save the last Saturday in June, next year, for us."

Beth said, "We've finally picked the date and found a place."

Rachel picked up her glass. "A toast to you."

"Make it to the gods of justice," Eric said. "We've put in for vacation time and hope we won't have to cancel."

Chris said, "The FBI will just have to get its priorities straight and cover all its bases so you two can tie the knot."

"Right," Rachel said. "I'm sure all you have to do is close all the open cases you have and call it a day."

Beth said, "I wish."

Eric agreed. "We're certainly going to try, even though the future can be fickle."

Beth put on her pouty face. "Don't be a killjoy."

"Okay. Okay." Eric raised his glass. "To us, best friends, and a perfect wedding."

Beth leaned in and kissed him. "Best toast ever. I promise, nothing will stand in our way."

Chapter 10 ▶ White House, Washington D.C.

Wednesday, 10 April, 8 a.m.
Isabel entered the Oval Office. "Good morning, Madam President."

Dani moved to the facing couches and sat. "What's the good news?"

Isabel settled into the opposite couch. "You're not going to like it," she said. "Not because you've heard it all before, but because it is going to be a huge factor if you're planning to be elected to a full term in office."

"I have the new figures." Isabel handed her a sheet of paper. "As you can see, joblessness is up. The corporate sector has not bought into our work on climate change initiatives."

Dani said, "Can't they see higher temperatures and extreme weather are affecting the entire work force's initiative, commitment, and focus?"

Isabel said, "They can see it, they just don't want to be taxed for it or make corporate changes to cut their carbon footprint. They're responsible to their bottom line and investor dividends."

Dani said, "If corporations fail to address the inevitable consequences to their increasing air, water, and earth pollution, they will be responsible for the death of millions, who used to be their customers. Profits will fade and the corporations will close. Why can't they see they are forcing a recession from which there is no return?"

Isabel said, "I've got a team working on strategies."

Dani nodded. "Will the budget address them?"

Isabel shook her head. "My sources say Congress is unwilling to increase the national debt or decrease military spending. Given inflation, they will, in effect, be decreasing funding across the board."

"Unacceptable."

"Unavoidable."

"I'm the President. Set up meetings with congressional leaders. This calls for some serious arm-twisting. Also, get me list of top business leaders with global influence. Finally, I want my team in here to figure out the best approach for positive outcomes. This may be our Zero hour."

"I'll get right on it." Isabel rose to leave.

"Wait," Dani said. "Has the FBI stopped the march in Kryller?"

Isabel looked down and shifted from one foot to the other. "They can't."

Dani jumped to her feet, fists at her side.

Isabel raised her hand, palm out. "Please don't yell at the messenger."

Her hands relaxed. "You're right. What's the problem?"

"Freedom of speech and right to assemble."

"White supremacists are domestic terrorists."

"Well, actually, and you know this, it did not pass the Senate. It is coming up again for a vote next month. Therefore, there can't be an arrest until there is an act of violence."

"I want to see the Director."

"He's going to tell you the same thing."

"Send him in. I want him to tell it to me to my face. I will not take 'no' for an answer."

"Yes, ma'am."

Dani said, "On your way out, please find Yosef and send him in."

Yosef Hassan, ex-military intelligence, walked in with confidence and a radiant smile. "Madam President."

"Nice coverage on 60 Minutes on your journey to the White House and bravery in apprehending the late President's murderer."

Yosef said, "The whole incident brings me no joy."

"You've made your position very clear. Good job." Dani grabbed her jacket and said, "Let's go outside for a walk."

Surrounded by secret service, they went into the garden.

Dani said, "In afterhours private discussions with the Senate and House leaders, we have agreed on an encompassing agenda supporting human rights on all levels. Passage is not going to be quick or easy."

Yosef said, "Yes, I'm aware."

Dani said, "I want to know who the unrest's true leaders and backers are in order to dispatch a covert operation to ensure the legislation passes."

"The FBI is your best bet."

"I don't want to bring this up to investigation status until I know more so my directive is comprehensive."

Yosef said, "Let me do the research and get back to you as soon as I have something."

They resumed walking. "Let's keep this under the radar."

"Are you thinking the late President's enemies are also your own?"

"Yes. We must be careful at all times."

Dani's private phone rang. She pulled it out of her pocket and looked at the ID and then at Yosef.

"I've got to take this. It's the twins."

He nodded, "I'll be in touch," and left.

Alone, she said, "Hello, guys."

"Mom, you're on speaker phone because we couldn't agree on who should tell you first so we're going to tell you together because otherwise you may get the wrong idea and say we can't when we want you..."

"Stop. Brevity when I'm at work."

Ivan, "You know how you said we could get our learner's permit at sixteen."

Isaac said, "She knows what she said. Let me talk."

"No, I've got this."

"Are you kidding? Get..."

"Boys, tick tock."

Isaac said, "Our security detail just offered to teach us."

"No."

Ivan said, "They promised to take us to a secure...what?"

"No."

The twins, in unison, said, "But Dad said..."

"What? You can't drive until you finish college or until I'm no longer President. You know that. It's in your Security Handbook." She ended the call. Another came in.

Dani looked at the ID and answered.

Terence, her husband, spoke before she could utter a word. "Did you really say no? They're sixteen and they'd be with their security detail."

"If we say yes, driving will dominate every conversation."

He said, "We're going to have to talk strategy. I happen to know they are all over the internet and picking out cars."

"They can't have a car until I leave the White House."

"Did you restate the handbook? I don't think their unformed brains remember anything adversely affecting their intended goals. Especially when money is no object. They're making a fortune programming for Chris Gregory. They don't need us."

Dani said, "They get a few bucks a month. The rest goes to their college fund, over which I have control. It's not a secret."

"It bears repeating. Tonight. At dinner." Terence said. "In fact, every night until they accept the truth."

Dani said, "Good. You're in charge of car conversations. I don't want to worry about them."

"Okay. Got it. I'll handle it. No cars."

Chapter 11 ▶ Chicago, Illinois

Wednesday, 10 April, 10:30 a.m.
Dressed in jeans, white T-shirt, and leather jacket,
Eric, wearing his aviator sunglasses, leaned against
his rental car and made a call. "Hey, Beth."

"Hey, yourself. I've been waiting for your
update."

"Using my private eye alter ego, I've been to
several men, women, and family shelters, and the
story is the same. Tavius Global supports them with
money and security. In return, the company gets to
see who's worth recruiting. If they find someone, a
Tavius Global manager sets up the interview and, if
all goes well, brings them to their new home."

Beth said, "Does it all appear above board?"

"Everyone Tavius Global takes from Chicago
shelters is assigned to the Chicago facility, so there's
no crossing state lines. Once the people are
employees, the company is free to assign them to any
facility."

"Eric, did you talk about money? What's the pay
scale?"

"Have no idea. However, I do have the brochure which makes working at Tavius look and sound like a perpetual stay at Disney World. Hell, I may leave the FBI and apply."

"Don't you dare," Beth said. "What do you plan to do now?"

"Good question. The Tavius Global people know the FBI is looking for Santiago. They allowed the Chicago team to hold interviews with her neighbors and co-workers."

"Do you know if they were at her workplace and in her living quarters?"

Eric pulled out his notes. "Our agents were confined to a small conference room in the visitor's center."

"Did they try to inspect the site?"

Eric flipped a couple of pages. "They requested access but were denied unless they had a warrant."

"The place we need to see is the Kansas facility and interview the Winnie Santiago **living** there."

"The problem is, getting a warrant would require specifics, which we don't have because we can't prove a crime was committed. They could claim the photo we have is not Santiago and the person in Kansas is."

"Maybe we're focusing on the wrong problem."

"Yeah, maybe. Still, we don't have enough to get warrant."

"We might have if we could get a look at Tavius Global's taxes."

Eric laughed. "I bet you've just solved our problem. We can get them for tax evasion."

Beth said, "No so fast. Proving it would require seeing their books, which would give us access to employees present and transferred."

Eric stepped away from the car. "Which would set up the murder investigation."

Beth said, "Get back here. We need to figure this out."

"On my way."

He turned to walk around the car to the driver's side when he saw them coming. Two men wearing security jackets bore down on him. Eric slid across the hood, opened the driver's door, and glided behind the wheel. Before he could lock them out, one grabbed the door handle, and the other pulled him out.

"Sir, may we have a word?"

Eric straightened and adjusted his glasses and jacket. "You're going to have to make an appointment." He handed him his Johnson's Private Investigations business card. "I've got to get to a client." He tried to turn back to his car. A man blocked him.

"Yeah, right," the security guy said. "Call your client and cancel. Tavius Global needs your expertise now."

Eric reached for his phone.

"Forget it. Let's go."

A black SUV pulled up. Eric couldn't see inside the darkened windows.

The security guy opened the door and said, "Get in."

The other one walked around the SUV and got in.

Eric, squashed between the two men, said, "Where're we going?"

The man on his left said, "Somebody wants to talk to you."

The car stopped in front of a massive gate. Once it opened, it proceeded around a traffic circle, and stopped in front of a building emblazoned with "Tavius Global Industries."

"Get out." The security team pulled Eric from the car and escorted him to the top floor and through a set of glass doors.

The secretary looked up and said, "He's waiting for you."

One man opened the oak door and the other brought Eric into the room. "Mr. Octavius, sir, meet Special Agent Eric Jerrod."

Behind a large polished desk, sat the owner and CEO of Tavius Global Industries.

Eric noted the man's silver cropped hair, gaunt square-jawed face, dark eyes, and aquiline nose.

Octavius said, "Leave us," to security, and "Sit down," to Eric.

Eric didn't move. He gave himself a chance to look around the room, smell the leather upholstery, eye the expensive furniture, notice the missing personal touches, and appreciate the entire wall of glass facing Lake Michigan. He finished assessing the room and returned the gaze of the man seated before him. "Mr. Octavius, why have your people kidnapped me?"

"Special Agent Jerrod, you were escorted here. Please sit."

Eric remained standing. The micro-changes in Octavius's face telegraphed annoyance.

Octavius leaned back in his chair. "While you posed as a private detective, we knew who you were minutes after you entered the first homeless shelter. We have the best facial recognition system in the world."

"I still don't know why I'm here."

"Tell me why you made the rounds of our shelter projects today."

"I am working on two missing persons cases."

"What do they have to do with Tavius Global?"

"I'm not sure. Your people did not allow FBI agents to investigate on site. I'm digging deeper into the backgrounds of those missing."

Octavius said, "We do not abide interruptions, FBI or otherwise. Life here is about schedules."

"FBI investigations are a priority. I can assure you, warrants are being prepared."

"I see no need for legal action." Octavius stood.

Eric did all he could to remain impassive when he realized Octavius's suit, a Brioni Vanquish II, was the same one actor Daniel Craig wore as James Bond.

Octavius said, "Perhaps I can help," with a hint of a smile to project his agreeability.

Eric decided to test the waters. "Great. I'd like to speak to Winnie Santiago's friends and co-workers."

"Is she missing?"

"She is one of our cases."

Octavius pushed a button and said, "Bring me the Santiago folder."

Seconds later, Octavius had the file in his hand. Eric said, "Efficient."

Octavius didn't even look up. Instead, he reviewed the information and handed it to Eric. "She seems to be well and working at our Kansas installation."

Eric opened the file. The picture paper-clipped to the employee data sheet wasn't the one Winnie Santiago sent the FBI. "I see. I'd like to interview her friends and co-workers here and meet with Mrs. Santiago in Kansas so I can close this case."

"You want access to both sites?"

"Of course, otherwise how do I get the information?"

"As I said before, our facilities are designed to protect the rights of all our employees. Outsiders are not allowed beyond the Welcome Center."

Eric said, "I'm not an outsider. I'm FBI. I work for you."

"An outsider to the company." Octavius walked over to the window, his back to Eric. "My people will take you back to your vehicle."

Eric said. "I'll be back with a warrant."

Octavius smiled. "If you can get one."

Chapter 12 ▶ Harrison, New York

Wednesday, 10 April, 10:30 a.m.
Lucy Kilmer was a free woman since her parole and year of supervision ended. No more FBI check-ins or check-ups. Her life returned to normal. Business flourished. She had a top-drawer list of clients and every seduction challenged her. She loved the stimulation and her ever-growing bank balance.

She emerged from her after-work-out shower and heard the chime—a work call. The message said, "Check the video."

Lucy fired up her computer and watched the news feed.

"I'm standing here, in front of a family homeless shelter in Chicago and talking with the manager who says shelters in the area are being investigated by the FBI."

The woman said, "Yes, they came in undercover and asked about our residents."

"Were you alarmed?"

"Of course. We are very careful to keep the information about the people who stay here private."

"Did the FBI say why they were investigating you?"

"They, and I mean one very specific agent, Special Agent Eric Jerrod, wanted to know about Winn – I mean a specific woman and implied we were selling our residents."

The reporter's hand-held microphone started to shake. "What do you mean by the word 'selling?'"

"You know, letting area businesses buy them to work at their facilities."

The reporter said, "Are they?"

The manager laughed. "Don't be silly. This is the U. S. of A. We don't do human trafficking in this country. The whole idea is preposterous."

The reporter didn't laugh. "This country has done slavery."

The manager said, "Another time. Another place. The FBI is clearly overstepping its authority."

"How?"

"The Chicago area shelters are here to serve the people. To give aid and comfort, housing, and food to the many who have been rendered homeless by forces they could not control. We are proud to be a community service, supported by the community. We are transparent in our operations and do not need the disruption caused by unnecessary government interference."

Lucy closed the computer. Eric Jerrod and Winnie Santiago almost mentioned in the same sentence. Couldn't be good. How did he connect with her? How did the shelter manager know? She thought it through. The manager had to be a Tavius Global plant. Eric must have gotten too close to the truth and Octavius planted this news story to shut down anyone who knew anything and might help unravel the Santiago transfer.

Under contract with Tavius Global, Lucy's seduction team arranged the transfer of the Santiago family. They did the pick-up and followed protocol.

Lucy muttered, "No way Eric will ever find out what happened."

To satisfy any doubt, Lucy called Ultan. "Any problems with the last seduction transfer?"

"Why do you ask?"

"There's an inquiry."

"They'll find nothing."

"Which team did you use?"

"All our teams, including you, were in operations. I used our first back-up, the Ninja. I have the documentation if you'd like to review it."

"No, I trust you. Just tell me, did the Ninja follow our protocols?"

"Yes. Winnie Santiago is gone and untraceable."

Chapter 13 ▶ White House, Washington D.C.

Thursday, 11 April. 9 a.m.

Dani focused on Yosef's report which he'd sent to her phone. The systemic undermining of her administration ran deeper than she thought. She'd have to take care of it or risk losing the upcoming election.

Isabel stood in front of the desk and cleared her throat. "Ahem. Madam President."

Dani jerked her head up and put the phone in her pocket. "Sorry, I didn't hear you come in."

"I have updates for you. Peter has landed safely in Anchorage."

"Good. What else?"

"The head of immigrant resettlement is sending a team to Kryller as well as the other resettlement communities to work out any issues with farm and people management, as well as community integration. All future reports will reflect onsite evaluations."

Dani said, "Anything else?"

"Here's a list and summary of bills coming up in the House and Senate. We'll discuss them at this afternoon's meeting. Let us know your priorities and our marching orders."

"Thank you, Isabel. I'll get on this right away."

Dani's private phone vibrated as Isabel left the Oval Office. She looked at the ID and took the call. "Octavius."

"Dani, I've got the FBI investigating my Chicago and Kansas City operations. Make a call and stop this arrogant intrusion into my business."

"What are they investigating?"

"One of my employees transferred to Kansas. An FBI investigator said he had reason to believe she didn't make it despite my proof she did."

"Why are you concerned?"

"My company cannot be, won't be, distracted by a fraudulent investigation which will disrupt operations and cast a shadow over my brand."

"The FBI are just doing their job. I don't see the problem. They're discreet. It happens all the time."

"Not to me it doesn't," Octavius said. "Dani, I run a multi-national conglomeration which requires a delicate allocation of resources. An investigation would have far-reaching consequences. In the end, it will wind up affecting me, you, the cartel, and the global economy. This is not something I should have to explain to you."

"I needed to clarify the problem in order to handle it from my end."

"No investigation. Take care of it."

The line went dead.

Dani looked at her phone. How dare Octavius talk down to her. They were equals. Wealthy. Powerful. Decisive. Controlling the global economy together. *He just talked to me like I was the manager of his government operations, not the United States' President. He just went too far.*

Dani pressed the button on her intercom. "Vicky, get me the FBI Director on the phone."

Less than two minutes later she spoke to the director.

Dani said, "I understand there is an investigation targeting Tavius Global. I have spoken to the CEO, and they are handling the issue internally."

The director said, "I'll take care of it, Madam President."

"Find out who initiated interest in Tavius Global and let me know."

"Right away."

Dani ended the call and leaned back in her chair. Octavius was the most meticulous man she'd ever met. He never asked anyone for anything. This investigation touched a nerve. He didn't call her out of anger—he called her out of fear.

Her personal phone vibrated again. She checked the ID and answered, "Hi, Peter."

"Ma'am, this is Sam Reynolds, from the State Department, Peter's friend."

"What's wrong? Where's Peter? Is he alright?"

"He is okay. We are at the Anchorage Regional Hospital. Peter fell and suffered a severe concussion. He initially lost consciousness but is awake now. The hospital has been great. They did x-rays, stitched the gash, and stabilized him."

"I'll order a plane and medical team to bring you both back to Walter Reed. Do you need anything else?"

"That'll do it."

"Stay with him."

"I won't leave his side."

"Good. See you both very soon."

Dani ran to the door, swung it open. Her staff froze. Dani said, "I want a medical team and plane to escort Peter Powell and Sam Reynolds from Alaska Regional to Walter Reed immediately. Peter's been hurt."

Her staff sprang into action and initiated the airlift. Now, Dani froze.

Isabel approached and whispered in her ear, "Come on, Dani. It's done. Elmendorf Air Force Base is in Anchorage. They'll make sure Peter gets home safely and as soon as humanly possible."

Dani nodded.

Isabel turned to Vicky. "Get tea, coffee, and snacks brought up asap." Vicky nodded and picked up the phone. To Dani, she said, "Come on. Let's go sit down. I'll call and check on progress. I know you'll feel better once Peter is in the air."

Dani nodded and allowed Isabel to lead her into the Oval Office. She sat down and stood up again. "Where's my phone?"

Isabel pointed to Dani's hand.

"I've got to call Sybil."

"Why don't you wait until we know when he'll arrive in D.C. We can arrange for her to be here. No need to worry her until then."

The kitchen staff arrived and placed the tray on the coffee table. Isabel thanked them and offered coffee or tea to Dani.

Dani stood and put her hand up. "No need to fuss. I'm okay. I've come to rely a lot on Peter and..."

"You don't have to explain. We've all be there."

Dani looked at the time. "We have a meeting soon, right. I haven't had a chance..."

"I'll reschedule. You sit down and relax. Have something to eat before you jump back into work."

Dani nodded. "Okay. You win. I can use some down time."

Less than fifteen minutes later, Terence arrived. "Isabel called me. Are you okay?"

"I'm fine. What are you doing here?"

"Isabel called me and told me what happened."

"I overreacted."

"You? Not possible."

Dani laughed. "I'm glad you're here."

"I've also got an update from Isabel," Terence said. "Peter's expected to land in D.C. around 11:30 tonight. He'll be immediately transported to Walter Reed. You'll be able to see him there."

"Good."

"Isabel is very organized."

Dani smiled. "It's why I keep her around."

"Food looks good. May I join you?"

Dani said, "Don't you usually eat with Bruce, your preferred partner?"

Terence shot her a look. "Don't go there. I care about you."

"Sure. Dig in. I've got to call my aunt." Dani used her phone. "Hi, Sybil."

"Dani, how nice to hear from you."

"Sybil, I've heard from Peter."

"In Alaska?"

"Yes," Dani said. "He's okay and recovering from a bad fall."

"I can leave for Anchorage in an hour."

"Not necessary, he's coming here. I'll have a helicopter waiting for you at the New York heliport at three this afternoon. Come down, stay with me, and we'll go visit him together as soon as he arrives."

Sybil said, "I will. See you soon."

Dani put her phone down.

Terence said, "Good. I'll meet her when she arrives. Get her settled. We'll see you at dinner." He took a bite of a sandwich.

Dani picked up a cup of coffee, took a sip, and looked at Terence. "Can I ask you a question?"

He nodded. "Go ahead."

"What do you know about Tavius Global Industries?"

"I'm a lawyer. I know everything about anything. You'll have to be more specific."

"What have you heard about their business model?"

"Tavius Global is dedicated to modeling a new work environment where the company cares for the workers and addresses their basic needs. Their premise says stress-free healthy workers are more productive, use their time efficiently, and, per person, reduce management and HR personnel. In other words, lean and profitable."

"That's the PR. Do you know if it's working? Have there been any outside studies?"

Terence leaned toward Dani. "What's got your interest and why?"

Dani leaned toward Terence. "You don't know the answer, do you?"

Terence smiled and sat back. "Not a thing. However, I'll do some discreet research."

Dani shook her head. "Not you. I can't have this come back to me."

Terence stood. "I have resources. No one will know. Don't worry."

As he walked out the door, Dani said to his back, "Not you!"

He waved without turning. "See you at dinner."

She knew in an instant she'd made a mistake.

Chapter 14 ▶ Gramercy Avenue, New York City

Thursday, 11 April, 11 a.m.
Rachel finished typing and leaned back in her chair. Zeus, on the floor by her side, raised his head. She looked down into his soulful eyes and smiled.
"You're right. I've been working all morning and it's time for a break."
Zeus whined.
"What do you think? A little lunch and a walk?"
Zeus jumped to his feet, tail wagging, and put his head on her lap.
Rachel gave him scritches behind his ears followed by a big kiss on the top of his head. "Come on. Let's go."
Zeus emitted a few whuffs and backed up. Rachel stood, stretched, and walked down the spiral staircase with Zeus beside her. Two-thirds of the way down, she paused when she saw Chris, phone to his ear, standing in by the windows, and silhouetted by sunlight.

Her heartbeat accelerated. That guy was her guy. Baby or not, she couldn't be happier.

At the bottom of the staircase, she walked up behind him and captured his body in an embrace. Chris put his hand over her forearms while he finished his call. He put his phone away and twisted to face her. "Everything okay?"

Rachel nodded. "Taking a break."

He hugged her. "Breaks can be fun."

She lifted her chin and they kissed. "You know what?"

"I'll bite. What?"

"We should go on vacation."

He laughed. "Our whole life is a vacation."

"No, really. Engage in some 'just us' time. In a different place with no demands."

He kissed her neck, behind her ear. "I'd call this 'us time.'"

Zeus whined and dropped to the floor.

Chris said, "What's up with him?"

"I promised him lunch and a walk."

Chris straightened and leaned back. "Good. I'll come. We'll get something to eat while we're out."

"What happened to 'just us'?"

"Zeus guilted me."

Rachel laughed. "You are such a pushover." She kissed him, grabbed his hand, and said, "Let's go."

Zeus bounded to the door, his tail wagging his body, before they'd even taken a step.

Chris said, "Wait. Did you check the tides?"

Rachel nodded. "We're at low tide. The streets should be dry."

Chris shook his head. "I don't know what's taking so long. The East Side is far more vulnerable than the West Side. The flood control structures should have been done by now."

"No politics. Let's go and have a nice lunch, come back, and nap afterwards."
He smiled and opened the door as Rachel put on Zeus's service dog jacket and leash. He said, "I love afternoon naps," put his arm around her, "with you."

"Rachel, are you listening?"

"Uh, sorry. I disappeared into the mural."

"Huh?"

"I never noticed it before. It makes the Mediterranean look like the top item on anyone's bucket list."

"Okay. You win. Let's talk vacation."

Rachel looked at him. "Seriously? Sometimes I can't tell if you mean it or not."

"How about Chicago and Lake Michigan?"

"How about Greece and the Mediterranean?"

"I'm going to Chicago. Why don't you come with me? You can shop the Miracle Mile. We can book a suite overlooking Lake Michigan and stay for the weekend. Sample all the five-star restaurants and maybe an improv show."

"Why are you going to Chicago?"

"C'mon Rachel. Just say 'yes.'" He took her hand in his and smiled his sexy smile, the one he knew made her heart sing.

She fell for it every time. "Yes. Of course."

He kissed her. "Now for my favorite dessert."

"Not so fast. What's going on in Chicago?"

"I've got a meeting with Octavius, head of Tavius Global Enterprises."

"A client?"

"Not yet. He's interested in my ultra-thin subcutaneous personal microchip tracker."

"For his entire empire?"

Chris laughed. "I won't know until I talk to him."

"You know I hate those SPMTs. However, this time, I promise to keep my mouth shut if you can arrange an executive tour of his complex for us."

"You want to walk around an industrial complex rather than be ready for me when I get back to the hotel?"

"Don't you want to see why he wants or needs your device?"

"Stop the bullshit, Rachel. Why the interest?"

"You know my new book is about workers' rights. Tavius Global is claiming to be pioneering an employee and environment friendly twenty-four-seven worker campus."

"I'm sure it's all online."

"It's not. Not one single article by a non-Tavius Global employed reporter. The glowing reviews are all internally generated. I want to see for myself. If this Octavius person has figured out the optimal situation, it should withstand outside scrutiny."

"As in you?"

"Yes, since the opportunity presents itself."

"This is sounding less and less like a vacation with a lake view."

"Chris, how long could it take? An hour? Maybe two? It's just us."

He rolled his eyes. "You're lucky I love you so much I can't say no."

She put her hand over his, licked her lips, and peered through her lashes. "Don't worry." Rachel lowered her voice. "I promise to make our post Tavius Global tour vacation not just good -- unforgettable."

"Check please."

Chapter 15 ▶ Federal Building, New York City

Thursday, 11 April, 12 p.m.
Beth walked into her office and found Eric at his desk, on the phone. She held up two handled paper bags and mouthed the word, 'Lunch.' She dropped one in front of him and took the other to her desk. She tried not to eavesdrop, even though Eric's voice seemed to get louder and angrier by the minute, until it got very soft and he ended the conversation. He turned to her. "I can't fucking believe it."

Beth said, "Tell me."

"Our warrant request for an on-site Tavius Global inspection has been denied. I explained in excruciating detail the importance of following up on a murder or, at best, a kidnapping across state lines."

"Our information could be a prank."

"When I sat in front of Octavius, he snapped his fingers and his secretary produced Santiago's folder before he could open his hand. He expected me and made sure the information contradicted anything Winnie Santiago could have written."

"Wait. Made sure? How could he know? In fact, he could be right."

Eric said, "He's not. When does the head of a corporation send his henchmen to force an investigator to have a sit-down in corporate headquarters with him so he can say there's no problem?" Eric poked in finger in the air. "'We've got a problem, Houston.'"

Beth nodded. "I agree. Did they say why we couldn't have a warrant?"

"No, they didn't. I tried to get clarification. They said 'no' to everything with a final order to leave Tavius Global alone."

"In those words?"

Eric took a breath. "What?"

"Did they use those exact words—'leave Tavius Global alone?'"

He thought a moment and nodded.

She said, "Meaning what?"

"Good question."

Beth's phone rang. She looked at the ID. As she said, "Good afternoon, Director" She looked at Eric, never taking her eyes off him while she listened. "We'll be there." She put the phone down. "We've been ordered to meet with the President."

Eric said, "I guess we'll get our answer."

Beth and Eric entered the outer lobby of the Oval Office.

Isabel introduced herself and said, "Follow me. The President will be with you in a few minutes." She led them into the Oval Office. "Please make yourself at home."

Beth and Eric walked in, and the door shut behind them.

"Quite the nice living room arrangement," Eric said, ambling over to the closest of two couches. "Do you think we should sit?"

"I don't know. It feels strange to hang out without the President."

"Do you think she'll remember us?"

"My red hair and your green eyes. How could she forget?"

Eric smiled. "I don't know, but you always make an impression on me."

Beth laughed.

A door opened.

The FBI Special Agents stood at attention.

Dani entered, saw them, and smiled. "You're Chris and Rachel's friends." She shook their hands. "I met you at their wedding.?"

Beth said, "Yes, ma'am."

Dani said, "Before we begin, I want you to know I've asked you here because I don't want anything we discuss to be repeated. I am, as you must know, working with the corporate community and I don't want to be identified as interfering with their turf. I need them on board for our environmental and worker initiatives."

Beth said, "I understand."

Dani smiled, "Now, please sit and explain why you're interested in Tavius Global."

Over the next few minutes, Beth told Dani about Winnie Santiago, and Eric told her about his research into the shelters and his meeting with Octavius. He ended with his last conversation with the FBI director.

Dani said, "I'm the one who asked for the investigation to stop. Octavius is a personal acquaintance, a huge donor, and claims to hold the key to restructuring the modern manufacturing workplace."

Beth said, "How does our investigation into a missing person change anything?"

"It puts doubt on the company and questions its ability to take care of its business and employees."

"It's a moot point if nothing's wrong and it's just a mix-up or prank."

Eric said, "The warrant I requested was for access to her records and her workplace to confirm there was a Winnie Santiago in Chicago and then go to Kansas, meet with her, and confirm the transfer."

Dani said, "Doubting Octavius's word."

Eric said, "I believe he put his faith in the document he read, trusting his staff completely. However, my experience says don't trust a piece of paper unless the information can be validated."

Dani said, "I'm sorry. My order stands."

Beth said, "Please. We have concerns. Santiago may be the only missing person case we've heard about, but not the only person missing."

Eric said, "Exactly. If it happened to be the first time an employee transfer went sideways, the company would have been happy to have us help find their missing person."

Beth said, "Madam President, no one is above the law."

Dani stood up and walked around the room, stopping behind the couch facing Beth and Eric. "What is your current case load?"

Beth said, "I monitor my agents in the National Missing Persons Division. Neither Eric nor I are working a specific case right now."

"Good. I want you to work this as a special project for me. There must be other ways to investigate without raising any red flags. I will let Octavius know the FBI has been stopped for now."

Beth said, "If we go poking into Tavius Global business, and he is as powerful as he seems, he will know."

Dani said, "I agree. However, I'm working on including our mega corporations in a strategic plan to end the stalemate on job and climate initiatives. Collecting data on invited members would be imperative if I'm to make my point. You two are going to be my researchers. Who knows what you may, or may not, turn up?"

Beth looked at Eric and stood up. "We will draw up a strategy and get it to you within the next two days."

"Perfect. I will invite the CEOs and have the meeting set by the time you get back to me. As long as no one is singled out and the same information is required for all, we have no dilemma."

Beth said, "Thank you, Ma'am."

Dani smiled. "I appreciate your cooperation on this. I'll have an office prepared for you. Wesley Warren is head of security. He and Isabel will help you any way they can. In fact, I'll have her find you accommodations close by."

Eric said, "Thank you, ma'am."

Dani pulled out her phone, tapped it, and put it away. Isabel knocked and opened the door. "Isabel, get the information you need from Beth and Eric to arrange for them to join us for a few weeks. Also, let the FBI director know they are on assignment here and to call me if there are any problems."

Isabel said, "Consider it done." She nodded at Beth and Eric. "Come with me."

As they were leaving, Dani said, "See you in two days."

Chapter 16 ▶ White House, Washington D.C.

Thursday, 11 April, 3 p.m.
Dani's Cabinet meeting lasted longer than she'd hoped. She heard the helicopter blades whirring outside--thwup, thwup, thwup, got out of her seat, and walked over to the windows. She watched the chopper land, and Terence, being his gallant self, stride across the lawn to meet Sybil. She trusted him to make her aunt comfortable. He had been very accommodating since she found out his secretary, Bruce, had taken her place in his affections. Their agreement was for him to stick it out with the family during her presidency. Afterwards, he'd divorce her and marry Bruce.

Her attention returned to the meeting. "Is there anything else open for discussion?" Looking around the table, eyes met hers briefly. She heard indistinct murmurings.

Dani let them squirm for a few seconds before she said, "Please keep your seats. As for the media, thank you for the coverage. Please leave us."

When the room cleared, she said, "I am going to spend the next two weeks in a hard, and I'm sure, tortuous road to ensure consensus on jobs and climate action with the House, Senate, and big business. I, or my office, will be requesting information from your agencies. Please provide it as a matter of course.

"You may contact me to confirm if you are in doubt. However, you are not to argue, block, or delay requests. You and your staff are to treat them as routine, and this request is not to be the subject of discussion or gossip outside the necessary lines of communication."

Dani stood. "I must have complete and accurate confidential information at my fingertips to encourage cooperation and break the stalemate decimating this country and countries around the world."

She looked around the table, establishing eye contact with each cabinet member. Done, she said, "Any questions?"

"Madam President," her predecessor's Secretary of the Interior said, leaning back in his chair with an "I know better than you" informal attitude. "I'm uncomfortable with your 'no questions asked' request. Every file contains confidential information, so I'd like to review your planned security process."

She stiffened, raised her chin, and looked down her nose at him. She raised an eyebrow and sharpened her tone. In her best "don't fuck with me" voice, she said, "Are you questioning my authority or integrity?"

The man flushed and sat up straight. "No, ma'am." He gulped and cleared his throat. "I'll personally bring whatever files you request whenever you want them."

She softened and smiled. "Excellent. Thank you, everyone, for your support and leadership."

All the members stood as she left the room, Isabel trailing behind her.

Isabel said, "Sybil is upstairs in your private quarters. Peter's plane is on schedule. Beth and Eric are all set. I'll have lists and strategies ready for you first thing in the morning. Have I missed anything?"

"Let Wes know Peter needs an escort from the airport to the hospital. I'll want to leave here with my family when the plane lands so I can be at Walter Reed when Peter arrives."

"I'll take care of it."

"Thank you, Isabel. I'll call if anything else comes up."

Isabel turned and Dani continued to the elevator and went up to her private quarters. She entered the living room and embraced Sybil. "I'm so glad you got here safe and sound."

Sybil said, "Have you heard anything?"

"They're in the air. We still have a few hours."

<~<~|~>~>

Dani, Sybil, Terence, and the boys arrived at the hospital at ten o'clock. Peter had a room assignment, but he wasn't there yet. The doctors insisted on a thorough admissions evaluation. The waiting seemed interminable until Sam joined them in the executive waiting area. "Everything's fine. Peter slept through the entire trip. He's awake and with the docs."

Sybil said, "I want to see him."

"Soon, I promise."

Dani said, "Will you tell us what happened?"

"Of course," Sam said. He pulled up a chair and told the story to the semi-circle of faces. "Peter and I, along with Ari, a scientist from Harim Labs, were in Anchorage, ready to drive to our destination, when a couple of vehicles blocked our path. A man with a weathered face walked up to us and thrust a card into my hand. It read: 'I represent the Inupaiq (ee-NYOOP-ee-ak), Village of White Bear, Bering Straits coast. Village elder, Tulok, extends invitation to visit.'

"He said, 'Come with me. Our people are sick. Our food is poisoned. Our home is disappearing. Help us.' I told him we had plans, but Peter wanted to go. So, our plans changed. We followed the Inupaiq vehicles to an airstrip less than fifteen minutes away, loaded our gear into a puddle-jumper and took a cramped, bumpy, three-hour trip to White Bear, Alaska.

"After we landed and unloaded our stuff, Tulok greeted us and apologized. He said, 'I am sorry for the kidnapping. I had to get your attention. Our community is desperate.

No one at the State Department or any other government agency wants to talk to an Inupaiq about climate change.' He waved his hands in the air, "No more business," and invited us to his home for dinner.

"The car-ride resembled a rollercoaster. Formerly straight roads buckled. The warming has exacerbated the upper permafrost cycle of freezing and melting. The ground shifts in every season. Government won't pay to fix the problems because they are never ending. Everyone on the peninsula is terrified they'll be cut off.

"Still, the view was amazing. As the road curved down to the village, we could see the Bering Straits. The buildings, no more than two stories, looked like the road. Some are straight, some tilt, some have cracked, and some have just collapsed.

"Every destroyed house leaves a family homeless. I asked about FEMA or government relief funds. Tulok said, 'We are considered Native Americans and not eligible for money. The insurance people say nothing built on permafrost is insurable.'

"After dinner, we went outside. The sea's saltwater smell permeated the warm air."

Sam paused and pulled out his phone. "Here, I'll show you."

Swipe. A fence askew and broken by heaving and freezing ground.

Swipe. A row of town houses split in two, one section higher than the other.

Swipe. An imploded tin roof structure.

Swipe. The distorted road.

Swipe. The General Store built on piles with extra shoring to offset the shifting ground.

Swipe. A gray barn-like structure balanced on the crest of an undercut cliff across the cove.

Swipe. The waves crashing against the earthen walls.

Sam said, "The piercing shrieks as metal tore and twisted like paper sounded like torture."

Swipe. The wreck fell into the sea.

Swipe. A large piece of precipice followed.

Dani said, "It is beautiful country. I had no idea the coastal Alaskan villages were in such dire straits. I have a feeling my agencies are protecting their budgets or using the money for other purposes. I'll make a mental note to check this out."

Sybil said, "What about Peter?"

Sam said, "He was walking around the peninsula's edge, undercut by the waves. Tulok shouted at him to move back. Peter waved his hands and pointed to the beach about 20 feet below him and half-way between us. I ran to him until I saw the mastodon tusk sticking out from sandy beach. I stopped to look. At that moment, Peter toppled over the edge and lay spread-eagle on the beach below."

Sybil audibly sucked in air and covered her mouth with her hands.

Sam reached out to her. "He's going to be okay. I know it. The Inupaiq were great. They did first aid, strapped him to a stretcher, and flew us back to Anchorage. We were met by an ambulance and taken to the hospital. We came here as soon as he was stabilized."

Sybil said, "How is he?"

Before Sam could answer, they all heard stretcher wheels rumbling in the hallway.

Everyone stood. Sybil ran to Peter. The stretcher halted. She said, "I'm going with him to the room. Give us a few minutes." The stretcher resumed its journey with Sybil holding her son's hand.

Terence said, "I'm taking the boys to the cafeteria. They need a break. This is pretty intense."

Dani watched them go and turned to Sam. "Is Peter going to be okay?"

Sam nodded. "He regained consciousness while I was with him. Doctors said he lost a lot of blood and has delayed cognitive responses. Doctors were conservatively optimistic. Peter's a fighter. He'll be fine."

Dani looked at him.

Sam said, "Promise."

Dani said, "Now, the truth about the Inupaiq."

Sam said, "I have to admit it's worse than I described. There's no running water on the island. Community is a real thing. No one wants to leave without everyone."

"Did you find out how much it would cost to move the village?"

Sam said, "Tulok said somewhere in the two hundred-thousand-dollar range."

"Not outrageous."

"It is to the state when dealing with indigenous peoples."

Dani said, "Please send me a picture of the business card the Inupaiq gave you. I will see what I can do to expedite a relocation plan for all the affected communities."

"Remember, they would rather die together than leave separately."

"I will. I won't forget," Dani said. "I'm going to Peter's room."

"Okay. I'll wait here for Terence."

Dani walked down the hall and turned when she saw Sybil standing with a doctor. Dani approached and said, "How's he doing?"

Sybil dabbed at her eyes with a tissue.

The doctor said, "He's been well taken care of. We have to watch him over the upcoming weeks to see how fast his brain heals from the trauma. We'll know more then."

The doctor left and Dani hugged Sybil. "He'll be fine. He has to bc fine."

Sybil stepped back. "Of course, he has to be fine. He's all I've got."

Dani said, "He's all we've got. He's the family business's CEO."

Chapter 17 ▶ Tavius Global, Chicago, Il

Friday, 12 April, 10 a.m.
Rachel and Chris, accompanied by Zeus, walked into their suite at their 5-star lake-view lodgings on South Michigan Avenue, Chicago, at eleven o'clock in the morning. Zeus plopped down in a sunny spot by the windows, placing his head on his paws.

Rachel said, "This is beautiful."

Chris said, "As promised." The bellboy brought the suitcases in, and Chris tipped him. "We have to leave here by 12:30. It's a short trip to Tavius Global on the map. Traffic could double the time."

"Are we set for the tour?"

"Yep. All arranged. You'll get to see all the innovations mentioned in the brochure and press releases."

"I'm excited. This could be the industrial-worker breakthrough the world is waiting for." She put her suitcase on the luggage rack between the dresser and the closet.

Chris said, "You're going to unpack now?"

Rachel paused and looked at him. "What did you have in mind?"

He smiled. "Many things. However, I'm starving. We need to skip the fun stuff and go to lunch."

Rachel frowned.

He laughed. "Not so bad. I've a reservation in the restaurant downstairs. We can eat, take Zeus out for a stroll, and be on time."

Rachel brightened. "We'll just have to postpone the fun stuff for tonight."

"You read my mind."

They sealed the deal with a kiss.

The car arrived on time and entered Tavius Global Highway at 12:20.

Rachel leaned forward in her seat to get a good look at the complex's walls. "You know, this place reminds me of a Hollywood studio complex."

Chris said, "Except the gates look like steel. They're as high as the wall and not very inviting."

Rachel said, "Or a prison."

The driver stopped at the gate. In less than a minute, they opened just wide enough for the car to pass.

Once inside, the car entered the Welcome Circle and stopped. Chris, Rachel, and Zeus got out. A tall, athletic woman strode toward them, wearing a red smock resembling a doctor's coat. They turned their attention to her.

"Welcome to Tavius Global Enterprises, Mr. Gregory, Miss Allen. I'm Francesca, Mr. Octavius's Personal Assistant and your guide. The tour will take approximately one hour. Mr. Gregory, your appointment is scheduled for three o'clock. I will have you back here with enough time to prepare for your meeting. Any questions?"

Chris said, "No, sounds good."

Rachel said, "Let's go."

Francesca said, "Please follow me." She did an about face and walked toward the Tavius Global Welcome Mall. "If you look on the entrance's far right side, past the Health Center, you'll see our transportation sharing center. Bicycles and roller-skates are primary. We have golf-carts for the disabled and anyone can use our cart-train. It runs the Main Street route, end to end, every half hour. It is all part of Tavius Global's commitment to reduce our carbon footprint. On our far right is a state-of-the-art Medical Center."

Inside the mall, she stopped at a door marked "Employees Only," and said, "Wait here."

The PA stepped inside for a minute and emerged with two royal blue smocks. "Put these on. They will identify you as corporate visitors." She reached into her pocket and pulled out two ID badges. "These are also for you. Wear them so you won't get mistakenly stopped by security. They also serve as a credit card if you'd like to purchase anything in the mall." She reached into the other pocket and pulled out another badge. "This is for Zeus in case you get separated. Attach it to his collar or his vest."

Rachel knelt. "Here you go, Zeus. Now you look just like me."

Zeus wagged his tail and licked her face. Rachel laughed and kissed his forehead.

Standing, she pulled out a pen and a copy of Tavius Global Enterprises accomplishments she found on their website. She looked at Francesca. "We're ready."

Their tour guide took them through the mall. Rachel insisted on stopping at intervals for to check out merchandise or a restaurant menu. When they emerged at the far end, they were in a manicured lakeside park. Rachel could see the whole cove, Lake Michigan beyond, and about fifty feet from the shoreline, a translucent floodgate spanned the cove.

"Wow," she said. "I didn't realize just how large this installation is."

Chris said, "Tell me about the floodgate system. I had no idea the tensile strength of plexiglass could withstand the force of battering waves."

"It is one of our patented ultrathick corrugated translucent products, set into steel casings pounded twenty feet into the lakebed. We are in the last test stages before releasing it to the world. It is designed to rise and fall so it stays five feet above the water level, which is expected to rise no more than twenty feet."

Rachel said, "When is the release date? Lake Michigan has already risen ten feet in this century. Something like this would save millions of lives if deployed along the coast of major metropolitan areas."

Francesca said, "We are in negotiations and the announcement will be soon." She looked at her watch. "Let's continue. Beyond this park, which is one of many, are the employee residences. They're built and completely furnished with eco-friendly materials."

To Rachel, the architecture resembled stacked shipping containers. She stopped at the entrance. "May I see an apartment?"

Francesca shook her head. "The layouts are in the brochure."

Rachel pulled out a brochure and opened it. "You're saying every apartment looks like a five-star hotel room with a kitchen?"

Francesca said, "Not all. We have studios, one bedroom, or two. Depends on how many people are in the worker's family."

Rachel said, "I'd really like to see one."

Francesca said, "If we have time, I'll see if there is an empty apartment we can view. Let's continue."

They left the apartment building complex and walked down the main thoroughfare. The streets were busy, filled with people walking, cycling, and skating.

The lake side property, Francesca explained, catered to the employees—housing, entertainment, sports complex, fitness center, parks, playing fields, and the school. Beyond all that is our private Port of Entry. On the other side of Main Street, bordered by the wall, were office buildings. "At the far end of this street," she said, "sit our manufacturing plants and the complex's operations center. Both have access to our above and below ground installations, as well as Lake Michigan."

Chris said, "Do you recycle all the water in the complex?"

"As much as possible. Some is filtered and purified for human consumption and most of what's left is brown water, which we use for all other purposes. Whatever sludge remains is treated before being stored and used as fertilizer."

"Will we get to the treatment plant?"

"Not today. We don't have time."

Rachel stopped, referred to the brochure, and said, "May we see a typical office space?" She referred to the brochure. "This says employee workspaces are well lit and ergonomically designed to stimulate and support worker productivity." She lowered the document and walked toward the entrance.

Francesca outpaced her and made it to the door first. "Certainly," and held it open for Rachel, Chris, and Zeus. She let the door swing shut and walked over to the receptionist.

Rachel couldn't hear the conversation and looked at Chris. "Why is it always such a big deal? She's Mr. Octavius's personal assistant… I don't know why she just doesn't…"

Francesca appeared. "We're going to the Information and Technology department."

Rachel wasn't sure what to expect, but it wasn't the stark beige and black open concept design with occasional low walled cubicles.

"This is the work area," Francesca said. "Through the door on the far wall, we get to the breakroom, which is off the main hallway. There's one on each floor."

As they passed a row of workers, Rachel heard a muffled noise, a weak cry, and a thud. She paused to looked for the disturbance. Retracing a couple of steps, she saw a woman on the floor. Zeus whined. "It's okay, boy." She released the leash and Zeus went over to sniff the woman. He licked her face, and she sat up.

"Good boy," the woman said, putting her arms around Zeus's neck. Using her chair for support, she stood and smiled at Rachel. "Thank you. I'm all right."

Rachel returned the smile. "Good."

Francesca intervened, put her hand on Rachel and said, "We must continue."

Zeus stared at the offending touch and emitted a low growl.

Francesca dropped her hand and led them from the office to the break room, which proved to be as stimulating as the workspace—bleak and functional.

Outside on the main street, Francesca said, "We have completed the tour."

Rachel said, "You haven't shown us the children's area?"

Francesca allowed herself a thin smile. "Our company operates on three shifts plus overtime if necessary. The children are cared for in our boarding school to give their parents time to meet their company-assigned goals, deadlines, and schedules. We find it's best to not interrupt the school's schedules or the children's attention." She looked at her watch. "We're running late. We must return to the administration building for Mr. Gregory's meeting with Mr. Octavius."

On the way, Rachel caught up to Francesca and said, "The PR touts Tavius Global's innovative approach to workers' rights. I'd like to talk with someone about that."

Francesca stopped and turned to Rachel. "Basically, everything we've seen is about worker's rights. They don't have more than one job or carry the burden of caring for their families. By providing housing, food, clothing, transportation, healthcare, laundry service, sports-exercise and entertainment, we ensure our workers have no financial issues or distractions. If they want to take a vacation, it's all-inclusive and free at Tavius Global resorts."

Rachel said, "A total and worry-free environment."

"We believe it's what every worker strives for. I'll see if there is a handbook after we get Mr. Gregory to his meeting."

Chris stepped away and pulled out his cell phone. He came back and said, "I'm not getting a signal and I have to check in with my office. Do I need to log onto a server?"

Francesca said, "While we do maintain a robust local server for the complex, the full internet is available on the executive administration floors. Follow me." She led them into the building, asked them to wait a moment while she stepped into the human resource office, promptly returning. "We will prepare a New Employee Welcome folder for you, which you can pick up on your way out."

She led them to the elevator, which opened to the CEO suite. Within seconds, her phone vibrated, and she saw Chris look at his. They had internet.

Francesca escorted Chris to the meeting and Rachel to the waiting area. "I've arranged for snacks, drinks, and water for Zeus. If you need anything else, please ask Mr. Octavius's executive secretary."

Rachel said, "Thank you, for everything. Your time, the tour, and all this."

Francesca nodded and said, "Unfortunately, I have to leave you at this point. Enjoy the rest of your day."

Alone, Rachel sat, and Zeus put his head in her lap. She smiled and petted him, closing her eyes to heighten the silky feel of his fur.

<~<~|~>~>

Chris walked into the CEO's office which smelled of oiled wood, leather, and a hint of pine. He didn't have to look for the owner and CEO of Tavius Global Enterprises. The silhouetted man stood in front of a large window, looking at a breathtaking view of Lake Michigan. As Chris approached, Octavius turned, remaining in the shadows, taking first advantage—he could see his visitor without being seen.

Gamesmanship did not impress Chris. Anyone who resorted to it showed a sign of weakness. At this meeting, it seemed out of place and uncalled for. He chose to ignore it and walked forward--his hand extended for a traditional greeting. "Mr. Octavius, I'm Christopher Gregory. Chris."

As the shadowy form approached to shake hands, the office lights brightened, "Octavius. Thank you for coming. Come. Sit."

Chris followed the man with cropped gray hair, trim, with the exception of a noticeable belly bulge, taut facial skin, and a controlled gait. He looked to be between sixty and seventy-five, instead of a very healthy eighty.

Octavius led Chris to a pair of highbacked armchairs, sharing a mahogany table supporting a pitcher of water and four glasses on a silver serving tray. He indicated which chair Chris should take and sat in the other—the one with the elevated seat. This set the agenda—establishing tactical advantage, power, and control.

Chris considered himself easy going, the kind of guy who would rather close a meeting with a handshake than a ninety-page contract. Still, intrigued, he ceded the first move to Octavius.

"Water?"

Chris raised his hand to decline. "Nice view." He shifted his eyes to the huge glass pane and did a partial room scan. There had been so little written about the reclusive Octavius, who occupied Forbes' 500 slot nine, he hoped there were clues in the man's choice of photographs, art pieces, and books, except none were on display.

"Thank you. It convinced me to buy this property. The changing beauty gives me peace."

Octavius poured himself a glass a water and took a sip. "Tell me, how did you enjoy your tour?"

"Very interesting. You seem to have thought of everything." Chris fidgeted in his chair. "We didn't get to see the areas supplying all the employee and facility services, nor did we get to see the manufacturing area." Chris stood, walked over to the conference table, and returned with a chair. "I hope you don't mind. I need something with more support." He placed it in front of Octavius and sat down. Now, eye to eye, he said, "Still, I'm honored we were able to see what we did."

"Tavius Global Enterprises, Chicago, is a huge facility. Next time, we will plan another tour with your interests in mind."

"You are very kind."

"Let's talk business." Octavius put his glass down. "I have five facilities like this one. Two are completed and three are in process. I employ thousands of workers at each site, and it is becoming increasingly difficult to keep track of them."

Chris said, "I thought the ID badges worked great."

Octavius rested his elbows on the chair's arms and brought his fingertips together. Peering over them, he said. "A great idea supplanted by yours, the subcutaneous microchip ultra-thin tracker, or as you call it, SMUTT."

"It does the exact same thing as your ID badges."

"There is a critical difference. Your technology eliminates the removal option—forgetting, losing, and lending—and still lets people walk around, shop, and dine without impeding their freedom. What's it going to take for me to buy the system from you?"

"You're not talking about an installation—you're talking about buying the whole SMUTT business?"

"Correct," Octavius said. "I've too many employees to negotiate a fair per person, or per thousand, or even per ten thousand units. It would be in my best interest to own the system and hire you as a consultant."

"Not possible. I have contracts with the government and other entities much like yours."

"Sign those contracts over to me. My company will service them. You would no longer have to carry the great burden of manufacturing and quality control since I already have the space and workforce."

Chris stood. "Octavius, thank you for your interest. I'm not prepared to sell at this time."

Octavius remained seated. "Not even for two point three billion?"

Chris smiled. "No. Not selling at any price." He looked at his watch. "My wife and I have an evening planned. Thank you for everything."

Octavius raised one eyebrow and lifted his chin. Through a thin smile, he said, "This is not over. We *will* talk again."

<~<~|~>~>

Rachel never heard Chris approach. She heard, "Ready?" and her eyes flew open. Zeus jumped to his feet and put his paws on her lap.

Chris laughed. "Did I startle you? You two looked pretty sweet snoozing together."

"I can't believe I fell asleep."

"At least you'll be rested for this evening's outing." He held out his hand.

Rachel took it and stood. "What are we doing?"

"I'll tell you in the car."

They rode down the elevator unaccompanied, stopped off at Human Resources to collect the New Employee Welcome packet, and got into the waiting car.

The driver went around the circle, paused at the large steel gates, waited for them to open wide enough for them to pass, and exited the complex.

Rachel took a deep breath and opened the packet. Chris put his hand on her arm. "Wait until we get back to our room. In fact, if it's a no work vacation from here on, wait until we get home."

She looked at him. His eyes were searching the vehicle. She understood, without his saying a word—there were listening devices imbedded in the vehicle. "You're right. Time to party."

He smiled. "We've about two hours until our dinner reservations. Best Indian food in the area."

"Yum. And then?"

"We're off to prime seats at the famous Second City."

Rachel hugged him and kissed him. "You are the best."

He kissed her back and said, "You owe me big time."

Rachel giggled. "Can't wait."

Chapter 18 ▶ Bethesda, Maryland

Saturday, 13 April, 9 a.m.

A couple of days after Peter's arrival at Walter Reed Medical Center, Dani and Sybil walked into his darkened room. A nurse handed him a cup of meds. He downed them in one gulp and gave her back the cup. As the nurse passed them, she said, "He's sensitive to light and sound," and left.

Dani said, "Hi, Peter. You're looking better."

Peter smiled.

Sybil moved a chair close to the bed and sat down. She held his hand and said, "How are you doing today?"

"Okay, Mom. Not great, but okay."

Sybil said, "Have you talked with the doctor?"

Peter said, "There's like three or four docs who have seen me. They talk a lot, but I can't focus. If they repeat everything often enough, I'm sure I'll figure it out."

Dani said, "Do you remember anything about the accident?"

"No. I only know what Sam told me. The first thing I remember is waking up here."

Sybil said, "You don't have to think about it at all."

Peter smiled. "Don't worry, Mom. My problem is I can't think."

Dani changed the subject. "What are the meds for?"

"They help to control my headaches."

"Is there anything I can do for you?"

Peter said, "No. Not right now. I just need to rest."

Dani stood. "I'll leave you to it."

Sybil said, "I'm staying."

Dani said, "Stay as long as you like. Call me if you need anything. Terence and the boys will be stopping by later."

<~<~|~>~>

Back in the Oval Office, Dani pulled up Yosef's report on the forces blocking her agenda and undermining her election chances.

She read, "People are willing to sacrifice the general population's health and welfare to keep President Dani Vanderhagen Mitchell from serving another term. Powerful. Female. Assertive. Knowledgeable. All negatives to the oligarchs used to calling all the political shots."

Dani had come up against this before with a lot less to lose. It had to be handled, although she wasn't sure how. She pulled out her phone, called Yosef, and asked him to meet her in the rose garden—the only place she was sure no one would overhear her conversation.

Ten minutes later they were on the lawn, facing the river.

Dani said, "That was quick."

"I happened to be in the building."

She said, "Do you think the Potomac Park Flood Levee will be able to protect the White House and key depositories as river levels continue to rise with its cresting potential increasing exponentially?"

"Good question," Yosef said. "Shall I investigate?"

"No. Just wondering."

"Did you want to talk about my report?"

"Yes," Dani said, "it is deeply troubling. I had no idea the forces were so dense and determined. I need deflecting strategies to deal with each of them."

Yosef said, "Do you want to play nice or get down and dirty?"

"Isn't there a middle ground?"

"So, Madam President, nice is not a given."

"Yosef, can you give me three levels of action by tomorrow?"

"Noon okay?"

Dani nodded. "By the way, be sure no one has access to the report."

"Of course. It is on a private server outside the government control, and only you and I have access to the information."

"Excellent. See you tomorrow."

She watched Yosef leave and pulled out her phone. Looking at her contacts, she couldn't decide who to call. She knew Peter's cartel position would be jeopardized while he remained in recovery. Losing the Vanderhagen-Powell-Mitchell place at the table populated by the eight wealthiest conglomerates in the world was unthinkable. Who could she trust to vote her interest? How could she manipulate the very people denying the climate crisis for financial and political gain?

Having no answers, Dani sighed and put her phone away, deciding to talk with Peter the following

day. One way or another, she had to figure out a way
to deal with it.

<~<~|~>~>

Yosef Hassan left the meeting, got in his car, and
drove to the Tidal Basin. He parked. He breathed
deeply for several minutes to slow his heart rate.
His excitement stemmed from learning the job he
had been training for since he joined the Israeli
army at eighteen was about to commence.

Calm, he exited the car and walked to the Tidal
Basin's edge. His earpiece in place, he pulled out
his phone and found the contact he wanted. An
annoyed voice answered. "What do you want?"

Yosef said, "Sorry, my friend, wrong number."

Seconds later, the call came. "Good to hear
from you."

Yosef said, "It's time."

"You know this how?"

"The President wants information to blackmail
the leaders of industry."

"This is true?"

Yosef said, "She asked me to find out what it
would take to force them to support her agenda and
her massive climate change deal."

"Will she use what we give her?"

"Not clear. I believe she would prefer not to
threaten them. It is more like a last resort."

"Maybe. We will hold back the best parts until
and if she needs them."

Yosef said, "Any word from the team?"

"Rumblings at Tavius Global. Will keep you
informed."

"Good."

"We will send you tidbits. You will report how they are received. Understood?"

Yosef said, "And then?"

"If our goals align, we will send more."

The call ended. Yosef pocketed the phone and clasped his hands behind his back. He stood tall, chin up, as he surveyed the basin. The Mossad was his lifeline. Together, they would end the apocalypse threatening life on earth.

Chapter 19 ▶ Chicago, Illinois

Saturday, 13 April, 10:30 a.m.
Chris and Rachel spooned on the bed. Zeus watched from the couch.

He said, "You know, this vacation idea of yours has merits." He kissed her neck.

"We have to get up, don't we?"

"I've got tickets to the Brookfield Zoo."

Rachel sat up. "Why didn't you say so?"

Chris laughed. "I'll jump into clothes and walk Zeus while you shower. When I get back, I'll order breakfast and shower. By the time I'm done, the food will be here."

"Good plan."

As Chris leashed Zeus, he felt something odd inside the dog's collar. "Rachel."

She appeared at the bathroom door, holding a towel around her. "You called?"

"Did you tape an ID onto Zeus's collar?"

"No. Why? What did you find?"

Chris knelt to disengage the paper without destroying it. Successful, he stood and opened the folded note.

"What does it say?"

Chris read it out loud. "Find Winnie Santiago."

"Where did it come from?"

"I have no idea." He handed the note to Rachel. "A souvenir." He grabbed the leash. "See you later."

<~<~|~>~>

After her shower, Rachel wrapped herself in the hotel-provided thick bathrobe and walked into the bedroom while she dried her hair. She spied the Welcome Packet on the table. She sat down and looked at the contents. Before she finished, she reached for her phone and photographed every page. As an afterthought, she photographed the note.

Rachel finished as Chris and Zeus returned.

"No work," he said. "Remember?"

"You told me about outright rejecting an over two-billion-dollar offer. Wasn't that work?"

"No. Neither was your emphatic agreement with my decision."

She sighed. "I have to say the Tavius Global complex gave me the creeps."

"See? Not work, a conversation."

Rachel gave him a sideways glance. "Your rules are fishy. Still, I'm done. Watch. I'm putting everything away in its packet, putting the packet in the bottom of my suitcase, and closing my suitcase. No more work."

Chris knitted his brows, folded his arms, and tapped his toes. "You admit to work?"

Rachel answered by moving toward him, doing her best sultry stripper imitation, untying her robe's belt, and putting her hands around Chris's neck. "Just a few minutes of reading. Can you ever forgive me?"

He slid his hands around her body and kissed her. "Maybe."

She started undressing him. "This one time?"

"Only if you wash my back."

His clothes marked their path to the shower.

They finished dressing in time to admit room service. Chris fished his wallet from his dog-walking pants while the server set the table and laid out the service. Rachel disappeared into the bathroom to fix her hair.

She returned, ready for breakfast, fed Zeus, and expected to see Chris seated. He wasn't. "What are you doing?"

He put his finger to his lips. "Sit down, the food looks great." He had a device in his hand and waved it over the walls and the lights.

She didn't hear any beeps. "You did a good job ordering. These are some of my favorite things."

Chris stopped and put the scanner away. "We're clear. I didn't want to take any chances."

"Did you check last night too?"

"Of course."

"Because you saw one in the car yesterday, when we left Tavius Global, didn't you?"

Chris nodded. "Strange because it wasn't there when we left the hotel."

"Did you find one in our room last night?"

"Yes. I didn't tell you because I didn't want to ruin the evening."

"I'm surprised we got bugged at all. Didn't whoever's behind this know you were a security expert?"

Chris smiled. "I guess they figured since you and Zeus were with me, I'd drop my guard. They didn't know I keep a mini-scanner on my keychain and an app on my phone."

Rachel said, "It's creepy living in a big brother world."

"Unless it's the only world you know."

"Like everyone at Tavius Global's compound."

"Yes."

Rachel said, "We need to get out of here."

"You bet," Chris said. "But first, I'm starving."

They dove into the food and devoured every morsel of eggs, home-fries, bacon, French toast, breads and muffins basket, fresh fruit compote, orange juice, and coffee.

Rachel popped the last wedge of cantaloupe into her mouth and said, "Yummy."

Chris got up. "I called a different car service and they're downstairs."

Rachel said, "Ready Zeus?"

The dog ran to her and sat at attention. "Good boy."

She leashed him and put on his vest. "Wait. I have to get my windbreaker. It's in the suitcase." She flipped it open, pulled out the jacket, and said, "Chris, the packet from Tavius Global is gone."

"I'm not surprised. Tavius Global seems to be closely monitoring who says what about their operations and what they consider internal documents."

"Why would they care?"

"The facility is a pilot for restructuring mega-corporations around the globe. There are trillions to be made."

"It takes a lot of paranoia to think two people have the power to bring their operations to a halt."

"Oh, I don't know. You're a writer and the President's friend."

Rachel shivered. "Stop. I don't want to be afraid or look over my shoulder. I've been there. Done that. I was on the Ayatollah's hit list until he died. I can't live in fear again."

Chris put his arm around her shoulder. "Don't worry. You won't have to. I'm here."

Chapter 20 ▶ White House, Washington D.C.

Sunday, 14 April, 10 a.m.

Terence and Sybil were already at the breakfast table when Dani arrived. She looked around and said, "Where are the twins?"

Terence said, "Good morning. Sleep well?"

"Okay, I admit I'm a little testy. I've got the dilemma plague—lots of problems which have solutions which could be worse than the problems themselves."

Terence said, "Did you want our input on anything?"

"Not at this moment. First, I have to speak with Peter."

Sybil said, "I'm sure he's doing better today. He's sleeping a lot. However, the doctors assure me it's normal with certain kinds of concussions."

Dani said, "Did they say when they'd release him?"

"They're waiting for him to have what they call a 'normal' morning. Eat, talk, walk around, shower, dress, you know, stuff like that."

"When do they think it will happen?"

"Any day now."

Terence said, "You can't rush or force it. If you do, he'll be released too soon, and his complete recovery will take longer."

Sybil said, "How do you know?"

Terence smiled. "Played football. Concussions happened. Often players were sent right back into the field. The last time I played, I went down. Knocked out. I couldn't remember the game when I woke up. So, I quit. Just like that. Done."

Sybil said, "Good to know. I'll be prepared."

Dani turned to Terence. "Where did you say Isaac and Ivan are?"

He sipped a cup of coffee and looked over the rim at her. "I can say they're definitely not in their room."

"Hmm. What else?"

"They had a good breakfast. Eggs, juice, toast, and a couple of pancakes."

"Interesting and evasive. Terence."

He used his napkin to wipe his mouth. "I can't give you their specific location because they're with their security detail."

Dani's fork stopped mid-air and dropped to her plate. "Driving lessons. They're taking driving lessons."

Terence said, "I am not in a position to confirm or deny."

"They're sixteen. They can't drive until after my Presidency."

"They know."

"So, what are they doing driving?"

Terence reached out and placed his hand over hers. "Dani, you asked me to handle the driving and car thing. Remember?"

She nodded.

"So, relax. I'm handling it."

"This is not what I meant."

"Still, it's my job and I'm doing it in my own way. They're our children, and you've got enough on your plate."

"Okay. Okay. Still, I want to see them at breakfast. Deal?"

"Deal."

Sybil said, "Well done. I'm proud of you."

Dani laughed. "It helped having you here. It probably saved us from an all-out war."

Sybil said, "Always happy to help."

"I'll help you in return and take you to the hospital."

<~<~|~>~>

Dani watched as Peter greeted his mother with open arms. When he hugged her, he said, "Good to see you, again. As you can tell, I'm much better today."

Dani said, "I can't tell you how relieved I am. I've been very worried."

Peter smiled. "Don't waste your time. I'm from tough stock."

Sybil said, "Did the doctors say you could come home?"

Peter said, "They're going to give it another few days so they can see how I'm doing weaning off the meds, so they can adjust the doses I'll need when I leave."

Peter swung his legs off the bed, stuck his feet in hospital slippers and stood. "Follow me to the lounge. I'm told there's coffee and Danish."

The three, followed by Dani's security detail, went to the lounge, and sat at a corner table. They had the room to themselves.

Peter said, "Dani, did Sam give you the story about our Alaskan trip?"

Dani nodded. "Yes. I've already initiated rescue operations."

Peter said, "Their quick action saved my life. They need your intervention to save theirs."

Dani nodded and said, "Before I go, I want to know if you're well enough to continue working with the cartel roundtable. We have crucial work to accomplish, and I have to know if I can count on you."

"Absolutely. I have a slight problem with double vision, focusing, and occasional headaches, but it's all under control."

Dani looked at Sybil. "Would you please give Peter and me a few minutes?"

Sybil said, "Of course. I can hear the gift shop calling my name."

Dani watched her leave and turned to Peter. "Have we bought up over fifty percent of the land options put up for sale to date?"

"Yes. I did the trades before I left."

"When is your next video meeting?"

"Thursday."

Dani said, "We don't have much time to initiate strategy to bring everyone around to our climate agenda. It means they have to be okay with shelving their 'shareholders first' philosophy and going with 'stakeholders first.'"

"Whoa. I'm not even sure I'm on board with that."

"What do you mean?"

Peter said, "Our holdings are heavily invested in African mining operations. I haven't tried to change the appalling conditions because we only have months left before we to have to halt all underground mining and maybe a year left on our strip-mining operations contracts. It's getting way too hot to work. People are dying on the job from heat-prostration and insufficient water availability."

"When one door closes, another opens."

"The hemp project will minimize the impact to our portfolio, I've invested in sustainability operations and resources. We will be a top hemp producer nationally and maybe even worldwide as soon as you make it a preferred crop."

"What about Octavius?"

"He'll be second. Even if he's first and we're second, we still stand to make a fortune."

Dani said, "True. Still, I need businesses to commit to their community—local and global. You have to help me on this, even if it means shutting down the mining operations."

Peter said, "Let's say we hypothetically stop today. What do we do with the people? Unless you take them in, they have no place to go, no housing, schools, or transportation."

Sybil returned and Dani stood up. "Thank you, Sybil. I'll leave your son to you while I return to my family and whatever surprises await me."

Peter said, "Goodbye, Dani. Don't worry. We're in good shape. Do whatever you have to."

Chapter 21 ▶ Gramercy Avenue, New York City

Sunday, 14 April, 2 p.m.

Chris walked into their apartment, released the travel bag, and stretched his arms over his head. "I loved our vacation, but it's great to be home."

Rachel hugged him from behind. "Great time. Loved every minute except for the 'spied on' part." Before he could turn, she released him and ran for the stairs. "Order in for tonight. I'm good with whatever you choose."

"Wait!"

Rachel stopped on the third step and turned her shoulders. "Wait? Why?"

"First, let me do a bug scan." Chris walked over and flipped a switch twelve inches above the light switches. The toggle turned red as a buzzing noise filled the apartment. Seconds later, it turned green. "We're clean."

Rachel said, "What did you want to talk about?"

"I want to know what's so important we can't take the time to decompress, and I mean together?"

"Tavius Global. My book. An article for the Sunday paper."

"You're not going to write about our tour, are you?"

"Of course. Tavius Global Enterprises plans to make a fortune on a business model from the 1890's, which, if accepted, will enslave workers all over the globe."

"You can't write about Tavius Global."

Rachel came back down the stairs. "I can, and I am."

"Don't. I'm asking. We were given the tour as a personal favor. Besides, I'm still in negotiations with Octavius. Your fervor might cause irreversible consequences."

"Negotiations? I thought you refused his offer."

"I did. This isn't about money. It's about power and control. He won't take my refusal as an answer. He will keep upping the ante until I agree."

"Are you kidding me? You're playing a pissing game with that cretin?"

"I prefer chess. I need to stop him from ever controlling SMUTT."

Rachel said, "What does his business model have to do with you? People have to understand what's behind his brochures touting a workers' utopia."

Chris moved to the couch and sat down. "I don't want him to focus on you. The man is capable of anything. He can go after me as much as he wants. He can't destroy me. You, on the other hand, are vulnerable." He patted the cushion. "Come here. You'll have plenty of time to attack his hypothesis. I'm just asking you to wait."

"I can't. I want to get my first impressions out there before he can start his global campaign to enslave the world."

"Rachel, you and I both know there are two kinds of people in this world—those who have choices, and those who don't."

"Don't you dare tell me Tavius Global *is* going to save the world."

Chris patted the cushion again. "Please sit with me. I want to have a discussion, not a fight."

Rachel stiff-walked over to Chris and sat next to him like a rigid doll.

Chris put his arm around her shoulders. "Really? You don't even want to listen to me?"

She softened. "I am reluctantly listening."

Chris pulled her closer to him. "Look. You have a choice as to how you live your life. It's not a privilege most people have. Octavius has a huge operation going to address the concerns of people who do not have a choice. He's giving them a place to work, an apartment, healthcare, sports and entertainment, and a whole shopping center. His employees are living the middle-class dream and protected from any climatic apocalypse. For them, this is a good thing."

"A benevolent despot offering a secure prison."

"Still, you have to agree it's better than living in fear on the street."

She pulled away from him and stood up. "Tyrant."

"Stop." Chris got up to face her. "You're getting all worked up over nothing."

"Really? Nothing?"

"All I did was ask you not to write about Tavius Global Enterprises until I've neutralized him."

"You're going to stop him?"

"I have to. Octavius is a gamer and must win. I don't like games. So, I want to win this one for all the reasons you mentioned."

"You want me to shut up and be nice so you can show him who's got the bigger dick?"

Chris jumped to his feet. "Zeus, let's go for a walk." He looked at Rachel. "I need some air."

Rachel watched him leave, grabbed the nearest pillow, and dropped to the floor. She screamed into it before assaulting it with her fists. Drained, she sat back, leaning against the couch, clutching the pillow to her chest. Calmer, she realized it didn't really matter whether she wrote about it today, tomorrow, or next week, since her book wouldn't be published for months. Her confrontation with Chris was nothing but a clash of ego.

She rose to her feet. The green security toggle caught her eye. "My phone. Where's my phone?" She felt her pockets and looked for her purse. She spied it on the steps with her phone just visible. Jerking it out, she checked her Welcome Packet document photographs. They were still there.

She sighed with relief and ran up the stairs to her office. Within minutes, she'd downloaded the images to a thumb drive, which she backed up to another thumb drive. When she felt her data was safe, she deleted the images from her phone. One drive she hid in her pencil holder, and the other she placed in a plastic baggie and slipped it into the pocket of Zeus's service dog vest hanging by the door.

Mission complete, Rachel wasn't sure what do to next. She decided a vodka tonic would hit the spot, prepared it, and sat in the living room waiting for Chris and Zeus to return.

They walked in sooner than she expected. Chris unleashed Zeus and put a bag on the kitchen counter. When he looked up, they locked eyes.

Chris said, "Feeling better?"

Rachel said, "I am. I may have overreacted. I see red when anyone says 'no' to me."

Chris poured himself a drink. "Noted and remembered."

She said, "You've also got me thinking about security. Do I need an internet-independent computer with a thumb drive port and my word processing app?"

Chris smiled. "You mean one not easily hacked or accessed."

She nodded. "All the tracking devices have made me completely paranoid about people trying to access my work."

"Rachel, we are on the most secure network and server available. I know because I built it."

"If you're right, why can't I write about what I want?"

"Write about anything. However, just to be safe, just don't copy, send, or publish it anywhere."

Rachel sipped her drink.

Chris plopped down next to Rachel. "You know Octavius will get SMUTT anyway."

"As long as it's not from you. I don't want us to be any part of what he's building. It didn't work before and it's not going to work now."

He said, "Even if he's saving lives?"

"It's an illusion," Rachel said. "Trust me. There has got to be a better way."

"And, if not?"

She turned to look at him. "We'll figure it out."

A phone buzzed. Rachel and Chris each reached for theirs.

She said, "Maybe someday, Mr. Tech Guy, you can change your phone alert to a different sound."

He said, "Or, for the millionth time, you let me teach you how to do it yourself."

It was her phone. "Hi, Beth."

"Eric and I are downstairs."

Rachel looked at Chris, he nodded, and she said, "Come up."

Chris ordered another take-out while she got up and opened the door. "What's going on?"

Eric walked over to the bar and made drinks for Beth and himself.

Beth said, "We're going to D.C. to work on a special project for the President."

Rachel said, "Congrats. Sounds exciting."

Eric brought the drinks over. "We'll be working in the West Wing. Our entire stay is being underwritten. It's like a holiday."

Beth said, "Except we'll be working."

Chris knelt to fill Zeus's bowl with dog food.

Rachel said, "Can you tell us on what?"

Eric sat down next to Beth. "We're looking for a Winnie Santiago."

The dog food pellets hit the floor, bouncing around like hail in a rainstorm. Seconds later, Chris appeared. "Wait." All eyes followed him. He walked over to his desk and put on the white noise-signal disrupter and background music. "I have to do this for now. Tomorrow, I'm having this whole building inspected, tested, and upgraded." He picked up his drink, sat in a side chair, and said, "Okay, Rachel, now you can tell them."

Chapter 22 ▶ Bethesda, Maryland

Sunday, 14 April, 6 p.m.

Dani arrived at the hospital around six, after the patients' dinner time. Through the open door to Peter's room, she saw Sybil and her son deep in conversation. She paused. Her aunt looked like a sporty Katherine Hepburn in her slacks and silk shirt, close cropped hair, and slim build. She smiled. More than just looking like Hepburn—Sybil also had the star's on-screen toughness.

Sybil had walked away from the Vanderhagen family to pursue her own dreams and follow her heart. Lidia, her deceased wife, had brought her great joy in life and immense sadness in death. Peter's accident had snapped her out of mourning. Her strength returned.

Peter, on the other hand, reminded her of everyone and no one. He had a pleasant, non-descript face. If he wasn't leading the parade, you'd never notice him in it. It gave him a great advantage in his work. People never found him intimidating and often made the mistake of underestimating his intelligence, drive, and determination.

Dani valued his even temper, sharp mind, and photographic memory. He was indispensable to her, Sybil, the family, and PRAISE. They were all lucky to have him.

Dani knocked on the doorframe and walked in—her security detail stayed in the hall and flanked the doorway. "Greetings, family. I've come to check on you and give Sybil a ride back to the White House."

After a short visit with the two of them, Dani said, "Sybil, before we go, please give Peter and I a few minutes."

When Sybil left, Dani said, "Are you really ready to go home?"

Peter said, "I feel great, and the meds help the headaches."

"Have you given any thought to what we talked about, you know, getting support?"

Peter lost his smile. "I did." He picked up the newspaper from the rolling table. He poked a news story with his finger. "Do you want to tell me what this is about?"

She glanced at the headline and read it aloud. "Congress has called for an end to the Afghanistan war." She looked at him. "I don't understand."

Peter sat up straight and swiveled so his legs dangled off the bed. His eyes narrowed and he pointed at her. "This is your doing. You weren't supposed to do this until the September before the election."

"What are you talking about?"

"You screwed up. Afghanistan is, was, our backup to Africa."

He leaped out of bed and grabbed her by the shoulders. "All the mining operations, all the minerals, all the control. We were supposed to sign next month in exchange for ending the war. We were getting a piece of the mining operation and a percentage of gross profit. You ending the war was to be our bargaining chip."

"Peter, calm down. I don't, didn't know."

Dani stood. Peter didn't loosen his grip. She said, like parent to child, "Peter, let me go. You're hurting me."

The Secret Service agents at the door ran into the room and pulled them apart. It took both men to loosen Peter's vice-like grip. Released, Dani walked out as Sybil rushed past her.

Peter's face darkened, his brows converged, his eyes narrowed, and he bared his teeth. In a frenzy, he pointed at Dani and screamed, "You bitch!"

Dani, safe in the hallway, watched as Sybil ran to her son, trying to fight off the agents and calm Peter down. Hospital staff ran into the room. Peter, spittle forming at the corners of his mouth, resisting restraint, shrieked, "You've ruined us. We're fucked, and it's your fault." The nurse found a moment to administer a shot of sedative. His face went from rictus to relaxed in a matter of seconds. His body lay immobilized on the bed.

The nurse turned to Sybil. "He'll be fine when he wakes up." Turning to the agents, she said, "You can go. We've got this. He'll be fine."

Outside the room, Dani said, "Get me the doctor *now.*"

The Secret Service escorted her to a private sitting area where Sybil joined her.

Dani looked at Sybil. "Did you know about this altered behavior?"

"I knew he could have some impulse control issues. This is the first time I've seen it."

The doctor entered the room and addressed the two women. "I'm sure you have questions, but I have one for you before we start. Did Peter play sports?"

Sybil said, "Yes. He got all kinds of athletic awards in school."

"High school and college?"

"No, just high school. Why?"

"Did he play any contact sports like football, soccer, wrestling, or hockey?"

"Not all at the same time, but he did try them all. He gave them all up when he went to college."

The doctor pulled up a chair and sat with Sybil and Dani. "As you know, Peter suffered a severe concussion. He's been having headaches, light-sensitivity, and focus issues. We have him on medication therapy to minimize the disruption to his life. His symptoms are not going away immediately. It will take time—anywhere from two weeks to two years."

Sybil said, "I had no idea. Peter said he's doing great and wants to come home."

The doctor nodded. "What he said is true."

Dani said, "Something else is happening, isn't it?"

The doctor said, "We are observing a certain emotional instability and on one other occasion, we witnessed an incident similar to what happened today. While it's highly unusual for such immediate presentations, we think Peter has Chronic Traumatic Encephalopathy, or as it is known, CTE."

Sybil's face drained of color.

Dani put her hand over Sybil's. "That's permanent. Right?"

"There are therapies and activities to help to diminish the symptoms, but the damage is permanent and progressive."

Sybil's eyes reddened. "Are you telling me Peter is never going to get better?"

The doctor said, "In the long term. However, I believe extending his stay here for healing and learning how to manage his changing brain would benefit him and everyone concerned."

Sybil covered her face with her hands and sobbed. "I just can't lose another. First my wife and now my son. It's not fair. I don't think I can bear it."

Dani put her arm around Sybil's shoulders. "How long do you want to keep him here?"

"Another two to three weeks."

"Could he get this care in New York?"

"Yes. However, because we deal with a lot of veterans with PTSD and CTE, we are uniquely qualified. Therefore, I'd recommend not moving him."

Dani said, "We'll talk this over and let you know. Is Peter awake?"

"No. He needs to sleep for a while." The doctor stood, "If there is anything else, don't hesitate to contact me." He gave them his business card and left.

Dani turned to Sybil. "Come. Let's go. Peter's asleep."

"No."

Dani said, "We're going home so you can rest. I'll make sure you have a driver when you want to come back."

Sybil composed herself and gave a determined head toss. "I'm staying. If I need or want anything, I'll call."

Dani let her be. She had to leave. *Who could replace Peter?*

At the doorway, Dani stopped. Her security detail did some fast back-peddling to avoid crashing into her.

She returned to Sybil and said, "I have a job for you."

"Oh no you don't. My job is my son and running PRAISE."

"I think you're going to love this particular assignment."

"Really?"

"I'd like you to take over Vanderhagen Holdings while Peter recovers and represent us at the cartel table."

Sybil laughed without humor and lowered her voice. "You've got to be out of your mind. My father and brother were nothing more than hitmen to manipulate the world economies."

Dani said, "You, Peter, and I are the last Vanderhagens. My sons, who might qualify, are too young. I can't do it because I'm President. Peter can't do it because he is, at the moment, unreliable. I'm afraid strong, capable you is our perfect option."

"Absolutely not. The cartel killed my husband and, just last year, my wife. I refuse to help them do one goddamned thing." She turned her back to Dani.

Dani got up close and whispered in her ear, "Would you do it to get even?"

Sybil spun to face Dani. "Absolutely."

"First you get operational details, passwords, access to documents and reports from Peter. The retaliation strategy must remain between you and me. We can discuss it over the next couple of days. You and I will be an amazing team."

Sybil hugged Dani. "Thank you. This is the first time I've felt truly alive since Lidia's murder."

"Good, because you and I are going to save the world."

Chapter 23 ▶ Israeli Embassy, Washington D.C.

Sunday, 14 April, 11 p.m.
Yosef Hassan stared at the mirror--Yakov Handelman stared back. Yosef's jet-black wavy hair and eyebrows were flecked with gray with his sideburns even grayer. He had added a steel-gray brush mustache to his normal two-day facial growth. Contact lenses changed his blue eyes to brown.

His alter-ego worked at the Israeli Embassy in a small office marked "Broom Closet." Surrounded by the best security available, he worked with his handler in Israel without his usual concerns about being overheard.

His usual shift ran from eleven pm to seven am as duly noted on all work reports. In truth, he used the space as necessary. Here he could relax and not worry about his immediate safety.

Once he settled in, read emails and newspapers, he called Lev. It would be eight in the morning, Israel time.

"The President is ready to commit to the UN Climate Directive. She must convince the heads of fossil fuel, agriculture, clothing, mining, timber, recycling, and building industries to forego old practices and put their efforts into maintaining clean air and water while going green and supporting sustainable products and processes."

"Finally."

"She asked me to find the underbelly of these multinational corporations so her appeal to their support has bite if she needs it. This means names and dates."

"Accidents?"

"Not unless nice, with a backup of implied threats, fails."

"Do you have a target list?"

"I have ours. I'll get the President's list today, cross-match them, and get back to you."

"Later."

The line went dead.

Chapter 24 ▶ White House, Washington D.C.

Monday, 15 April, 8 a.m.

In the Oval Office, Dani rocked a pen with her fingers. It made a tapping noise on the yellow legal pad on the desk.

Isabel stood in front of her. "Do you want to go over your agenda for today or skip it?"

Dani said, "Let see it before I answer."

Isabel produced a list and placed it on the desk. "These are the people who have asked to meet with you. Let me know your preferences, and I'll set up a schedule."

Dani nodded.

Isabel said, "What are your items, so we can prioritize them?"

Dani leaned back and started counting on her fingers. "I have to meet with the special FBI taskforce. I need the list of congressional members who haven't signed onto my environmental initiative.

Isabel said, "Shall I add a list of their vulnerabilities?"

"Yes. After we discuss them, set the meeting up and include the House and Senate leaders."

"You mentioned the corporate leaders last week. I've started a list."

"Good. I'm interested in corporations who refuse to support my environmental plan."

"Understood."

"Finally, I want to meet with the government agencies with a vested stake in getting everyone on board."

"Got it."

"Oh, there's one more thing. I want to meet with Sybil Powell sometime later today. She's going to let me know when, and I'll forward the time to you."

"How's Peter doing?"

"He's recovering nicely, although he could be out of commission for six months or so."

"Tough break."

Dani said, "Please get started. I want to see the FBI team as soon as they arrive."

Isabel made it halfway to the door when Dani said, "Wait. Here's the appointment list. I've added Yosef Hassan. Schedule him in as soon as he arrives." She paused. "Have the kitchen send up fresh coffee and a cheese platter."

Before the kitchen delivered the coffee, Beth and Eric arrived.

Dani used a remote control to initiate background music and another to initiate interference with anyone's listening capability.

She turned to the Special Agents and said, "I am so glad you're here. I have a specific task for you, and it must be done without attracting any attention. Requests for files should be imbedded in a larger request or directly through me."

Beth said, "We understand. We've done this work before."

Dani said, "I'm sure. However, your target is massive, powerful, influential, well-connected, and secretive."

Eric said, "Tavius Global Enterprise."

"Yes. It's up there in the top ten globally."

Beth said, "Is this because Mr. Octavius wouldn't allow us to investigate a missing person at his Chicago location?"

Dani's eyes flashed. "Octavius used me, with not-so-subtle threats, to stop your inquiry."

Staff came in with coffee and a snack spread.

After they left, Dani said, "Octavius believes his money put me in office and therefore he controls my decisions. While the first part is true, he was a big donor, the second part is false. I make my own decisions. However, I believe I need him, as a leader in the corporate sector, to carry out my plans for the country within my timeline. I want you to find the leverage I need to force him to change his mind."

Eric said, "We do have some new information. Our mutual friends, Rachel and Chris Gregory, recently took a modified and orchestrated tour of Tavius Global's Chicago installation."

Beth said, "The workers are given everything they need except the freedom to access the worldwide internet, leave the facility, or resign."

Eric said, "Rachel and Chris weren't even sure if the workers had cash accounts. Their ID passes are scanned for purchases, of which the company keeps track, but the employees don't seem to carry any debt."

Beth said, "Or, earn any equity. No money. No savings. No escape."

Dani nodded as she took in all the information. "Have you come up with an approach?"

Beth said, "We think we can get a much better sense of what's going on through Tavius Global's tax returns and payroll reports, and any other compliance documents filed with the federal government. If we can get to the Illinois State Attorney, we can also check on any complaints which may have been filed."

Dani said, "I'm going to send you a list of other companies I'm interested in. You can ask for the same info on all of them. No one will know which, if any, are being targeted."

Eric said, "Understood."

Dani called Isabel. "Send Wesley in."

She ended the call and continued. "Also, I will arrange to get signatures for any documents which require one." Dani heard a knock on the door. "Come in."

Dani said, "Wesley Warren, Head of White House Security, this is Beth Neilson and Eric Jerrod, FBI Special Agents. Beth and Eric are working on a project for me. It is covert and any leak could be disastrous. I want them in a safe room. No listening or visual surveillance. Please give them any assistance they require."

"I've already secured a space and will make sure they are undisturbed, Madam President."

"Good," Dani said. "Also, give them my private number."

"Will do."

Dani watched them leave. She listened. When the door latch clicked into place, before she could relax, she felt a chill and tingling sensation up her spine. Pressure. She knew all the pieces had to be in place because she wasn't going to get a second chance.

Chapter 25 ▶ Gramercy Avenue, New York City

Monday, 15 April, 8 a.m.
Rachel flung her arm across the bed to extract her morning kiss from Chris's lips. She got a big slurpy Zeus kiss instead. "Eww, Zeus."

The dog whined and licked her again.

"Okay. Okay. I'm up."

Zeus jumped off the bed and sat on the floor, his tail wagging in expectation.

Rachel looked at him. "What's going on?"

Zeus whuffed.

"Where's Chris?"

Zeus went to a four-point stand and barked.

Rachel put on her robe and followed Zeus into the living room.

Chris and two guys from the second floor were checking wires, connections, electronic devices, and stuff she knew nothing about.

Zeus ran to Chris who turned toward Rachel. "Sorry if this racket woke you. I couldn't sleep. I kept taking apart, restoring, and upgrading the entire system in my head until I drove myself crazy. At 3:27, I had to start working on it."

"Have you had breakfast?"

"What time is it?"

"Eight-ten."

Chris looked at his team. "Sorry guys. I didn't realize. Go take a break. Can you come back at nine?"

Murmurs of "No problem" followed the men out the door.

Rachel had the coffee perking and bread ready when Chris slid onto a stool at the counter. "What can I get you besides coffee? Eggs? PB&J? Bagel with cream cheese, lettuce, onion, and tomato?"

"I'll go with the bagel and take Zeus downstairs for a potty break."

"It'll be ready when you get back."

As the door closed, Rachel's phone buzzed, and she took the call. "Hi Dani. This is a surprise." She put the phone on speaker so she could listen and prepare breakfast for Chris.

Dani said, "For me, also. I just finished talking with Beth and Eric. They told me about your trip to Chicago. I want to know more about it."

"If you've talked to them, you know everything." She opened the fridge and pulled out the fixings and olives stuffed with pimentos for an extra punch.

Dani said, "I want your impression. Are people at risk working for Tavius Global?"

"Depends what you mean."

"Rachel, what's going on? I've never heard you so evasive."

"I'm sorry, Dani. We're having security issues at the moment. May I call you back?"

"Private line. I'll be waiting."

Chris walked in, filled Zeus's water bowl, and fed him. "Who was that?"

"Dani. I didn't want to say anything because I knew my phone hadn't been checked yet." Rachel handed her phone to Chris who opened it and removed the SIM card, replacing it with a new one. "Good. Now we can eat."

They sat at the counter, eating, each quiet with their own thoughts.

Rachel put down her bagel, took a sip of coffee, and turned to Chris. "Were you thinking about Octavius and SMUTT?"

"No. As far as I'm concerned, the matter is settled. I meant what I said. He will, however, contact me in the next few days. Octavius is the kind of man who doesn't take 'no' for an answer. I'm sure he wants to own it and lease it to companies all over the world."

"Spread the joy and make billions."

"Pretty much. Why are you so interested?"

Rachel said, "I shudder at the thought of workers being tracked during every micro-photon of their life."

"Buckle up. This technology is happening."

"But you don't have to be at the center of it and he does."

Chris laughed. "I told you. It's not about the money, it's about winning. His offer equates to the first move in a chess game. He expects me to play because he believes I can't walk away."

"So, what are you going to do?"

"I already told you, nothing." Chris grinned and took her hands in his. He leaned forward so they were nose to nose. "Are we good?"

Her answer drowned in his kiss.

Chapter 26 ▶ White House, Washington D.C.

Monday, 15 April, 10 a.m.
Dani and Sybil sat in the Oval Office, taking advantage of coffee and snacks.

Sybil said, "I wanted to see you before I went to the hospital to talk with Peter."

"How's he doing?"

"Yesterday, I left before he completely recovered from the sedative. He still doesn't remember anything about the accident."

"Just as well," Dani said, "since he can't do anything about it."

"He's going to get better. I've been discussing protocols with his doctors, and we think, with work, he'll be able to manage at close to normal."

"I'm so glad for Peter and you."

"I'm not sure how Peter's going to feel about all this." Sybil sipped her coffee, put the cup down, and said, "Before I start interrogating my son, please let me know what areas I need to concentrate on."

Dani said, "Peter knows all about the Vander-hagen interests and investments, and he knows where the documents are to back them up. You'll have to familiarize yourself with where we stand regarding each portfolio and ongoing projects. Peter sits on a weekly call with the other cartel members and submits reports as well as evaluates everyone else's reports. He needs to explain to you how and when to access the call, the process, the reports, and decisions."

Sybil smiled. "I'm a quick learner. Don't worry."

Dani said. "There is one thing he might not know and it's not trivial. No woman has ever been a part of this group. The members manipulate global trade and politics. Their money, influence, and connections run deep. They don't ask for loyalty and secrecy, they expect it. Your father, your brother, and now Peter, enforce it."

"I may have to rethink my decision."

"I understand," Dani said. "However, you do have help—the Ninja at the Philadelphia house works for the Vanderhagen family, both as housekeeper and cartel enforcer."

Sybil said, "You're telling me, if I give removal orders, the housekeeper will carry them out?"

Dani nodded. "This is important. You have to act like your father and think bigger. If we don't break down this wall of control and manipulation, we will never be able to enact the huge changes we need to make to combat the world's economic collapse due to cataclysmic weather events and the human fallout as millions are driven from their homes and economies collapse."

Sybil said, "Is my goal to get them to support your initiative, based on UN studies and the Paris Agreement, or throw a monkey wrench into their operations?"

Dani smiled. "I knew you'd be the right person. If you can, get them to support the sweeping actions I'm presenting within the week and influence global action to ensure the best positive outcomes."

"Good, I'd rather save lives than end them."

"First, though, is to insist you're the person, the anointed person as it were, to represent our interests and maintain our influence."

"I'm a Vanderhagen. Period."

Dani nodded. "Also, make sure they're aware you've many family secrets which you have never shared because you stand in solidarity with, are loyal to, the cartel."

Sybil said, "I'm going to have to be polite and professional to those fuckers who used my wife, Lidia, and her dream of an internationally recognized art gallery, to hide their money laundering operation, and wound up killing her."

"Yes."

"I'm going to have to rehearse. I'm going to be at the table with the fuckers who engineered the demise of Tawanda by destroying the whole refugee community."

"Yes."

"Then, they killed my pompous brother, James."

"Yes."

Sybil tossed her head and stood. "Dani, don't you worry about a thing. I will sit at the cartel table, and I will bend them to my will. Nothing right now would give me more pleasure."

Dani smiled, "Of that, I have no doubt."

Dani's day sped by. Meetings and authorizations kept her occupied. She took a breath at three-thirty and realized Rachel hadn't called back. With a twinge of

annoyance, she pulled out her phone, and relaxed.
Rachel had called back, several times. She hit redial.

"Hi, Dani. Busy day?"

"You bet. How're you doing?"

"Working on my book. It's taking shape, so I'm
stoked."

"Tell me about how you happened to know of
Winnie Santiago."

"During our tour of Tavius Global, someone
must have slipped the note into Zeus's collar. I didn't
think anything about it until we talked with Beth and
Eric."

Dani said. "They are still looking into her
disappearance, and possibly others. Do you think
there's anything illegal going on there?"

"I don't know enough to answer. However, I do
think the people I saw signed employee contracts
willingly. They lead structured, comfortable lives
separate from the outside world. Everyone is literally
walled in. It's clean, well kept, and amenities are
available and used by everyone. In short, it's a gilded
cage. I didn't see any evidence of actual money. I
have a sneaking suspicion the management
indoctrinated the workers with the quid pro quo, 'You
work for us, and we'll take care of you.'"

"I see."

"Don't get me wrong, if it didn't have this 'Big
Brother' feel, and the employees were free to come
and go, with access to the open internet, the concept
is good and green. They wouldn't need cars, because
they live across the street from work and within two
miles of parks, gyms, and entertainment centers.
Shared bikes, roller skates, electric carts, and an
electric bus system cover transportation. All in all, a
very minimal carbon footprint."

"Did you meet Octavius?"

"No, Chris did."

"What happened?"

"He offered to buy Chris's tracking technology."

"Interesting."

"Chris said 'no.' We don't think it will end here. Chris said Octavius's a gamer, and the offer, his first move. We'll see."

"Hmm. Interesting," Dani said. "When are you coming to D.C.?"

"No plans right now."

Dani put her phone away and swiveled to look out the windows. She heard a knock on the door and returned to her desk position.

Isabel and Yosef walked in.

Dani said, "What do you have for me?"

Isabel said, "Lists of U.S. people, companies, and foundations who are seen as against any climate action."

Dani said, "Corporate and Congress."

Isabel nodded. "I've even split them up into categories to help you set up meeting agendas."

Dani said, "Isabel, you're amazing. I'll go over these tonight and we'll talk in the morning."

Yosef said, "I too have lists and information, perhaps on a deeper and more global level. When you are ready, we can compare."

"Thank you, Yosef. I'll call you when I'm ready."

Yosef said, "I will be ready when you are," and left.

Isabel said, "I also want you to know, the FBI team is on the job, and I've expedited every request."

"Good," Dani said. "Perfect. Thank you. Any word on the coordinated presentation?"

"The memo went out. I expect to get a response by tomorrow as to the delivery date."

Dani nodded. "I'm done for today. I need a break. If you need me, I'll be in the family suite."

Isabel paused at the door and looked back at the President. "It looks like we are in for some very interesting times."

Dani laughed. "Indeed. Hold on. As they say, 'it's going to be a bumpy ride.'"

Chapter 27 ▶ Gramercy Avenue, New York City

Tuesday, 16 April, 11 a.m.
The spectacular spring day drew every New York City inhabitant outdoors. Rachel couldn't remember when the streets were so crowded and the hum of life so loud. She could feel Zeus's pressure against her leg. Even though people were giving him a wide berth, it wasn't as much as usual.

At the first corner, she felt inclined to turn around and go home. She stopped when rays of sunlight warmed her face. It felt wonderful and compelled her to continue to the East River walkway. The high tidewater lapped at the structure's edges without submerging it. A good day.

Rachel had once been so fearful being outside alone, she hadn't left her apartment for months. Zeus changed all her life. He provided her with all the support and protection she needed to enjoy her freedom. In tribute to him and her thoughts, she reached down to pet the dog.

While in the bent-over position, a runner jostled her, causing her to lose her balance. Zeus stiffened and his seventy-five pounds of muscle took her weight, preventing her from falling to the ground. She righted herself and led them to a bench so she could catch her breath.

Zeus leaped up beside her, sat, before laying across her lap. Rachel hugged him and leaned back, petting his caramel head. "Zeus." The dog's tail thumped on the seat. "I can't remember a time when anyone has been so confident as to ignore you." More tail thumping. "The good news is we're both alright." This time, Zeus licked her cheek. "Good boy. Let's go. After our walk, we'll pick up lunch."

Zeus jumped down and they rejoined the parade of people.

Not long after, a runner bumped into her again. She didn't lose her balance like the first time, but her anxiety ramped up. "Come on, Zeus, let's go back." As she turned, someone bumped with enough force to cause her to fall into the closest person's arms. Zeus yelped.

Rachel apologized to the man who held her upper arms, too long and too tightly, and wrenched herself free. Her heart pounded and she gasped for breath. Zeus herded her to the side and shielded Rachel from the passersby. She leaned against the railing and calmed herself by identifying images in her field of vision and repeating them over and over.

Her panic subsided. She knelt to assure Zeus she was fine. She petted his head, his back, and ran her hands down his sides. He whined. She looked down at her hands. She pulled out her phone with one and stared at the blood covering the other.

"Chris, I'm maybe two blocks away on the river walk. Someone stabbed Zeus."

"Don't move. Put pressure on the wound if you can. I'll be right there."

Rachel cradled Zeus in her arms, his head resting in the crook of her left elbow and talked nonsense to comfort him. He wagged his tail and licked her tears between attempts to nuzzle under her right arm. She shushed him, holding him tighter so he wouldn't wiggle so much. He whimpered and whined. "It'll be okay," she assured him. "Help is coming."

Chris appeared and knelt next to her—his arms laden with bandages. He ripped open gauze squares and put the pile on the dog's wound. "Hold this." Rachel held them in place, pressing them against Zeus's body.

Chris produced a roll of gauze and unwound it to secure the squares in place. "That'll have to do until we get him to the vet." He scooped up the dog and Rachel followed him—until she couldn't.

<~<~|~>~>

Chris cursed under his breath. "Who would stab a dog? Why the fuck would anyone stab a dog? This dog is family. Why would anyone want to hurt my family?"

He took a breath once he laid the dog on the back seat. He patted him on the head. "You're going to be okay, Zeus."

He expected Rachel to dive under his arm and slide in next to Zeus. She didn't. Surprised, he turned and held his arm out so she could take his hand. Confused, he turned expecting to see her. She seemed to have disappeared. He scanned the crowd, noticing a small group had collected around something on the ground.

Chris ran over and elbowed his way to the center. Rachel's inert body lay crumpled on the ground. He got his arms under her body and, operating on pure adrenalin, he picked her up. He made it to the car, put her next to Zeus, and jumped into the driver's seat.

He pulled out his phone to call 911 to alert police to the assault and the emergency room to expect him with two victims, one of them a dog. Ready to pull out, he realized a police car blocked his. The officer stood by his driver's window.

"Sir, may I see..."

Chris interrupted him. "I've got two injured, possibly dying, victims in the back seat. Either siren me to the emergency room or get out of my way."

The officer's eyes shifted from Chris to the inert bodies behind, widening as he realized the crisis. "Okay, sir. Follow me."

The policeman ran to his car, flipped the lights and siren on, and took off, Chris right behind him. The streets were brutal, jammed with cars, trucks, and busses. Messengers wove in and out of traffic, and jaywalkers seemed to materialize out of nowhere. Chris cursed them all which helped to offset his panic.

At the entrance to the emergency room, staff spilled out, opened the car, and put Rachel on a stretcher.

Chris pointed. "The dog too."

Someone in white started to argue.

Chris threw caution and decorum to the wind. "If you don't fucking take the dog, I will personally pull the trillions of dollars I've invested in this hospital and make sure you never work in this city again."

A doctor rushed past them. "Do it. Get the dog in here right now.

Chris followed the entourage inside and demanded an initial report from the doctors. Staff tried to calm him, "Please Mr. Gregory, we need you to calm down, do the paperwork, and be patient."

"I want to know if my wife is dead or alive."

"Please Mr. Gregory, the doctors will come out as soon as they know anything."

"I don't need a doctor, send a nurse, or anyone who knows anything."

"Please Mr. Gregory, you're not helping."

"I want to know about my dog."

"Mr. Gregory, please!"

Chris paused. He felt a huge presence next to him and turned. The security guard, who made linebackers look like children, said, "Sir, I must ask you to wait outside."

Chris turned to the receptionist. "Call Johnson. Tell him it's Chris Gregory."

She made the call, hung up and said, "His secretary said the hospital administrator is in a meeting."

Chris resisted the guard. "I have every right to be here," and pulled out his phone. He tapped a few times and said, "Johnson, I'm in the emergency room. I need status reports on my family. Make it happen. Now."

"Sir, I need you to come with me."

The receptionist looked at him oddly and said, "Wait a minute," to the security guard.

Chris said, "What?"

She nodded to the lettering over the emergency room doors—The Christopher Mark Gregory Emergency Services Wing. "Are you him?"

He gave her a crooked smile. "I promise you a raise if you find out what's happening."

Johnson arrived as she jumped out of her chair. He looked at her and said, "Sit." He pointed at Chris,

"You, come with me." To the guard, he said, "I've got this."

Chris followed him through the "staff only" double doors and into an empty recovery room. Johnson turned to him. "You've terrified my entire staff. I'll be surprised if they stop shaking by tomorrow."

"Status."

A doctor joined them. "Mr. Gregory, both your wife and dog will be fine. They were both stabbed by a very sharp, long, thin, needle-like stiletto. I don't think either felt anything, which caused the problem—a slow leak. I don't know how your wife realized the dog was bleeding, but it probably saved both their lives."

"So, they're alive, right?"

"Yes, they are both stable and in surgery." The doctor looked at the wall clock. "Give the surgical team time to finish up. Figure on seeing your wife in thirty minutes."

Chris sighed and dropped into the only chair in the room. "Oh my God. I thought I'd lost her."

"She'll be fine."

"What about Zeus?"

"The dog's going to be fine. He did great in surgery. You can see him now, although he is a little drowsy."

Chris turned to the hospital administrator. "Thank you, Johnson. Thank everybody for me."

Less than a half hour later, Chris joined Rachel in recovery and accompanied her to a private room, staying with her until she fell asleep.

With a sense of relief, he went outside her room and called J & J Security. "Jack, Rachel and Zeus are at the hospital. Same room. Starting now, I want twenty-four-seven coverage. I won't leave until you get here."

Chris returned to Gramercy Avenue, told Nikolai what happened, and went up to the apartment. He poured himself a single malt Scotch and called Beth. "Put me on speaker, this is for you and Eric." He recounted the morning's events and reported both Rachel and Zeus were on the mend. "I expect them home tomorrow or the next day."

Beth said, "Are you sure it was Tavius Global?"

"Who else would want to hurt or scare me?"

Eric said, "What can we do? There isn't a shred of evidence to connect the stabbings to Tavius Global."

"Rachel and I have talked it over, and I am going to release the technology tonight. It'll be open-source, and anybody can adapt it to their own needs, taking Octavius's dream of controlling my work out of his reach."

Beth said, "He's not going to be happy."

"What can he do?"

Eric said, "Anything he wants, including ruining your reputation and shutting down your entire business."

"We'll survive anything he throws at us. I have no need to play his games, nor do I want to."

Eric said, "I can't believe you're walking away."

Chris said, "I'm not. Rachel and I will cooperate with you in any way we can to shut down his 'revolutionary' concept for industrial sites, which is no better than a dressed-up prison."

Beth said, "We're looking into it as we speak."

"Rachel's convinced, and I'm not at all sure why, that Octavius uses undocumented and possibly slave labor. She thinks he could play a part in the Canadian First People's high disappearance rate, as well as refugees from Africa and South America via Mexico."

Eric said, "Did she have an anesthetic induced vision?"

Chris chuckled. "I'm not at all sure how her brain works but I've learned to trust her instincts."

Beth said, "Okay. Good heads-up. When she's up to it, have her call me."

Eric said, "Chris, this is not over. Watch your back."

Chris ended the call, took another sip of his drink, and showered.

Refreshed, he sat down at the computer. It took him three hours to design the open- source release. Satisfied, he packaged the code, keeping the directions simple and easy to follow. He sent the announcement to his International Computerized Universal Inc., ICU for short, security team.

He instructed them to upgrade company security and make sure we are ready to repel an all-out hacker attack. Next, they were to upgrade all client systems to the new version which could handle the tracking system and put them on high hacker security alert.

Immediately, he got "On it" responses.
He replied, "Text me when it's ready."

<~<~|~>~>

In her hospital bed, Rachel, recovered from the surgery aftereffects, was on her e-pad. She looked up and smiled when Chris walked in with one hand behind his back and a huge bouquet of roses in the other.

Zeus whined.

Chris said, "I miss you, buddy," and shifting his gaze to Rachel, "I missed you more."

Rachel gave him a pouty look and said, "How much?"

He revealed his hidden hand holding a brown paper bag. "This much."

Inside the bag, she found two large ice cream containers and one doggie size. She looked at him. "With everything?"

He grabbed one ice cream sundae, removed the top, and handed it to Rachel. "You bet." He grabbed the other for himself, and lowered Zeus's treat to the dog's waiting mouth.

Two spoons into the confection, Rachel said, "You are definitely the best."

After three heaping spoons of sundae, Chris put the container aside and said, "Move over." He laid down next to her, his arm around her shoulders. "Tell me again what happened."

Rachel recounted the jostling and pushing incidents. "Never happened before on any of our walks. People are pretty much afraid of Zeus. Then, from out of nowhere, it happened again. Maybe three or four times in succession. It seemed once I lost my balance, I couldn't get my bearings, even with Zeus as support."

"I believe you were targeted to let me know how vulnerable I am."

Rachel stared at him for a moment. "Octavius."

Chris nodded. "After you left, Octavius doubled his offer. I refused—again."

"Did he threaten you?"

"Not exactly. He said, 'the third time's a charm.'"

"If he's expecting you to sell to protect me from further harm, don't you dare."

Chris kissed her. "That's my girl."

Rachel said, "What are you going to do?"

"I'm planning to release the SMUTT technology as open-source code. Everyone will have the access and opportunity to build a tracking device on their own. In effect, I won't own it so I can't sell it. Nobody profits. It's all set to go public if you agree. So, what do you think?"

"You know I hate the whole chip idea, but if it's going to happen anyway, do it."

Chris smiled. "I knew I married you for a reason." He picked up his phone and saw the message, 'Ready.' "I'm calling my tech guys." He went to speed dial and tapped. To the voice on the receiving end, Chris said, "It's decided. Release the specs as we discussed." He ended the call, looked at Rachel and smiled. "Done."

"What did you mean 'as we discussed?'"

"I'm releasing everything except the chipboard's composition. Producers can figure out what works best for their application all on their own."

"Octavius will be pissed."

"True." Chris stroked his chin. "We'll have to watch our backs."

Rachel said, "Better, let's see how we can work with Beth and Eric to end his private prison empire."

"Way ahead of you. Already talked to them and they're on board."

"Tomorrow it's going to suck being Octavius." Rachel loaded her spoon with more ice cream.

Chris put his hand on hers. "I'm not sure if he's going lash out or not."

"I know."

"Know this too. No matter what happens, you and I are set. We don't and will never have to worry. We will always be okay."

Chapter 28 ▶ Harrison, New York

Tuesday, 16 April, 11 a.m.
Lucy ate lunch to the TV news as background noise
and read news updates on her phone. At the end of
her meal, she shut off the TV, put away her phone,
and walked to the sink to do dishes. As she passed the
police scanner, she turned it on. Among streaming
information was a stabbing report.

She put the dishes away and dried her hands.
Passing the scanner, she reached out to shut it off
when she heard the victim's name—Rachel Allen
Gregory. She froze, listening for a few more seconds
to find out the receiving hospital's name.

Lucy called the hospital, pretending to be a
registered physician. No luck. The nurse, wise to the
various scams of nosy non-relatives, said, "I'm sorry.
You are not on the patient's approved individuals list.
Please contact the family for updates."

Knowing she could hack the hospital computers,
Lucy poured herself a bourbon and sat down in her
easy chair and wondered how much she really cared

about Rachel Allen and why. Her body responded to the alcohol. She put her feet up and her head back, letting memories flood her brain.

Her first, and only, love had been Theodore Donovan—Ted—smart, handsome, and committed to making the world a better place. He founded PRAISE, Positive Response by Action to Institute a Safe Environment, a prestigious, well-respected operation, to help neighborhoods. Over time, his horizons expanded and soon PRAISE served the global community.

Lucy met him at Columbia University—they were classmates. He was the big-man-on-campus because his casual manner, easy smile, and lackadaisical approach put everyone at ease. He kept his accomplishments low key, so few knew he earned top grades.

Lucy, on the other hand, kept to herself. Her demeanor was controlled, self-contained, and cold. No one flocked to her side, although her brilliance permeated everything she did. She remembered sneering at Ted, disgusted and jealous at the same time. Graduating as an actuarial accountant meant everything to her, including never seeing Ted again. That is, until he asked her to go for a coffee with him, in the school café, in front of everyone.

Ted changed her life. She became his alter ego—the surrogate to carry out his secret vigilante operation to permanently remove undesirables who have escaped the law. He called it "seduction" because he would seduce a target with an offer they couldn't refuse. All walked willingly into a bloodless, painless death.

Lucy sipped her drink. It would have been perfect, heaven, except for one thing.

Ted's one and only love was Rachel Allen, who never reciprocated.

Lucy put down the glass and sat up. If Ted were here, he'd tell her to protect Rachel. Find out who tried to harm her. Seek retribution. But Ted's dead. She reclined again. Took another sip. Decided she didn't feel anything. However, for Ted's memory, she'd find out what happened to Rachel and do what she could without expending too much energy or exposing her operation.

Except for the one time the Ninja stepped in to save her unconscious ass as per cartel orders, she, and only she, looked out for Lucy Kilmer. She closed her eyes and fell asleep.

Later, Lucy read several newspapers' reports on the attack. The word "stiletto" kept appearing, not the usual knife. It jarred her. The Ninja kept a staff spear tucked close-at-hand. She had seen it once and it looked exactly like a stiletto. When she brought the Ninja on board, Lucy had to impose her seduction methods on a person who depended on the spear's swiftness and accuracy. However, it was understood the Ninja operated as an independent contractor and free to work with anyone willing to pay the price.

Her gut told her the Ninja had attacked Rachel.

She put out a digital tracker app to locate any articles on "stiletto," "ninja spear," "long thin knife," "Rachel Allen," and "Christopher Gregory." By the weekend, if not sooner, she'd know everything she had to know to move forward.

Chapter 29 ▶ Tavius Global, Chicago, Il

Wednesday, 17 April, 6:15 a.m.
In his penthouse apartment on the top floor, adjacent to his office, Octavius began his day with a forty-five-minute ride on his cardio-cycle. It cleared his head and toned his lean body, save for a bit of a tummy which emphasized the slight curvature of his spine and gave the impression his butt stuck out.

The imperfection marred his perfection perception, and he repeatedly asked his doctors for a remedy. After tests, their conclusion: all part of the aging process. Frustrated, he ordered the removal of all the mirrors in the workout room.

Done with his exercise ritual, he threw a towel around his neck, sat down, and picked up his e-pad. He checked his schedule, national and global media headlines, and made several notations. He checked the time. He always showered at seven. With a minute to go, Octavius caught a glimpse of a story featured in a tech column. "New Open-Source Code Available."

His phone chimed seven o'clock. A slave to routine, he saved the article and hit the shower.

Thirty-minutes later, showered and dressed, he entered his office and walked to the massive floor-to-ceiling windows. Lake Michigan stretched to the horizon and sparkled as the morning light skimmed the surface. Taking a moment to appreciate a power greater than his own calmed him.

His secretary knocked on the door and stood guard while a waiter walked in and set a tray on the desk—two dishes with silver covers and a tea-cozied tea pot—and left.

Octavius took a bite of toast dipped into a scrambled poached egg, pulled out his e-pad, and brought up the article he saved earlier. The moment he realized Chris Gregory had given his program away for free to the global community, he bit his tongue.

In pain and fury, he punched his intercom and demanded his secretary corral his top three company advisors and two trusted vice-presidents for a mandatory nine o'clock meeting.

He hung up without waiting for her response. He jumped to his feet and started pacing to displace the volcanic energy building in his body. After a few minutes, he tore off his jacket, tie, and shirt, and kicked off his shoes. Octavius dropped to the floor and did rapid-fire pushups until he collapsed.

Rolling onto his back, he laid on the floor. When his breathing normalized, he got up, collected his clothing, and entered his private restroom. Clean, dressed, and in control, Octavius emerged ready to meet the day's challenges.

The summoned were in their seats.

Octavius stood at the head of the conference table and said, "You all are aware I made an offer for ICU's tracking program, SMUTT."

Heads nodded.

"Rather than sell to me, Christopher Gregory gave it away. It's now free and available to anyone. Thoughts?"

The advisors pointed out Tavius Global could also use it. Plus, since it was free, not only did the company save money, but it could easily customize the program for its specific needs. Their collective opinion supported a win-win scenario.

Octavius said, "Sharing is not owning. While saving a few billion, I've lost trillions."

No one moved a muscle.

"This is not a win. I've lost and Christopher Gregory owes me."

Silence.

Octavius put his hands on the conference table and glared at each person. Straightening, he folded his arms across his chest. "I want Gregory investigated, and if he has something, anything, as valuable as SMUTT, I want it."

Chapter 30 ▶ White House, Washington D.C.

Thursday, 18 April, 9 a.m.

Beth sat deep in the maze of boxes and files. She heard Eric walk in and said, "It's about time."

"Hey, give me a break. I've been collecting data, testing theories, and working this case."

"I hope you brought me a coffee."

"I did—hot and just the way you like it," Eric said. "Where are you? There are twice as many boxes as yesterday."

Beth raised her arm and waved her hand. "I know. More come every hour. It's nearly impossible to keep track. However, I got lucky and found an anomaly."

Eric wound his way through the tight aisles. "Found you," he said and sat beside her. "Here's your coffee. Tell me what you've got."

"A connection between employee stats and net profit reporting. I'm seeing profits rise, although the number of employees remains static. I have a strong feeling something is out of whack. We've got to put together worksheets and look at gross and net profit reported, number of employees, payroll, taxes, and cost of goods."

Eric said, "Anything else?"

"Tons, but we can't forget why we started all this."

"Winnie Santiago."

Beth nodded. "If, as we suspect, there's something going on in the employee sector, we have to find it to get a warrant to do an in-depth analysis of Tavius Global's tax returns."

Eric fired up his computer and said, "Give me a minute and we'll get started."

"Set up a spreadsheet for each company. I expect comparable data will show the problems—if there are any."

Five hours and three cups of coffee later, they stared at the spreadsheet.

Beth said, "Save and duplicate this. Store the original. We'll use the copy."

"Done. Have you noticed anything?"

Beth shook her head. "We've got five years of returns in front of us and absolutely nothing looks out of order to me."

Eric leaned back in his chair. "Maybe we're too close?"

Beth gave him a sideways glance and leaned back. "What do you see?"

"Nothing."

"You're right. Each year is almost a carbon copy of the one before, ignoring fluctuations in sales, global markets, and cost of goods."

Eric said, "Almost like a programmed, computer-generated report?"

"Except, it wouldn't be true if it pulled actual information from all the inhouse systems."

Eric moved closer to Beth. "You're thinking a second set of books."

"Yes, but we don't have the expertise to prove it."

Eric pulled out his phone. "I'm going to get a couple of forensic Certified Public Accountants in here. They'll know how to pinpoint the problem."

"Good," Beth said. Her phone buzzed. She listened and said, "Have to go see the President."

<~<~|~>~>

Dani welcomed Beth and introduced Sybil, who walked over and embraced the Special Agent.

Beth flushed. "I'm not sure I deserved such a greeting."

Sybil backed off. "You absolutely do. I can't thank you enough for all the care you took in Lidia's case. I was out of my head with worry, fear, and, once you found her body, grief."

"Fortunately, we got it sorted. I hope you're doing better."

"I am, and happy to be working with you."

The women sat down around the tea, coffee, water, and pastry laden coffee table.

Beth said, "Have either of you talked to Rachel or Chris?" The other two women shook their heads. "Yesterday, Rachel and Zeus, who are fine by the way, were stabbed by someone with a stiletto."

Dani and Sybil peppered her with who, when, and why.

Beth shook her head. "All I know is they'd both be dead if Rachel hadn't noticed Zeus's wound and called Chris, who broke all speed records getting them to the hospital."

Sybil said, "Who would want to hurt them?"

Beth said, "I've checked with the police. There's no evidence identifying the attacker."

Dani stood and paced the room as Sybil poured coffee and Beth chose a chocolate chip cookie. "I wonder. Could this have anything to do with Chris's announcement to open source his chip tracking software?"

Beth nodded. "I wouldn't be surprised. Octavius tried to buy it."

Sybil sipped her coffee. "Are you thinking Octavius ordered the attack?"

Dani froze. "That bastard." She turned to the women. "I bet he did. He doesn't take 'no' for an answer."

Beth said, "Still, we have no proof to tie him to the stabbing."

Dani sat down. "True. Beth, tell me how your research is going? Are you making progress?"

"We opened a new line of inquiry just before you called. Eric's calling in a team of forensic CPAs. I hope we'll have something very soon."

"Good. Thank you. Let me know when. I appreciate your coming up here. Sybil found out you were in the building and wanted to say hello."

Sybil smiled. "I'm sure we'll see each other again."

Beth's phone buzzed. She looked at the ID. "I've got to go. Please excuse me, Madam President."

Dani nodded and Beth left. Turning to Sybil, Dani said, "Let's walk around the garden."

Outside, Sybil said, "You know, it very well may be Octavius who targeted Rachel. He is the cartel's managing partner. He ordered Lidia killed when she wouldn't launder their money. This is almost the same scenario."

Dani said, "We have to be careful dealing with the cartel. There is nothing they won't do to protect their control. Based on what you've told me, if there's trouble, they kick out the problem and continue, adjusting as necessary."

Sybil said, "Vanderhagen Holdings is part of it and therefore vulnerable. Peter must have a plan B. If not, I'll work one out with him. Maybe a plan C as well."

"Good idea. We can't be too prepared."

Sybil said, "I'll be on the next cartel call."

Dani smiled. "Even though I'm the President, he treats me as his assistant. Don't let him pull that shit with you."

Sybil said, "I won't. I have leverage. He's the sole owner of Tavius Global. I will bring national headlines and charges against him and the cartel members for killing Lidia."

Stepping off the path into the grass, Dani took off her shoes and wiggled her toes. "Remember when we were young—carefree?"

"Barely."

"Sybil, I'm not sure going in with a threat is the best approach."

Her phone buzzed. She looked and saw a text message from Yosef. "Octavius got sued big time by the last oligarch he crossed. He's not looking to make waves while he's preparing his big announcement about Tavius Global Chicago."

She raised her eyes. "I have a better plan."

"Tell me."

"Octavius is our chief competitor, along with China and India. Our involvement is through many layered companies, so our trading doesn't set off alarms."

"Secrets," Sybil said, "have never served me well."

Dani gave her a sharp look. "It's going to have to be your middle name until Peter is well enough to return."

Sybil put her hands up in surrender. "Peter and I will strategize. I'll be ready. In fact, I'll call Octavius today and explain I'm the only person capable of protecting the cartel's and the Vanderhagen interests while Peter recovers."

Dani put her shoes on. "Let him see you hold equal power and know your stuff."

Sybil smiled. "Don't worry. I will and I do."

Chapter 31 ▶ Bethesda, Maryland

Thursday, 18 April, 10 a.m.
Sybil left the White House and went to Walter Reed to talk with Peter. She found him sitting up in bed working on his computer. "I see you're feeling better."

Peter looked up. "Pretty much. There doesn't seem to be enough medication to deal with my headaches. Doctors say it may take months or even years before they're gone."

"We'll deal with it," Sybil said, "one day at a time." She walked over to the bed and looked at his computer screen. "What are you working on?"

"I've brought up the worksheet the cartel uses at the weekly meetings so I can explain it to you before the call tomorrow."

She pulled up a chair, sat, and said, "Let's do this."

Peter explained where he got the numbers for the Vanderhagen Holdings and gave her access to the ledgers.

He said, "We look at profit and loss as well as our balance sheet." He showed her how to run the reports. "The last thing we do is compare the current report to the last one and identify the changes with a plus or minus percent."

"So, no one ever gets to see the actual numbers, just the variables."

"Exactly. Next, we compare our changes with the cartel's total changes, and determine if we are in line with the fluctuations. If there is a negative deviation, we determine the cause and make adjustments."

"Adjustments?"

"A rethinking and necessary realignment of leadership and policies of governments whose economies are not performing as predicted."

Sybil stood up and went to the window. "Within the cartel structure, you're the adjuster. You take care of the messy side of all this."

Peter nodded. "Coups, disappearances, accidents, governing philosophies, and trade manipulation."

"Are these discussed on the call?"

"Once we know who, where, and what, members may offer information and suggestions."

"Does anyone question the numbers dictating adjustments?"

"Not since I've been in the calls. Octavius, the current chairman, dominates the call. No one, to my knowledge, has questioned his assessments."

"Have you arranged the adjustments determined by the cartel?"

Peter said, "That's what the Vanderhagens do. I knew all about this going in and believe I've helped keep stability in the world markets."

"I see."

"Mom, you don't have to do this."

"Yes, Peter, I do."

"Let me do the call."

Sybil said, "No. This is something I have to do myself."

He handed her the "cartel" phone, and she left.

Outside the hospital building, Sybil followed the signs to the Green Road, a healing woodland space the Hospital provides for patients and their families. She needed to clear her head to enter the world she'd fought against her whole life—a world of privilege, abuse, bullying, misogyny, and entitlement which saw itself above the law.

The Executive Director at the PRAISE Foundation, she oversaw the disbursement of millions of dollars to ease the suffering of peoples denied their human rights by the very governments driving them into poverty. The Presidents, dictators, and elected officials were caught between their own greed, their people's needs, and the cartel which put them in office in the first place.

She looked at her watch. She had to call Octavius to introduce herself. Her dueling responsibilities did not have to be examined now.

Sybil laughed and spoke to the wind. "It's a good bet he won't even talk to me. I've got nothing to worry about."

Returning to Peter's hospital room, she saw him sitting in the recliner, watching TV, and eating his lunch. She closed the door, pulled over a chair, and sat down next to him.

Peter looked at her and said, "Hi, Mom. How'd it go?"

"I didn't make the call. I thought about everything I wanted to say and realized it might not be the best approach."

"Interesting and unexpected."

Sybil sat facing him. "I know. I'm trying out a new perspective."

Peter said, "Uh-oh. You being flexible can't be good. Do you want me to make the call?"

Sybil smiled. "You read my mind—if you're up for it. I'll be here on stand-by."

"No problem. Close the door." Peter used the remote and turned the TV off. He took the phone from Sybil and called Octavius. Once the phone started ringing, he put the speaker on.

"Peter," Octavius said. "How are you feeling? I heard about your fall in Alaska."

"I'm much better than I was, but I'm still not operating at one-hundred percent. It's the reason for this call. I've asked my mother, Sybil Vanderhagen Powell, to fulfill my position and responsibilities until I'm able to return. She's a Vanderhagen and the best person to look after our interests and the cartel's."

Octavius ran true to form. "I'm as uncomfortable with a woman on the call as I know the other members will be."

Peter rose from the chair, his face flush with anger. "Look. I have the right to appoint my successor. It's my decision, and I don't give a rat's ass who likes it or not."

Sybil ran to his side and grabbed the phone out of his hand and pointed him to the chair. She mouthed, "Sit down."

She spoke into the phone. "Hello Octavius, this is Sybil. Peter's brain injury has affected, among other things, his impulse control."

"I see."

"I am in constant communication with him and prepared to do whatever is necessary to maintain, control, and grow the Vanderhagen and cartel fortunes."

Octavius said, "Be prompt," and ended the call.

Sybil looked at the phone and said, "What a rude man."

Peter said, "You didn't have to do interrupt. I was doing just fine." He sipped ice water. "To your point, Octavius can be a prick."

Sybil said, "Regardless, I'm on the cartel call."

Peter shook his head. "He was way too easy, Mom. Norms are established. No variations. Something's happening at Tavius Global or with Octavius personally. I can feel it."

"I believe you. However, until we know what, there's not much we can do."

Peter nodded. "Be here an hour before the call so we can go over some key issues."

"Don't you trust me?"

"You, Mom, absolutely. Octavius, not so much."

Chapter 32 ▶ Gramercy Avenue, New York City

Thursday, 18 April, 1 p.m.

Rachel stepped into their apartment with her arms uplifted to embrace the space. "I'm so glad to be home."

Chris said, "Don't get too excited. The doctor said you need rest."

"I'm fine. I've been resting for two days."

"Very funny," he said. "Let's get you to bed, and I'll bring you some tea and those English dark chocolate digestives you love."

"How about I rest by having tea on the couch instead?"

Chris shook his head. "I don't know."

Rachel walked into his arms. "I know you're worried about me. I promise I'll be good. Please let me feel normal again."

They kissed and he relented. "Okay, go sit down and put your feet up."

When he turned his back, Rachel walked over to the staircase and put her foot on the first step.

"No stairs."

She turned. "I need my computer."

"Work is not rest."

"Chris, stop fussing."

"Okay, okay. Maybe I'm overthinking the doctor's orders." He walked over to her. "Sit. I'll go get your computer."

"With the power pack."

Chris pointed to the couch. "Go."

Once Rachel settled down, Zeus limped over to her and laid down on the floor, his head on her foot. She sipped the tea and munched on a biscuit. Within minutes, overcome by a wave of exhaustion and heavy eyelids, she fell asleep until big slurpy kisses awakened her.

She opened her eyes and saw Zeus staring at her. She smiled. His big pink tongue licked her again.

Rachel reached out and petted him.

Chris said, "We've just come back from our slow walk. He wanted you to know how much he missed you."

She looked at Zeus. "I missed you, too. You're such a good boy."

Zeus's tail whipped back and forth.

Rachel sat up and stretched. "What time is it? How long did I sleep?"

"Four hours, give or take," Chris said from the kitchen. "How do you feel?"

"Fine. Rested. You were right." She spied her computer on the coffee table. She reached for it. "I have to get to work."

"What do you mean 'get to work?'"

"Octavius can't come after us without a fight."

Chris finished up in the kitchen and joined Rachel on the couch. "I can't imagine what you're thinking, but there is no way to fight Octavius without serious consequences."

Rachel said, "He tried to hurt you by killing Zeus and me. He's responsible, and he needs to pay for it."

"Them's fighting words, Mrs. Gregory, considering you're in recovery for two weeks."

"Do you think I should do nothing?"

Chris put his arm around her. "Releasing the code as open source, in retaliation for his attack on you, hurt his pride and pocketbook—a two-fer."

"It was a great idea on your part."

Chris said, "The best part is, he didn't win. He didn't get to make a fortune on reselling and leasing it or making it a proprietary part of his model community."

She put her head on his shoulder. "Well, when you put it that way..."

"It's the only way to put it."

"What if I wrote an article on his model industrial complex?"

"Why bother?"

"To expose his scheme to enslave the world's workers, especially in his fabricated world."

"Absolutely not. You'd be like waving a red flag in front of raging bull."

"People need to know what's going on."

"You don't even know what's going on. An hour-long tour isn't enough research before you tear apart an idea."

"The idea's been around since the 1800's, and in similar models since the agrarian age started, and farmers didn't own the land they worked. All Octavius has done is dress it up."

"All good until you mentioned Octavius."

Rachel sat up straight. "You mean the historical perspective would be okay with you?"

Chris laughed. "Why not? Isn't it in the book you're working on? If people are going to be able to evaluate what's happening today, it's a good idea to first give an historical point of view."

"Absolutely." She threw her arms around him. "You're the best."

Chapter 33 ▶ White House, Washington D.C.

Thursday, 18 April, 5 p.m.

Beth, Eric at her side, sat across from the FBI forensic CPA Gilbert Abrams and his assistant. She said, "Tell me what you've found."

Abrams spoke for the pair. "We have one definite problem and two highly suspicious problems."

Eric said, "What's definite?"

Abrams handed them a folder and said, "Here's the documentation. You can follow as I explain the short version. When you divide the national average annual revenue per employee into the company's reported revenue, the answer should match, or at least come close to the number of reported employees, within a count of ten, plus or minus."

Beth said, "What did you find?"

Abrams said, "Tavius Industries Chicago has under reported almost half its employees. Now, I realize there's no reporting for robots, which have replaced any number of people, but I'm basing my numbers on their tax filing and the averages reported by other companies similar in size and industry."

"Is it a simple mistake or are we looking at fraud?"

"I can't be sure at this moment," Abrams said. "It looks like the Tavius Global accountants just reproduced the tax return from the previous year and applied published percentage indices without remembering to update the employee information."

Eric said, "So no one would have noticed in the first filing, because the discrepancies would have been within or close enough to the variation."

"Pretty much. However, over time, the difference is impossible to ignore."

Beth smiled. "We've got them. A warrant will be a no-brainer for the judge. We will have access to the site and do a physical count, as well as verify the listed employees are, in fact, working there."

"Don't rush," Eric said. "What about the two suspicious problems?"

Abrams said, "The Chicago site, as well as others, lists an inordinate number of consultants who were well paid for undisclosed services. While it may be on the up and up, my experience says something underhanded is going on. For example, they might be supplying underpaid immigrant workers who go unreported, or black-market items."

Beth said, "The company sits right on Lake Michigan. They have their own port, airstrip, railway stop, and road system. This means they operate virtually unchecked."

Eric said, "If there is a port of entry, U.S. Customs has authority. Although, if Tavius Global is breaking any rules, bribing officials would be no big deal."

"I agree. This leads me to the other suspicious problem—human trafficking."

Beth said, "You think they are buying people to work in their manufacturing plant?"

Eric said, "We know about climate refugees, forced to migrate by drought and heat. They are prime targets for kidnappers and slave traders, especially along coasts and borders like U.S. and Mexico, U.S. and Canada, and Africa."

Abrams said, "If true, which I suspect it is, Tavius Global may have set themselves up as a distribution hub for human trafficking. There's much money to be made by using and selling illegal workers. Companies often hire the unscrupulous people running such operations, often identified on company tax forms as 'consultants.'"

Beth said, "Everything we've talked about is theory. I need tax filings and background information on several of these 'consultants' to make our case. To take down Tavius Global, we have to know what we're looking for and be sure we'll find it."

Abrams said, "We're on it."

Eric said, "I'll get on the shipping info and dig up info on land and air access to the site as well." To the CPAs he said, "Let me know which consultants you select. I'll do their background checks."

Beth said, "Sounds like we have a plan. I'll get the President to sign off." She pulled out her phone and texted Isabel. "Can the President see me now?" Seeing the answer, "yes," she stood up. "I've got to go. Don't say anything to anyone about what we've found or what we're working on."

Five minutes later, she arrived breathless at Isabel's desk. Dani's Chief of Staff nodded. Beth took a few seconds to breathe and, composed, entered the Oval Office.

Dani looked up from her computer. "What have you got for me?"

Beth left the Oval Office a little dazed.

Isabel said, "Are you okay?"

Beth nodded.

"Good, because Eric is meeting you here."

Eric appeared as if on cue. "C'mon, Beth we have to go. They want us at the FBI crime lab."

Beth said, "We're not on duty."

"It wasn't a request," Eric said. "He took her arm and led her to the building's exit. "By the way, what happened with Dani?"

"We had a weird conversation. She listened as I explained, asked me some questions to be sure she understood. Said she'd think about it overnight and get back to me in the morning."

"Sounds reasonable. What's the weird part?"

"It wasn't what she said, Eric. It was more about how she said it. She's normally very decisive. Something's happened. This Tavius Global investigation may be way bigger than she thought."

Eric put his arm around her, pulling her close. "We will know soon enough. For now, we can only do our jobs. The big guns make the decisions and take responsibility for the outcomes. Let the President do her job." He kissed her. "Let's find out what's happening here, have dinner, and enjoy the rest of the evening."

She kissed him. "I like the way you think."

At the building's entrance, Beth said, "FBI Special Agents Neilson and Jerrod for the coroner."

They waited less than five minutes. A man walked toward them. "I'm Dr. Bob Koenig, a forensic pathologist working with the coroner. Follow me." He led them to a large room, with tables lined up in three rows. On each table were skeleton remains. "These bodies were pulled out of a New Jersey wetlands sanctuary, fed by the Delaware River, across from Philadelphia."

Beth said, "How many?"

Dr. Koenig said, "We have identified fifteen separate individuals. There may be more coming."

"Out of curiosity, did one of them surface? I mean, how?"

Dr. Koenig said, "From the report, the sanctuary is protected. There are a series of raised walks visitors use to explore limited areas. Recently, with the head waves, and the changing water levels, wrapped plastic bags became visible. The contents are what you see here."

He walked down one aisle and half-way down a row. "We are in the midst of tagging, testing, and identifying these individuals."

Beth said, "Why are we here?"

"Two reasons. First, one body had a ninja staff spear tip in one of the rib bones. It resembles a stiletto tip. Second, it is the only weapon we can directly associate with a body—this body."

Beth said, "That's the second time in two weeks I've heard about such a weapon."

Koenig nodded. "Me too. It's not your run-of-the-mill choice. It's an up-close attack. Feels personal."

"What's the other reason?"

"This." Koenig held up a badge of some sort.

Eric said, "Is it an ID?"

Koenig nodded. "We've pulled the name—Winnifred Santiago." He looked at Beth. "I know you're head of Missing Persons. We are using your open cases to identify these bodies."

Beth turned to Eric. "There's a huge disconnect between where she disappeared and where she wound up." She looked at Koenig. "Have you identified others?"

"So far, we've identified seven. Five were men. All seven were either in politics or business. There is no evidence specifically identifying the murder weapon. Besides the weapon, they have one other thing in common. The last time anyone saw them, they were all going to a week-long business event."

Beth said, "You mean scheduled?"

"Yes. Nothing seemed out of place. No one appeared distressed. It's all here in our follow-up interviews with co-workers and families."

Eric said, "Sounds familiar, Beth."

She said, "Yes, it does. We have a serial murderer with no obvious leads."

Eric gave her a crooked smile. "No obvious leads—yet."

Chapter 34 ▶ White House, Washington D.C.

Thursday, 18 April, 8 p.m.
Dani, her family, and Sybil finished dinner. Conversation felt awkward, as if each person struggled to find a topic separate from their thoughts. The twins disappeared as soon as they finished their last bite of dessert. Dani, Sybil, and Terence sat in the living room sipping after-dinner drinks.

Terence said, "I'd like to know what's going on. I have never been in a room with you two where you've been this quiet. Give."

Sybil said, "I'm just worried about Peter. He's not coming along as fast as I thought he would."

"Be patient. He has the time to rest, so let him. Peter is not the guy with a nine to five job."

"You're right. Still, he does have responsibilities. They require a level of focus and action he's not ready to assume."

"You're talking about Vanderhagen Holdings?"

Dani said, "Yes. Sybil is going to step in for Peter until he is ready to resume his role."

Terence said, "So, what's the problem?"

Sybil sipped her drink. "I'm bracing myself for what happens when I ask my questions."

Terence emptied his glass. "What could possibly happen?"

"Since no woman has ever sat in on this call tomorrow, and nobody seems to question items on the agenda, I expect a hostile reaction."

Dani said, "Why? What did you find?"

Sybil said, "Their growth indices don't consider actual consumer activity. In other words, their numbers and decisions are based on false assumptions."

Terence said, "Interesting. Sounds worth talking about."

Dani said, "Even though it's not a realistic indicator, they're probably using the Gross National Product and adjusting for other variables."

Sybil said, "Or the numbers, as they are, hold a secret known only to those on the call. I'll check with Peter in the morning."

Dani said, "I also wrestle with knowledge concerning the cartel."

Terence said, "Stop. I don't want to know anything about this. Ladies, I leave you to your business."

After he left, Dani said, "Do I share it and possibly breakup the cartel, or let it be so we can continue to benefit financially from its leadership?"

Sybil said, "The cartel is poison. They killed Lidia. If you've got something to take them down, use it." She stood. "I have to get some sleep. I must be ready for this call tomorrow morning."

Dani stayed seated and said, "Good night. See you at breakfast."

Alone, she sipped her drink and stared into space. *If Octavius oversaw the human trafficking, he's out.* She'd make sure of that and make the most of the necessary power shift.

The immediate question to the cartel is are they all complicit in human trafficking, she suspected Vanderhagen Holdings was. On paper, she knew she had divested her share. Still, it could mean bye-bye presidency and hello jail.

She took another sip. Her phone buzzed. She looked at the ID. "Hello."

Yosef said, "I have some information."

"I'm listening."

"The Mossad is tracking smuggling operations moving more than a thousand units."

"Units?"

"Any combination of humans, animals, plants, and freight."

"I see."

"They track point of origin and port of call. I will text you those ports of call in the U.S., including the one on Lake Michigan at Tavius Global."

"Are the other companies identified?"

"Yes. I will text you the whole list."

"Impressive."

"Anything else?"

"Not now. A lot to digest. Good work."

"I will contact you when I have more."

Chapter 35 ▶ Bethesda, Maryland

Friday, 19 April, 7 a.m.
Sybil exited the elevator and stepped into the hallway. She glanced into the solarium. Peter stood by the window. She approached him, gave him a hug, and said, "What are you doing up so early?"

Peter said, "They get me up at six every morning to take my vitals. What's your excuse?"

"I wanted to go over the call's specifics. I'd like to appear as if I've done it a hundred times before."

"I figured you might have questions. Let's do this."

Sybil took Peter's arm. "Have you had breakfast?" He shook his head. "Come on. Let's go back to your room, get you some nourishment and medication while we talk." By the time they reached his room, his breakfast tray sat on the rolling-table.

Peter said, "Perfect timing," and collapsed on the recliner.

Sybil wheeled the table to him.

Peter laughed. "Okay. I'll eat and you talk."

Sybil sat on the bed, pulled out her e-pad, and opened the files she flagged last night. "First, do cartel members know who has a vested interest in which industry?"

"Sometimes yes. Sometimes no."

"Does anyone question the information each member adds to the spreadsheet?"

"Not that I've heard."

Sybil bit her lip. "So, everyone on the call believes they can tell what's going on by the numerical entries and the final calculations?"

Peter nodded.

Sybil said, "They must have a lot of trust in each other."

Peter sipped his coffee and put the cup down. "A trust driven by self-interest and profit. As long as each is doing well, they leave it up to Octavius and the spreadsheets for an overall global analysis."

Sybil handed Peter her e-pad. "I've used the codes you gave me. Something is keeping me from accessing the site."

Peter entered the codes. "Entry denied. Access may be tied to my IP address. Hand me my computer."

Sybil did, and he went through the same processes again. "I'm in."

"Go to the spreadsheets used for the meeting. See if you can view the formulas behind the calculations."

Sybil watched as he tried to access the set-up information. "Are you locked out?"

"Yes. Octavius has made it proprietary."

Sybil sat, facing her son. "This means this forecasting tool has determined our future without our understanding what factors are considered. I find this more than a little disturbing."

"Mom, it works. It's been working for years. We're only interested in the global picture to make sure economic goals are met. If anything is out of alignment with our projections, we decide how to correct the problem, and take care of it."

"As you've already explained."

"Did I explain the Vanderhagens are the watchdogs--your dad, brother, me, and if I can't do it, you? We are the fixers. We make sure whatever must happen happens. That's what we do. What you may have to do."

Sybil's body stiffened. She'd suspected all along her father had Lidia killed. Now, for the first time, she knew for sure. "Peter, have we ever questioned our role in this?"

He shrugged. "Never. It is what it is. We stave off recession, power capitalism, and ensure currency, trade, manufacturing, and investments remain strong. The cartel is a good and necessary organization keeping the world safe and the economy strong."

Sybil wasn't so sure.

<~<~|~>~>

In Chicago, Octavius prepared his office for the cartel call. He clicked a button on his remote and the office door locked. Another click engaged the white noise machine to ensure privacy from listening devices.

Today, as the cartel's chairman, he prepared to initiate the online meeting. He opened his computer, double-clicked on the sharing application, and waited. The cartel members logged in within seconds. Their images appeared on the screen and his appeared in a circle at the lower right. Octavius counted each connection click—an old habit to make sure there weren't any unauthorized listeners.

Octavius stared at his image and adjusted his position to look as powerful as possible. At seventy, the face he saw looked fifty. He jutted his chin out a little more and sat straighter. With the appearance of looking down at the others, he began the meeting.

"Welcome. Today, Vanderhagen Holdings is represented temporarily by Sybil Vanderhagen Powell. If anyone has issues, talk to me privately. Let's begin." Octavius cleared his throat. "Reports." The screen changed to a spreadsheet matrix.

One by one, each member updated their own numerical data. After the last entry, Octavius pushed the "CALCULATE" button. Preset formulas produced detailed graphs and charts of global issues and trends. "Comments?"

Silence.

Octavius said, "Good."

Sybil said, "I have a question."

Peter, who insisted on being in the room as a backup, shook his head, put up his hand, and mouthed, "Mom, don't."

She ignored him.

Octavius said, "Is it relevant to the purpose of this call?"

"I think it is. After going over our records and the cartel data, the totals seem out of sync with the real effects from natural and political disasters. May I inspect the calculations behind the on-screen results? I would like to know what factors drive the conclusions."

"Mrs. Powell, I must refuse. They are proprietary and for our discussions only."

"Then, Octavius, please explain how we keep profits high while there are over one-hundred-forty-thousand climate migrants who have no food or jobs due to fire, flooding, and drought? Explain how our profitability graphs continue to trend upward while millions have no access to potable water, clean air, shelter, food, education and healthcare?"

"It is not important how, Mrs. Powell."

"Without a comprehensive glimpse into the process, how can I, in fact, all of us, trust the information? With each wave of destruction, there are fewer and fewer customers—people just don't have the resources to buy or store goods. Still, we get richer as the poor get poorer. Isn't it clear we are digging our own graves?"

"Enough, Mrs. Powell. This is your first call. Don't force me to make it your last." Octavius cleared his throat. "Further comments?"

Sybil said, "Octavius, you don't get to say 'enough' to me. Even though you run the call, we are all equal members. I will persist until you or other sources provide the information."

Octavius didn't give her the courtesy of a reply. "This call is finished."

Octavius waited for each line to disconnect, counting the tones, and waiting two minutes before he hung up. His compulsive need to know that no one monitored the call staved off his paranoia.

Chapter 36 ▶ White House, Washington D.C.

Friday, 20 April, 10 a.m.
Beth entered the Oval Office.

Dani greeted her without getting up from the chair behind her desk. "Good morning. I'm sorry it took so long for me to get back to you. It's a major action and I had to give it serious consideration."

Beth said, "Not a problem. Do you need more information?"

"No. You were very clear. I agree, we need more evidence to make our case."

"I forgot you were a lawyer."

"Many do. They think I'm President because I was in the right place at the right time. Their tendency to underestimate me often works to my advantage."

"Madam President, I bet it does. However, regarding our evidence, the CPAs are working to gather proof to support their analysis. Eric is doing background checks on our targets, and I am working the agencies.

"What I need is your authority to keep digging without going through normal channels. My fear is Tavius Global will find out and clean shop before we can get our warrant."

"How many tax years have you looked at?"

"Five so far."

"Go back ten." Dani stood and walked around the desk.

"I agree. What about access to information?"

Dani said, "Give me your list and I'll clear it. Meanwhile, keep me up to date on your progress. We can't have any slip-ups."

Beth said, "Understood."

As she left the room, Dani's private phone buzzed. Yosef. She said, "Hello."

Yosef said, "I have news. The Mossad has intercepted three ships correctly targeted as slavers. However, one escaped our net—the Olivia Bay."

"Where is it headed?"

"It lists Tavius Global as its port-of-call and flies under a Cypriot flag."

"How much time do I have?"

Yosef said, "Two weeks until it enters the St. Lawrence Seaway and goes through two U.S. Customs and Immigration checkpoints—the first is at the Ogdensburg port, and the second happens a week later when it docks."

"Send me the info."

"Texting now."

Dani said, "Good work. I'll weigh my options."

Yosef said, "Let me know if you need more info. The world is counting on you to do the right thing." Dani ended the call and texted Beth. "You've got to have warrants and be ready to execute on-site in nineteen days—May 9th."

Chapter 37 ▶ White House, Washington D.C.

Saturday, 20 April, 8 a.m.

During breakfast, Dani noticed Terence and the twins were quiet. The teenagers' eyes darted from parent to parent as they shoveled in enough food for a small army.

She waited for someone to say something until she couldn't. "Okay. Something's going on. I can feel it. Isaac. Ivan. Is this the first time you've eaten this week?"

Isaac said, "We're sixteen. Eating is what we do."

Dani said, "Uh-huh."

Ivan said, "He's right. We're growing and we have to feed the machine."

Isaac said, "Hormones, Mom. They're killing us."

"Terence, are you going to tell me?"

"We were hoping you could take some time off and go with us to the park."

"Do you need me for a ribbon cutting?"

He shook his head. "Just for a family day."

"Come on you guys. You know I can't just roam around a park. Our security contingent alone would fill almost half of it."

Ivan said, "Mom, you could wear a disguise. We all could."

"Really? What kind of disguise would you wear?"

The boys spoke together. "Motor bike racing suits and helmets."

Dani looked at Terence. "I suppose you'd be wearing the same thing since you'd all be on the same team."

Terence had the good sense to look like he'd been caught. "Uh, yes." Suddenly, he brightened. "We even got the whole get-up for you."

Dani put her hand to her chest and widened her eyes. "For me?"

Isaac stood on her left and Ivan on her right. "Mom, it's going to be so much fun. No one will know who we are, and you'll get to watch us race four-by-fours over a dirt track. It's going to be the best day ever."

"Have you figured out security?"

Terence said, "We have given it some thought. The security detail has checked the speedway and will be dressed as our team's mechanics. Cecil's coming and he'll have standard security."

Dani said, "Cecil who?"

"What do you mean?"

"If you're referring to the Vice President, Cecil and I can't be in the same place at the same time."

Terence groaned. "I forgot. I really messed up."

Dani patted his hand. "Not so terrible. What if Team Mitchell wears head cameras? I'll have the tech guys set up a multi-view screen and I'll watch and be able to talk to you."

Isaac said, "So, we can go?"

Dani smiled, "Of course." She got two hugs and a kiss on each cheek, followed by a rundown of what to expect. "Family time is a good thing."

Dani remained at the table after her men had deserted her for guy-talk. As she sipped her coffee, she silently thanked Terence for thinking of Cecil and called her Vice President. "Hi, Cecil."

"Madam President, how nice to hear from you."

"Cecil, I want you to know I appreciate you running interference for the family at the park this afternoon."

"No problem. I am happy to help."

"Talk to me about the bipartisan coalitions you're building."

Cecil said, "It's so important to have both sides of the aisle working together if we are going to achieve your administrative goals."

Dani heard the "your" reference. A not-so-subtle position statement. She wasn't going to let him off so easily. "Because of your 'can do' enthusiasm, I'd like you to take charge of one our key projects."

"I'm at your service. What can I do?"

"Get the EEA, Emergency Environment Act, passed as soon as possible."

"Madam President, my effectiveness is primarily in the Senate."

"You are too modest. I know you've been working with people in the House of Representatives. Please coordinate a leadership meeting in the conference room by this Thursday to strategize how to get the EEA passed as soon as possible."

Cecile coughed and cleared his throat. "That's going to be a challenge. The major corporations continue to balk at any significant changes to their process or profits. I've had very little success in delivering the bigger picture."

Dani said, "Cecil, if anyone has the clout to do this, you do. I am available to you, day or night, to get this done. Let me know what you need. I'd like to see it passed by May 15th."

"Three weeks?"

"May 21st."

Cecil said, "June first. I know I can get it done by June first."

Dani smiled. "Thank you, Cecil. Let me know tomorrow what time on Thursday. Oh, one more thing. Please start the ball rolling by talking about the EEA in your opening remarks at the park this afternoon?"

She ended the call and wondered how soon Cecil would call his puppet master and financial backer, Octavius. He wasn't her choice. She had been thrust into the presidency and forced to accept those already holding elected and cabinet positions. Cecil, who stepped into her position as Vice President, was picked by a committee of insiders, and she bowed to their advice.

Dani learned of Cecil's connection to Octavius within weeks of his appointment. From the cartel's point of view, the match improved the cartel's influence. Dani was a Vanderhagen, and Cecil could be bought. They controlled the top two elected offices in the United States and could push their agenda forward without worrying about exposure.

The cartel found she wasn't a pushover. Dani chose to distance herself and her decisions from the cartel. Cecil, who had the perfect mix of attractiveness, charm, and presence, she manipulated like tool in her toolbox, neither friend nor confidant. She kept him, and Octavius, as far away from the Oval Office as possible. She would need Octavius's broad influence to pass the EEA and Cecil might be the one who could sell it to him.

"Dad, we're ready." The twins ran into the room.

Dani laughed. "My goodness. You two look so handsome and professional. Are you really my sons?"

Terence marched in. "Team Mitchell reporting for inspection."

Dani rose and bowed. "I am awed in your presence. May you go out and slay speed records, capture ribbons, and above all, be safe and don't kill yourselves."

Chapter 38 ▶ West Memphis, Arkansas

Monday, 23 April, 9 a.m.
A perfect day graced West Memphis, Arkansas. Eric and forensic CPA Gilbert Abrams drove up Route 40, past the motels and hotels and twenty-four-seven entertainment extravaganzas at the casino and racetrack. All served the interstate traffic.

Gilbert said, "Keep going until the intersection of Rt. 40 and Rt. 55. We should see a mostly abandoned shopping center. Turn in there. Our guy is in the open store."

Eric found the place. "Vargas Consultants." He parked right in front. The sign said "open," despite the dusty glass and dim interior light. "Are you sure we're in the right place? I don't see how this could be a million-dollar operation."

"Patience, my friend. Our target has made himself as innocuous and invisible as possible. He has just enough presence to defend and justify his tax return."

"I checked his background. He appears to be just another dude trying to support his family."

"Not my first rodeo, Eric. Watch and learn."

The pair exited the car and entered the store. Five feet in front of them, a reception counter blocked their path.

A bell sat in the center with a faded note, "Ring for Service." On the right side was a hinged flip panel which, when opened, allowed access to the hallway behind it.

Eric rang the bell three times before a thirty-something woman appeared. "May I help you?"

Gilbert said, "We're here to see Domingo Vargas on business. Here is my card."

She took the card, made a call, and lifted the counter partition. "He will see you. First door on the left."

They walked into a small windowless office with a high functioning ventilation system. Vargas's cigar smoke seemed odorless. Vargas didn't stand. He motioned for them to sit.

Gilbert said, "Thank you for seeing us. This is my associate, Eric Jerrod."

Vargas nodded. "I have appointments. What can I do for you?"

Gilbert opened his briefcase and pulled out a folder thick with papers kept in place by a metal fastener at the top. "Mr. Vargas, we are from the IRS and here to verify the information you reported on your last income tax statement, which you prepared yourself."

"Yes. I run a very simple business. A few expenses and a modest profit."

Gilbert looked through the pages. "Correct. However, we are more interested in your gross profit.

We are here to make sure you're not part of a money laundering scheme we've uncovered in this region."

Vargas looked shaken. "Money laundering? I don't even wash my own clothes. I would never do such a thing."

"I see. In that case, would you explain how your million-dollar gross income morphs into the pittance of net profit you claim?"

"My consulting business is strictly supply and demand. People tell me what they need, I find and supply it. Some items can be expensive. My clients pay me in advance. After expenses, there is nothing left."

"You have documents for all your transactions?"

"Of course."

"May I see them?"

Vargas narrowed his eyes. "Do you have a warrant?"

Eric pulled it from his pocket and handed it to Gilbert, who gave it to Vargas.

Vargas read it and said, "I'll be right back with the information."

Eric stood. "I'll come with you."

Vargas tapped his forehead. "I forgot, it's in here." He pointed to the safe. "I'll get the documents."

Eric moved to stand next to the safe, draping his jacket behind his gun. Vargas's eyes widened and perspiration rolled down his temples. In pulling out the documents, he made a show of proving he had nothing else in his hands.

Eric said, "Please close the safe."

Vargas complied and pushed the papers toward Gilbert, who looked at them one by one. After the sixth invoice, he stopped. "Mr. Vargas, what is the content of these items called containers?"

"I don't know, and I don't ask."

"If it is drugs, whether you're aware or not, you are complicit and will be prosecuted."

"It's not drugs."

"Uninspected foodstuff? The Federal Department of Agriculture would hold you responsible for not reporting this. It could mean a lot of jail time."

"No, not food."

Gilbert said, "I find it interesting you are familiar with what isn't being transported."

"Enough," Eric said. "Can we see one of these containers and look inside?"

Vargas said, "I don't see the actual contents. I arrange for pick-up, make sure the numbers are correct, and forward them for delivery."

Gilbert said, "We can't leave without a fuller explanation."

Vargas pulled out a handkerchief and wiped his brow.

Eric said, "I have another theory. Want to hear it?"

Vargas didn't say a word.

"I'm wondering why, you, a contractor for Tavius Global Enterprises in Chicago, have an office here in West Memphis, in a dying mall, in, what looks to me, the middle of nowhere?"

Silence.

"Now, if I take out my phone and plug this place in a map app, the biggest claim to fame of your location is the intersection of Rt. 40 and Rt. 55."

Vargas, mute, looked down at his hands.

"Ask almost anyone why it's significant and I'll bet they'd say it is the major route for transporting illegal immigrants from Laredo, on the Texas border, up the Mississippi Valley to Chicago. Did you know about that, Mr. Vargas?"

No answer.

Gilbert said, "How does it work? Your clients, like Tavius Global, pay you cash to hire and pay illegal immigrants? You get a ton of money, pay them bare minimum promising them free food and lodging. Your handlers oversee them and, when their time is up, bring them back. Looks to me like you make a fortune, hide most of it, and Tavius Global can claim they know nothing about short-changing these workers or the government. Do I have that right?"

Vargas, hoarse from dry mouth, said, "I want my lawyer."

Eric nodded. "I'll bet you do. Make the call." At the same time, he called the FBI agents standing by. "We're clear. Come in and lock this place up. We'll need whatever you find. Also, without any fanfare, put this place under surveillance to apprehend any cargo trucks checking in or on runs. We want to close down this trafficking operation outpost without alerting the others involved. Understand? No one knows." He ended the call.

Gilbert packed up, looked at Eric, and smiled. "All in all, a good day."

Chapter 39 ▶ Harrison, New York

Monday, April 23, 9 a.m.
Lucy sat on her bed surrounded by research. She picked up the piece of paper closest to her right hand—an early on-site police report on the recent discovery of a serial killer's graveyard.

With every plastic wrapped body found, more were discovered. The forensic pathologist on site noted an injury in the shoulder blade on the first skeleton exhumed—smaller than a bullet, rounder than a knife, more like a knitting needle or a stiletto of some kind. No bodies had been identified.

She found another article, written by a reporter. "Under any other circumstances, the graveyard would never have revealed its secret. As protected wetlands, it had legal protection from human intrusion. No one could have predicted the changing weather patterns would dry the topsoil, burn the vegetation, and transform the area into a desert."

Lucy reached for another random page— Theodore Xavier Donovan's obituary. She smiled. She had written it, calling Ted an "American treasure" for his philanthropic work through PRAISE and listed his awards and achievements. At the very end, she noted Rachel Allen's appointment as the new CEO of PRAISE, directing all inquiries be made to the organization.

Writing his obit wasn't all she did. She made sure all his pending projects calling for a seduction removal of criminals and political roadblocks were fulfilled. Finally, she erased any and all digital evidence pointing to any involvement with any of their operations from Ted's computers, phones, files and safes. As far as the public knew, Ted Donovan was a saint.

While he relied on her from the day they joined forces, Ted always kept her in the background—a casual acquaintance. Still, Lucy found herself more than a little surprised Ted didn't mention her in his will. She had never gotten a call from Ted's lawyer. It had nothing to do with money. Ted paid her better than well. What she craved, more than money, he never gave her—a sign she mattered to him.

Rachel knew she mattered. He gave her PRAISE.

Lucy sat back, wondering if maybe he'd given her even more. Maybe he had given Rachel something which should've been hers—a memento, or a personal keepsake, something, anything. Motivated, she went to the probate court's website, found, and requested a copy of the will. After paying the fee, she waited for the email. It appeared less than five minutes later.

Ted named Rachel as executrix. No surprise. But the warehouses he gave her were. Ted never mentioned them. They were his secret. *Well, not any longer.*

Determined to find out why those buildings were important, she got dressed, put on a wig, a hoodie, and stuffed oversized sunglasses in her hip pouch. She drove to the New York City docks on the Lower West Side and found the warehouses.

The three attached buildings were locked. Lucy saw no evidence of use. No tire treads or parking lines. Cobwebs hung from the lights attaching to the metal siding as well as the doors' upper corners. Windows were painted. Undeterred, she walked around the structures, looking for any chance to see inside. Here and there, through cracked paint, she could tell it was empty. No chairs, tables, boxes, wood scraps, or footprints in the dust.

Under her breath, Lucy said, "Come on, Ted. Show me why you bought this place." She turned the second corner and walked to the third corner where she found two garbage chutes.

Two large covered circular openings that must have had flexible tubes attached to funnel refuse into a bin. She tried to move one cover. It didn't give on the first try, but eventually it opened. Underneath, using her phone's flashlight, she could see the workings of a door. It didn't budge.

She tried the other garbage chute. The flap moved and revealed another. Her phone light played around the inner flap's edges, illuminating a set of four smooth recessed bolt heads at the three and nine o'clock positions. She'd need special tools to even try to budge the hardware. No way she was getting inside today. She terminated her investigation and walked away perplexed.

Halfway home, it hit her. She banged her hands on the steering wheel and said aloud, "Baffle! The second flap could be adjusted on the inside to allow garbage to be redirected. But where? Warehouses don't have basements. Unless," she smiled, "this one does."

Twenty minutes later, Lucy used an online real estate app and did a market value assessment on the property. She created her Real Estate Broker persona, Lola Klein, and a background for her anonymous client. Ready to do business, she made the call to the phone number filed with the will. "Hello, may I please speak with Rachel Allen?"

"Please, who is calling?"

"Lola Klein."

"I do not know this name."

"Who are you?"

"I am Nikolai Zukov. Is this helpful?"

"I'm sorry, I must have the wrong number."

Lucy ended the call and before calling again, checked the phone number against the document. "Rachel Allen, please."

Nikolai said, "Miss Klein, you have not told me your reason for calling."

"Mr. Zukov, is that the correct pronunciation?"

"Yes. Your business please?"

"I'm a private real estate broker and consultant. I would like to talk to Miss Allen about a piece of property she owns."

"Give me your phone number. If she wishes, she will call you back."

"555-212-5543."

<~<~|~>~>

Nikolai never received Rachel's personal calls on the concierge phone. When Lucy, as Lola Klein, called back, he pressed a "listen in" connection to Chris, who picked up.

When Lola Klein ended the call, Chris said, "You gave her a hard time."

"I do not like her voice."

"How many calls come for Rachel on your phone?"

"None. One, maybe a lawyer. I don't like lawyer's voice either."

"Good to know. Thank you for handling it. I'll tell Rachel."

<~<~|~>~>

Chris got up from his desk chair and walked over to Rachel sprawled out on the couch. He showed her the information displayed on his phone. This is the person Nikolai said wanted to get in touch with you."

Rachel looked at the name and the phone number. "I don't know this person and I definitely haven't seen this number before. Did you happen to check them out?"

"I did," Chris said. "The number is private, and the person just registered as a broker, with authentication papers pending. I didn't know you had any property for sale."

"I own the warehouses. My name must be on the deed. Wonder what someone wants with them? They sit on land only feet above the Hudson River. They'll be swamped and useless within two to three years."

"You could call her and ask, although I thought you didn't want to sell them."

Rachel gave Chris a quizzical look. "Why would you say that?"

"Oh, I don't know. Maybe because you nearly bit my head off when I wanted to use them."

"You didn't ask me first. I hate being taken for granted." She sat up and kissed him.

He returned the kiss and said, "Oh right, I forgot."

Rachel rearranged her body and sat. She called the number. "Rachel Allen for Lola Klein."

"This is Lola Klein. Thank you for getting back to me."

Rachel said, "What can I do for you?" She pressed speaker so Chris could listen.

"I'm calling about the warehouses on the West Side wharf. If you're willing to sell, I've got a client who would like to purchase them for cash, bills, or bank check, at fair market value."

"Really? Is your client aware they'll be flooded in three years or less?"

"Of course. Right now, his need is great, and he is motivated. If you accept the offer, we can do this by Friday. I have the power of attorney and will get the papers drawn."

Rachel looked at Chris. He shrugged. She said, "Send me your offer in writing and I'll consider it," and hung up.

Chris said, "If something is too good to be true…"

Rachel said, "It probably isn't."

"Bingo."

"We need to go check out the warehouses."

He smiled. "On the other hand, I wonder what it'll be like married to a millionaire."

Rachel held her arms out. "Come here and I'll show you what I've learned."

Zeus whined, put his head between his paws, and closed his eyes.

Chapter 40 ▶ White House, Washington D.C.

Monday, 23 April, 10 a.m.
Dani sat at the Oval Office desk mapping her public political agenda and private financial objectives to ensure a compatible timeline. This weekly exercise gave her the necessary clarity for juggling the endless pressure and workload—it organized the chaos. Afterwards, she ripped it up, put it in a metal bowl, and set it on fire.

Her private phone buzzed. After seeing the ID, she took the call and said, "Rachel, how are you feeling?"

"Much better. Chris's been fussing over me since I got home. It's oppressive."

Dani laughed. "I bet it's the reason you're doing so well."

"It's true. He's the best medicine I've got."

"Is there anything I can do?"

Rachel said, "Not right now. I called to let you know I have finished the book, and it's off to the publishers. We expect it to be released mid-to-end of

May. I've sent you a list of chapter headings. Review them, tell me which one you want to see, and I'll send it."

Dani said, "Okay. Got it. Let me look. Hmm. Send the two on unions."

"Will do."

"Anything else?"

Rachel said, "I've written an essay on the 1800's mining towns to accompany the book's announcement and availability date."

"When is it being published?"

"My publicist hasn't given me a date. Why? Is it important?"

Dani said, "Only if you're planning to attack Tavius Global. It's a smoldering giant that has to be contained until I have defenses in place to prevent a complete meltdown."

"Am I supposed to understand?"

Dani said, "I have plans in the works to encourage the end of wage disparity as well as immigration and immigrant economic absorption. The large corporations are not going to be happy at first. I expect Tavius Global will be the loudest objector."

"Hmm. I don't see any problem. It's just quick picture of life in a coal mining company town, both the good and the bad. As you know, if we don't learn from the past, we are likely to destroy our future."

Dani said, "I couldn't agree more. Thanks for the info. Talk to you soon."

After the call, Dani heard the ping of an email receipt. Before she could open it, another call came in on her private line. This time, she didn't say the name when she answered. "I'm listening."

"The Mossad has two operatives aboard. I will, under another name, board at Ogdensburg, the first

U.S. port on the St. Lawrence Seaway. If there is a plan to apprehend the ship at Tavius Global, we could avert any potential violence and/or casualties."

"When do you leave?"

"Next week. May 1st."

The call ended.

Dani stood and stretched. She picked up her empty coffee cup to get a hot refill. Before she could take a step, the private phone rang again. She saw the ID, dropped into her chair, sighed, and answered. "Good morning, Octavius."

Octavius said, "Not so good for me. I've been invited to a sit-down for the EEA. You know I've been lobbying against such bills for decades."

"I hope you'll come."

"To do what? Sit around with a bunch of useless so-called leaders with no vision or spine?"

"You have proven how effective lobbying is. However, it is time to do something. You've been working on this issue. I see you using this defining moment to assert your leadership."

"Don't suck up to me, Dani. Too much is at stake."

"Octavius, my political back is to the wall. Something must change. I want you to be a part of it."

"This June first deadline is crushing the Tavius Global Mid-Century rollout. I need until September to be ready to infuse the world with my new paradigm."

"Congress has to pass the EEA before it adjourns in August."

"Do it in September."

"No. This time we have to do it my way."

The call ended. Dani shook as she put the phone back in the drawer. She knew defying Octavius could have disastrous consequences. She took minor comfort in knowing he'd be distracted by the IRS and FBI long before the EEA deadline, and, she hoped, before he could exact his revenge.

Two days later, Cecil walked into the Oval Office. "Bad news. I've been on the phone and in meetings since we talked on Saturday. No one wants to sit down and work on passing the EEA. Corporations are against it. They've threatened to pull all campaign funding from anyone who supports it. When I pressed them about serving the people of this country, all I got is, "We're doing enough." The EPA is back, wildlife protections are back, and emission standards are back. We can't regulate everything."

Dani said, "More has to be done."

Cecil said, "It's certainly better."

"Better isn't enough because it's going to get much, much worse. This country must mount a campaign to protect itself from the human and industrial waste compounding by the day."

Cecil said, "Even when I spoke about new job opportunities and reintegrating climate-forced immigrants into their new surroundings with these jobs in the housing and service industries, I got nothing. It's been a much harder sell than I anticipated."

"Do you have a list of everyone you contacted?"

"Give me a moment." Cecil produced his e-pad and found the document. "Got it. I'm sending it to you right now."

Dani's phone pinged. She checked. "Got it."

Cecil said, "Before I go, is there anything else I can do for you?"

"Cancel tomorrow's meeting."

Cecil nodded left and Isabel entered. "He doesn't look happy."

Dani said, "Too damn bad. If this country is to have a comprehensive environmental act, I can't wait for him and his overlords. I'm going to have to do it by Executive Order."

Isabel said, "Do you want me to draw it up from your outline?"

"Yes. You and Terence. Give him a call. See if there's enough time to get it done by tomorrow. If not, let me know how soon I can announce it."

Twenty minutes later, Terence confronted Dani. "Are you out of your mind?"

Dani stood and walked over to the couch. "Did you want to discuss my plan?"

"If you go ahead with this Executive Order, you can kiss the election good-bye."

"Sit down. Let's talk about the election."

Terence sat across from her. "Are you thinking of walking away?"

Dani laughed. "Not without a fight."

"Walking away, though, nevertheless."

"If I run, I will be distracted from my job and have the media up my professional, presidential, and personal ass. I'm not so sure it's what I want."

"I thought we were a 'go.' Why this change?"

"While I'm the youngest President ever, I have the sense I'm seen either as too old school or so radical my leadership is either questioned or ignored at every turn."

Terence stood up and paced the room. "I don't understand. This is not a surprise. You knew it would be hard to inject such a progressive agenda."

Dani sighed. "Not this hard. I expected more support. I thought more people were looking for a new approach to surviving the growing catastrophes the country faces."

"Wait. This negativity is about other people's self-interest?"

"Cecil made it very clear no one wanted to enter the EEA minefield. I had Isabel call you because I needed to talk to someone rational who I trust."

He sat across from her. "Dani, I'm here. I support you 100%. You can do amazing things in the next four years."

"The truth is, I may have only seven months. I have to do as much as I can while I can."

"Nonsense. The American people will see your efforts on their behalf and elect you."

"An unknown at this point. We have to do the best we can right now."

"On it." Terence stood. "Tell me again, when do you want the EEA Executive Order?"

"I thought I wanted it A.S.A.P. However, let's do a thorough job on it and, at the same time, work on a workers' rights order." Dani pulled out her calendar. "In a week, it'll be April 30th. In two, May 7th. Will you have enough time to do both by then?"

"Yes."

"Good. Keep these under wraps. No leaks."

"Problems?"

"Maybe. At any point, if you become concerned, keep the boys home from school, and get Sybil and Peter to the White House. I don't want any accidents. We can protect everyone here."

Chapter 41 ▶ Bethesda, Maryland

Tuesday, 24 April, 10 a.m.

Sybil met Peter in the solarium. He was working on his laptop. She took a seat facing him. "You look like the picture of health. How are you feeling?"

"Better and better. The headaches are fewer and farther apart. I'm able to read in short spurts. My balance is returning as is my impulse control."

"What do the doctors say?"

"I'm good to go."

A deep voice in a white coat with a stethoscope hanging around his neck said, "Not exactly."

Peter laughed. "Okay, I may have exaggerated a bit."

Sybil said, "When can he leave, doctor?"

"He's made great progress. His stamina is up, his cognitive abilities improve every day, and his attention span has increased significantly. Peter is doing better than expected, although I'm not sure he'll reach optimal recovery for another six to twenty-four months. I would like to keep him here for a few more days before releasing him."

Peter said, "Hey, Doc. I thought we had an agreement."

"We might have, until a nurse heard you on the phone planning to climb Mt. Everest."

"A joke," Peter said. He looked at his mother, "A joke, Mom. I would never do anything that stupid."

Sybil put her hand up and, without answering him, addressed the doctor. "Impulse control issues?"

The doctor nodded.

Peter said, "So, two more days."

The doctor said, "Let's say, definitely by Friday." His pager went off. "I'm needed. Talk to you later."

Sybil looked at Peter. "Friday. Good."

"I'm not going home as a patient, Mom. I'm going back to work."

"With me. You're not ready to be on your own. We'll work together."

Peter arched his back and slammed the laptop shut.

Sybil raised an eyebrow.

Peter said, "Overreaction?"

She nodded.

He relaxed. "Then," he smiled, "working together it is."

Sybil pulled out her e-pad and pulled up a file. "Speaking of work, I've been doing some research because I don't like mystery numbers and I hate being manipulated."

"This process has been in place for years."

"That doesn't make it right—only accepted."

"What did you find out?"

She said, "Unless someone can prove otherwise, the final calculations are bullshit. I have tried to replicate them using every known economic index available. I've averaged and weighted the members' input. I've adjusted every which way and applied every reputable analysis index and formula. Nothing comes close."

"Why are you surprised? It's proprietary."

"Or it's not real. The formula is meant to distort the results."

Peter sighed. "Mom, you can go over this a million times. It doesn't matter. Members' profit margins are well over stock market averages."

"Peter, it does matter when he uses those calculations to activate government or personnel changes."

Peter raised his voice, "Mom."

Sybil put her finger to her lips, "Shhh."

He looked around and leaned towards her. She got closer to him. "Mom, we regulate the world economy, the distribution of wealth, and government stability. What we do works." Peter leaned back.

Sybil sat straight up. "What if what we do causes human suffering, intentional or otherwise? What if it works for us and not the other ninety-seven-point-four percent of the population? Is that okay? Are we doing our due diligence?"

Peter shook his head. "Stop. You're making assumptions."

"Am I? Did I make up the conditions in the Tawandian mines? In the refugee camps? Did I imagine the disappearance of Hope City or the annihilation of thousands into the sink holes?"

"What?"

"If you thought what happened in Tawanda was an act of God or a coincidence, think again."

Peter's eyes darkened. "You're wrong."

Sybil leaned in. "The Vanderhagens, my father and brother, and the cartel, orchestrated the whole thing. Nobody makes money when it goes to supporting the basic needs of an impoverished people. This shortsightedness will destroy us in the end." Sybil lowered her voice, tightened her lips, and narrowed her eyes, "I'm the Executive Director of PRAISE. I don't have to make anything up. I see it every day." She stood. "I'm not wrong."

She left before he could say a word. Peter's hands tightened on the only thing near him, his computer. He raised it above his head, let out a scream, and...

A nurse grabbed the laptop. Peter rose from the chair attempting to keep hold. When he lost the battle, he roared, picked up a table, and smashed it on the floor.

His phone woke him up. Peter, still dazed from the medication, lay prone on his hospital bed. His arm automatically felt for the phone. Finding it, he said, "Hi."

"How's it going?"

The voice brought him to his senses. Peter sat up. "Taxi?"

"Yes, my friend. I am traveling around the country checking the Tawandian immigrant communities. You?"

"I'm good. Recovering from a concussion. Just when I think I've got it all under control, something snaps. Still, I'm doing okay. Where are you?"

"At Dulles airport. I need to talk to you. Pick a place."

"I'm at Walter Reed in Bethesda."

"For how long?"

"At least until Friday."

"No problem. See you soon."

Peter put the phone down and fell back against the pillows and closed his eyes until he heard a commotion outside his door.

"Don't worry. I won't wake him. I'll be quiet."

Peter mumbled, "What's going on?"

"See, he's awake." Sam walked in. "Hey, partner. Here for a quick visit."

Peter smiled. "Sam. Good to see you. Taxi'll be here soon."

"Nice. A reunion. How are you doing?"

"Better each day."

"Want to take a walk and get out of here for a little while?"

They strolled The Green Project woodland paths. They talked about Alaska and sports before they seemed to run out of things to say.

Sam said, "You're not usually so quiet. What's going on?"

Peter said, "I got angry with my mother. She seemed to think everything that happened in Tawanda happened for a reason."

"I'm not surprised. Bad decisions yield bad results."

"No, not a bad decision. The destruction and abuse were intentional. Orchestrated. By a powerful group."

"To destroy Tawanda?"

"To control its resources."

Sam shook his head. "I don't want to believe that. Still, I have to say I'm not surprised, either. There are people who think the fires, floods, and droughts cleanse the land and keep the world population in check."

Taxi, who had walked up behind the men, put one hand on Peter's shoulder and the other on Sam's as he said, "Which is why not much relief reaches the affected populations, and civil wars appear to go unchecked."

After exchanging greetings, Peter said, "I want to know why I haven't connected the dots until now.

Taxi said, "Maybe you weren't looking."

Peter said, "Existing as an automaton. Just doing my job. Focusing on the mission. Following orders."

Sam said, "Welcome to the man-box realization."

"No. Can't be."

Taxi said, "Peter, face it. You either blocked, ignored, or accepted the prevailing privileged white man's theory on 'how the world works,' and did your part."

Peter collapsed on the nearest bench and let his head drop into his hands. "I've been fighting havoc I've helped create."

Sam patted Peter's back. "We are all complicit. Conditioned blindness. It's what we do next that matters."

Peter shook his head. "All those lives." He stared at the ground without seeing it.

He saw the Tawandian people refugees of an ongoing war for survival they didn't initiate or fight. In the camp, people were emaciated, hopeless, and living in squalor and filth. He recalled the smells of open sewage and death. Shelters made from scavenged bits and pieces found at building sites. Listlessness. Not much different than those working at the diamond mine. Poor diet. Long hours. Low pay.

Tears filled his eyes. He saw and reported. His uncle expressly told him not to change anything and find the individuals stealing diamonds from the company. In effect, ignore the root of the problem and deal with the consequences.

Sam patted him on the back. "Peter. Stop. You, we, saved a lot of Tawandians who are now living a better life here, in the States."

Peter raised his head. "I, we, could have done better, have to do better."

Sam nodded. "We will."

Chapter 42 ▶ West Side docks, New York City

Wednesday, 24 April, 11 a.m.
As Eric gazed at the warehouses with Beth, Rachel, and Chris, he said, "Do we have reservations for lunch, and I mean a nice place, with a snobby maître de, waiters, and a menu of delicious food I've never heard of?"

Chris laughed. "Done."

Eric said, "Good, because there is no other reason I'd have dropped everything in Washington to come up here and stare at these decrepit tin can buildings."

Beth said, "Except his obsession with Donovan and the sudden speedy no-questions-asked purchase offer."

Rachel said, "Eric, do you have a theory?"

"My only link to Donovan is his associate, Lucy Kilmer. Same initials as your customer's agent."

"No such thing as coincidences, right?"

"We'll see."

Chris said, "Or, it could be a straight-up legitimate offer."

Beth said, "Let's hope." She held out her hand. "Keys."

Rachel said, "I've got this," and walked up to the entrance, between the garage doors of adjoining buildings. She opened the door. "Here we go."

The four walked inside. Rachel became the tour guide. "This is where we found the car and a cabinet full of cleaning products." She walked to the door at the end and opened it. "This connects these two buildings and leads to a private apartment."

Eric said, "This is it?"

Rachel said, "Just as I found it, without the cars."

Eric checked the cabinet. "Empty."

Beth tried the door to the adjacent garage. "It's open." They followed her into the next building, and while she checked the apartment, Rachel and Chris sat on the bed.

Beth said, "There is nothing here worth the kind of money you've been offered." She looked around. Where's Eric?"

He appeared at the door and saluted. "Reporting in. I've checked the outside and found two garbage chutes bolted shut. They seem to go nowhere."

Beth said, "Something's wrong."

"I agree. There's got to be a basement."

Rachel said, "Where?"

Beth said, "If we can't find it, and we know it has to be here..."

Eric finished, "We have ourselves a secret door."

Chris stood up. "Nothing beats a good mystery."

Beth said, "Chris and Eric, check out the apartment. Rachel and I will go next door. Let me know if you find it."

Beth and Rachel stood ten feet from the wall with the two metal doors to the garbage chutes. Beth said, "The door on the right is what it's supposed to be." She walked over to it, opened it, and the outdoor cover swung open as well.

Rachel nodded. "Yes. No problem there. I'll open the other." She turned the handle, the round door opened, and a cover raised to reveal a chute into darkness. "This is different."

Beth looked and moved to the corrugated panel in between the chute and the door. "Let's look for a seam or a latch."

Eric's voice shouted out, "We found it."

The women rushed into the apartment.

Eric said, "Want to guess?"

Beth gave him a playful punch. "No."

Eric laughed. "Chris found it. I'll let him show you."

Chris walked over to the bathroom, pushed the door open, and released a hinge on the door frame. This allowed the linen closet to swing out into the bathroom and reveal a set of steps. "Voila."

Beth said, "Did either of you go down?"

Eric said, "Waited for you."

Beth said, "Rachel and Chris, you wait up here. If it's a crime scene, I don't want your DNA all over the place. Eric will take pictures and I'll send you a live feed."

While she spoke, Eric stepped on the staircase and found a light switch. He pulled his personal flashlight out of his pocket and switched it on. Beth did the same and followed him down into the basement.

She bumped into Eric who stood on the bottom step. "What's the matter?"

"I'm looking at a dehydrator with the last victim still present."

"Let's verify and call forensics. Keep it hush-hush. If Lucy is the person who wants this place, who knows how it will implicate her."

They walked over to a large glass box resembling an oversized fish tank. The bottom held an ash-like material shaped like a human.

Beth said, "This is a person."

Eric said, "Not a doubt in my mind."

She said, "If we touch or move it, the form will collapse."

Eric shone the flashlight above the tank. "So, the body would come down the shoot, fall into the tank, be processed, and the remains dumped, uh, pretty much anywhere."

Beth walked over to the industrial press. "Before the dumping, he must have used this to crush anything solid remaining in the tank."

Eric said, "When he was done, all he had to do was dump the evidence into the Hudson River. Son-of-a-bitch."

<~<~|~>~>

Friday morning, Rachel, Chris, and their attorney met with Lucy Kilmer, masquerading as Lola Klein, and her attorney.

As they looked over the contract, Rachel and Chris made some marks. Finished, Rachel said, "I'd like to withdraw the first building, which is only a garage, from the deal."

Lucy said, "No. Impossible."

"I will take less money."

"No. All or nothing."

Rachel and Chris whispered among themselves. Rachel said, "Fine. You can have all the visible floor to ceiling space, while I reserve ownership for any space not included in the presale inspection."

Lucy's voice went cold. "I am not here to negotiate. I want all the buildings, including the cellar."

"What cellar?"

Lucy said, "I inspected the property and did my due diligence. My offer and this contract are based on what I saw."

Rachel said, "Then we've reached an impasse."

"How about an extra two-hundred thousand and we close the deal right now?"

"One million."

"Seven-fifty."

"Eight."

Rachel pointed at Lucy and said, "Sold. Please make the checks out to The PRAISE Foundation."

Both parties signed the papers and Rachel got the PRAISE donation in a guaranteed cashier's check. She felt it only fair the money should go to Ted Donovan's favorite charity since the building belonged to him.

"By the way," Rachel said, "we did do our due diligence. We found the cellar, removed the junk, and left it broom clean."

Lucy jumped to her feet and slammed her palms on the table. Before she could utter a word, Beth and Eric entered the room. Her eyes widened and narrowed. "What the hell are you two doing here? This is a private…"

Eric didn't let her finish. "Miss Lucy Kilmer, please sit. We have some information for you. In the cellar, behind the stairs, we found the last box of personal belongings of several missing people. We ran each item through our fingerprint and DNA identification processes."

Lucy said, "I have no idea what you're talking about. I have never been inside any of those buildings."

Beth said, "I find that odd because we found evidence of your DNA."

Eric said, "Maybe you were Donovan's get-out-of-jail-free card."

Eric put her in cuffs and recited her rights.

Lucy said, "Bullshit. I want a lawyer."

He said, "Let's discuss this downtown."

Chapter 43 ▶ Bethesda, Maryland

Friday, 26 April, 11 a.m.
Peter got the doctor's okay to leave the hospital with
the caveat of no drinking, no driving, and no exertion
for the weekend with a follow-up on Monday. He had
to promise to rest. He agreed to everything because he
couldn't wait to leave. His mother would pick him up
after lunch.

Just as he zipped his duffle bag, Taxi walked in.
"Hey, what's going on?"

"Packing up. It's moving day."

"Soon, or do we have time to talk?"

Peter said, "Let's go down to the coffee shop.
They're discharging me somewhere between one and
three this afternoon unless they change their minds. I
had sort of a meltdown on Wednesday."

Taxi said, "I can see it has not been easy for
you."

Peter shook his head. "One day I'm standing in
Alaska's amazing light, on a precipice overlooking the
Bering Sea, and the next I'm stuck in a hospital. Not

only did I put a gash in my skull, I suffered a concussion. The gash is healed. The stitches are out. My hair has grown enough to almost hide the scar."

Taxi said, "But the concussion has been harder."

Peter nodded. "Much harder. I've had all kinds of therapy from vision to impulse control. Even yoga for reducing everything from headache pain to anxiety."

Taxi smiled. "It must all be working. You are looking good."

Peter laughed. "You're good medicine for me."

At the shop, they got coffee and pie, found a table in the corner, and settled in – backs to the wall. Peter said, "Sam would be proud of us being so tactical."

Taxi nodded. "Can we reach him if we have to?"

Peter pulled out his phone. "Hey, Sam. Can you meet Taxi and me at the hospital coffee shop?" He put the phone away. "He'll be here in twenty minutes. While we wait, tell me, what's been going on?"

Taxi told Peter about the issues in Kryller, Missouri, Mamadou's Journal, the fight, and President Mitchell's action to defuse a white nationalist uprising in the town. "Other new settlements had similar problems, but this was the worst. Since the President made community solidarity an issue, the other Tawandian centers have done much better."

Sam grabbed a coffee and sat down with them. "What'd I miss?"

Taxi gave him a big smile. "Good to see you, man."

Sam grinned. "So, tell me."

Taxi leaned over his coffee. The other men did the same. "I have very specific information regarding for-profit non-consensual human cargo."

Peter said, "Human trafficking?"

Sam nodded and said, "How did you come by this information?"

"One of my Tawandian friends got drunk and woke up on a slave ship docked in Tripoli, Libya. It was one of three stopped and searched by police. The fourth ship got away. The crew is armed. Their destination is the United States."

Peter said, "Did he tell the police?"

Taxi said, "He heard it from the police. Problem is, no one has jurisdiction in international waters."

Sam said, "Did the police tell the US Embassy?"

Taxi shrugged. "How do we find out?"

Peter said, "Why? What do you think we can do?"

Taxi said, "We can alert U.S. Customs or the U.S. Coast Guard to board the ship and free the five hundred people bound for slavery, as well as arrest the ship's captain and crew, and the companies engaged in the buying and selling."

Sam said, "Do you know the ship's name?"

"Olive something. It's flying a Cypriot flag, like the other three."

Sam said, "I can work with that. Do you have the day it sailed?"

"Some time around April 18th."

Sam used his phone to do the research. "I found an Olivia Bay, bound for the St. Lawrence Seaway, ETA May 2nd, and docking at the Illinois Port of Tavius Global, ETA May 9th."

Taxi said, "Good. We can tell U.S. Customs about the human smuggling. They can set the kidnapped people free."

Peter said, "Could it be that easy?"

Sam shook his head. "It's government. Nothing is ever that easy."

Taxi said, "What can we do in a week?"

Peter said, "I can speak to Dani, um, President Mitchell. She has the power to expedite any legal plan we come up with."

Sam said, "Let me check with the State Department and see if they even have eyes on human traffickers."

Taxi said, "As soon as you have answers, tell me what I can do, where I need to be, and when."

<~<~|~>~>

Peter, Sybil, and Terence were sitting in the White House living room enjoying drinks and hors d'oeuvres when Dani walked in. Peter jumped up.

Dani said, "Are you out or did you just get a weekend pass?"

Peter hugged his cousin. "I'm under weekend observation and if all goes okay, I'm discharged for good."

"Great news."

Terence stood and said, "What can I get you?"

Dani said, "My usual. Where are the boys?"

Terence handed her the drink and said, "Practice."

"For what? Basketball? Lacrosse? Track and Field?"

"Very funny. You know they've walked away from school sports ever since their escapades made headlines."

"So, where are they?"

"ATV practice."

"Inside or outside?"

"Why does it matter? You know they're really into this sport."

"It matters because," Dani looked at Sybil and Peter, "Octavius may be looking for revenge. I told him the environmental act would proceed without him."

Sybil took a sip. "Why are you surprised? The cartel will do anything to anyone to achieve its prime position. It operates on the fact it controls and equalizes the world's economy. If you stand in the way, you will be removed—one way or another."

Dani said, "I know the cartel is ruthless. I didn't count on it getting personal."

Sybil screamed, got control and said, in a low, steady voice, "Are you kidding me? They killed my wife. They killed my brother. That's why I'm here. Cross him, Dani, and you could lose everything."

Terence said, "Is it the EEA Executive Order?"

"Yes, Octavius is dead set against it."

"Should I pull the boys in from outside activities?"

"Yes, Terence, good idea. Maybe for a month or so."

"Don't worry. I'll handle it."

The chef announced dinner.

Peter said, "Wait, Dani. I have a question."

Dani paused and looked at him.

He said, "What are the chances of getting a slave ship bound for Tavius Global stopped by US Customs at the Port of Ogdensburg?"

Dani said, "How did you know about that?"

"Well, I..."

"Please don't say anything until we talk. How about first thing after tomorrow's breakfast?"

"Sure, I can wait."

"If anyone else knows, tell them to stop any and all inquiries until we have a unified understanding and plan."

"I don't know..."

"Peter, I mean it. Nobody talks about this. Period. If you need to make calls, do it now. Before dinner. This is confidential. On a need-to-know only basis."

"I'll try."

"Not good enough. Shut it down."

When Peter returned from making his phone calls, he saw Ivan and Isaac. As soon as they saw him, they raced to his side and hugged him.

Ivan said, "Great to see you."

Isaac said, "Glad you're out. Aunt Sybil said we've got the whole weekend."

Peter said, "You guys are the best. We'll make plans later."

Dani said, "Boys sit down. Peter, when you're ready, please tell us about Alaska."

Isaac said, "Did you hunt seals? Or, better yet, whales?"

Ivan said, "Did you eat blubber? Skin fish? Ride a dog sled?"

Dani said, "Twins, let Peter catch his breath."

Peter smiled, nodded, and dug into the food on his plate. After a while, he sat back, looked around the table, and said, "You know, you are my family. My only family. No sisters or brothers, aunts, uncles, or grandparents. It's good to be alive and here with you. I promise to do everything I can to preserve what we have."

Sybil patted her son's hand and gave Dani a sideways glance. "We all will.
"

Chapter 44 ▶ Tidal Basin, Washington D.C.

Saturday, 27 April, 10 a.m.

Peter met Taxi and Sam beyond the Franklin Delano Roosevelt Memorial on a bench overlooking the Tidal Basin. "We have to walk away on this one."

Taxi said, "You know I cannot."

"This ship is already on the radar. It's imperative it reaches its destination, so everyone involved with the transport gets taken down."

Sam said, "Meaning the buyers, sellers, and corrupt officials?"

"Yes."

Taxi said, "The ship is not docking at Tavius Global for at least two more weeks. We cannot let those people endure inhumane conditions in the cargo holds any longer than necessary."

"We have to," Peter said. "Once the government closes in, they will end this."

Taxi said, "This is one port in one country. These arrests, if they happen, only make a narrow dent in this billion-dollar industry. How many lives have to be sacrificed? 100? 500?"

Sam said, "We have to start somewhere. Interrogations will lead us to other players who can be dealt with later."

Taxi said, "Do you mean go after the whole industry?"

Sam nodded. "In for a penny, in for a dollar."

Peter said, "Back to the Olivia Bay. We're agreed? No action right now."

Taxi shook his head. "I do not agree to this sacrifice. I am not so trusting. I would feel much better if we could off-load the people. The ship could still finish the voyage without its human cargo."

Peter said, "I'll talk to the President again."

Sam said, "If she still refuses to talk about it, perhaps we could arrange an escort for the Olivia Bay once it gets through the locks. I am thinking a couple of tugboats."

Taxi said, "If the boat captain gets spooked, he might just sink the ship."

Peter said, "No way. Not with all those people on board."

Taxi said, "You do not understand. The kidnapped are not seen as people. They are a commodity to be bought and sold. The modern version of the slave trade serving the southern plantations for almost three centuries."

Sam said, "I figure the captain and crew are white guys transporting around five hundred Africans. Not very many when you consider the thousands lost in Tawanda. Regardless, I think Taxi's right. They'll sink the boat."

Peter said, "Do we have to make the choice to capture the slavers or save the people on board?"

Taxi said, "We do not know enough to do anything yet. Peter, you go back to recovery. Sam, we have to inspect the process of a ship leaving the Atlantic and traveling the locks to the Ogdensburg Port, going through customs, and on to the Great Lakes."

Sam nodded. "It's the only way we can make our operation look like it belongs."

Peter said, "Okay. You can take care of it. Let me know how much money you need. I'll make sure you have it." He stood. "I've got to get back. Again, don't mention the ship or its destination." The friends shook hands. "I hope all we're talking about is a pleasure cruise on Lake Michigan."

Sam started to leave but changed his mind. He turned to Peter. "I work for the State Department. You and the President are cousins. If she finds out we've been ignoring her wishes or doing things behind her back, there's a good chance she'd throw us in prison."

"We need to..."

"No," Sam said. "We need to tell her we won't interfere, just be observers once the ship enters the Great Lakes."

Peter nodded. "I'll talk to her."

Taxi said, "You make this okay. Prison for ignoring Presidential orders is not an option I am comfortable contemplating."

Peter said, "Don't worry. It's going to be okay. I promise."

Chapter 45 ▶ Gramercy Avenue, New York City

Sunday, 28 April, 9 a.m.

The weight on her chest and the wet tongue on her face woke Rachel up from a deep sleep. Zeus's deep brown eyes seemed to search her soul looking for the answer to, "why aren't you up, dressed, and ready to play?"

Rachel hugged the dog. He smelled of fresh air and treats.

Chris called out from the kitchen, "Hi honey, I'm home."

She smiled at the image of Jack Nicholson's manic face alerting his family to the horrors to come and said, "I'm coming."

He said, "Be quick. The croissants are warm, the coffee is hot, and your article in the op-ed section is on fire."

Rachel jumped out of bed, ran to the bathroom, and donned her sweats. Without combing her hair, she burst into the living room, eyes searching for the paper.

Chris said, "Don't panic. Sit on the couch. I've got the paper and breakfast."

Zeus heard the magic word, ran to the kitchen, and sat by his placemat.

Chris said, "Good boy," and put the pellet-filled dog dish down. "Okay, Zeus. It's yours." Zeus gobbled it down.

Rachel feigned a childish pout. "What about me? I'm sitting and waiting too."

Chris laughed. "Good try. Zeus does it better." He carried the tray to the coffee table, set it down, and handed Rachel the paper, pre-folded to her article. "Here you go," and sat next to her.

Even though she knew every word by heart, and Chris had read it earlier, she read the first sentence out loud. "Even though slavery has been around since the first conquest, the 1800's coal mining towns moved workers from the agrarian to the industrial setting."

Holding the business section, Chris looked at her and said, "I particularly liked the part where you say, rather than a US dollar-paid hourly wage, workers were subjected to a closed economic token system." He read from the article. "Workers were paid in tokens, which could only be spent in owner-controlled banks, stores, schools, and town. Owners spent their profits where they lived, often outside the community and state."

Rachel said, "Why? Too much? Too close to Tavius Global?"

"No one would know to even make that connection. Octavius hasn't announced his revolutionary social order."

"Think he'll be offended?"

"I have no idea. He's got to see you've got a book to sell, and your article leads right into your premise." Chris returned to the business section.

"So, what did you think?"

"I liked it," Chris said without looking up.

Rachel poked his arm. "Just like?"

"No, more than like. I loved it."

Rachel smiled, leaned over, and kissed him. "That's my guy. One good review is all I need. I'm starving."

<~<~|~>~>

Octavius spent an extra half hour exercising to dissipate the unease he felt. First, he lost the rights to SMUTT by being outmaneuvered by Chris Gregory, and now Dani would move forward on her environmental plan with or without him.

As a global leader, he could not tolerate being defied once, much less twice. He paced in his office, finding no relief from the expanse of Lake Michigan's sparking water. He grabbed his phone and called Cecil and said, "What's the EEA's status?"

"Sir, it's Sunday morning."

"Status, Cecil."

"I'm in church with my family, sir."

"Leave."

Octavius could hear the repetitive "excuse me" as Cecil worked his way out of the pew, heavy breathing, and the massive doors squeaking, followed by bird calls.

"Sir, I'm outside with my security detail."

"Status."

"I don't know anything more than what I reported. I set up the meeting. No one wanted to go against you and the other massive campaign donors. So, I cancelled the meeting. The President wasn't happy. I think she's planning something."

Octavius said, "I want you to find out what's going on. I'm the guest speaker at the upcoming Global Economic Conference. I don't want any surprises. Let me know no later than Monday, May 7th. The conference is May 11th." Octavius hung up without waiting for an answer.

He paused, took three deep breaths, and assessed his state of being. He shook his head and went into pace mode. Pulling out his phone, he called his executive assistant. "When can you be in my office?"

"Thirty minutes."

"Twenty."

Octavius sat down and used the time to review the cartel's spreadsheet numbers. He made a point never to second guess himself. Still, Sybil Vanderhagen Powell's words sat in the back of his head. Could she be onto something? *It's true there is a world-wide recession. It's also true we are growing richer while others grow poorer. Is it possible?* The thought of being wrong drove his need to prove he was right.

He copied the whole financial electronic workbook to a new file, closed the original, and studied the formulas. He brought up Federal stats to adjust the totals for various inequalities, starting with the "10 deciles of Income," which adjusts household income by dividing it by the number of consumers in the household. He frowned. He found other parameters, such as suicide rates, underemployment, and infrastructure issues.

The variations altered his original totals by a significant margin, and not in a good way. He leaned back and contemplated his options. Seconds later he resumed pacing. Aloud, he said, "I will not be bested by some woman who thinks she knows everything after only a few minutes of study." His words didn't comfort him. More pacing. "Dammit. If I choose to acknowledge the human factor, it will cost us a fortune." He walked over to his computer, saved the file, and shut the machine off. He needed time and distance to evaluate his options.

A knock on the door and his Executive Assistant, Ferguson, walked in, briefcase in hand.

Octavius said, "Sit."

Ferguson followed instructions.

Octavius said, "Why haven't I heard about actions against Christopher Gregory?"

"Sir, the investigation is ongoing."

"It's taking too long. Get me something ASAP."

Ferguson reached into his briefcase and brought out a folded newspaper. He pushed it toward Octavius. "Sir, have you seen this?"

Octavius snatched the paper from the table and walked over to the window light. He scanned the article, ripped the paper in two, and tossed it into the wastepaper basket. "Another woman who thinks she knows better than I." He sat down across the table from Ferguson and said, "Thoughts?"

"Sir?"

"I want to end the productive life of Mr. Gregory and his wife."

"Do you want me to make a call?"

"No. First, we have to strip them of their integrity. Then, seduce them into retirement." Octavius leaned back and folded his hands across his chest, "Attack Gregory's company. Destroy ICU's reliability and offer Tavius Global Security as the best alternative."

"What about Rachel Allen?"

"Put up counter arguments in the comments to her article. We can also address positives in our upcoming announcement. Somewhere in the material put a spin on "new world solutions are often reimagined old-world failures." Get me a copy of her upcoming book. We can do a subversive media attack before it launches."

"I will take care of this," Ferguson said. "Anything else?"

"Let me know when it's done. After they wallow in their total misfortune for a while, we'll get rid of them."

"Yes, sir." Ferguson stood and closed his briefcase. "One more thing. One of our contractors has failed to deliver their quota of workers."

"Take them out and get a replacement. I've made it clear from the start; at Tavius Global, there are no second chances."

Chapter 46 ▶ White House, Washington D.C.

Sunday, 28 April, 10 a.m.

Dani returned to her residence for her second cup of coffee and to check on Peter. He entered the dining room as she sat. Smiling, she said, "How are you feeling?"

Peter said, "I'm doing well and glad to be hospital free."

Dani said, "Where's Sybil?"

"She's working. Between the cartel and PRAISE, she feels pulled in a million directions."

Dani nodded. "I know how that feels. There is never enough time in the day." She sipped her coffee and observed Peter. "Did you want to talk about something? You look relaxed, but your energy is high."

Peter laughed and sat down. "I never saw myself as an easy read."

"You're not. I'm just a very smart lady. Tell me."

"It's about the ship and its human cargo."

Dani's voice hardened. "It is not up for discussion."

"Many of those people are refugees from Tawanda. How can we save some and let others die?"

"The Olivia Bay must complete her voyage as is. Do not get involved."

"Perhaps we can..."

"Do nothing. Do not alert the U.S. Customs, inspectors, police, port authorities, any staff workers, or the Canadians. Do not go anywhere near this ship. Not in the Atlantic, the seaway, or the Great Lakes. Do I make myself clear?"

"Yes. Very. What I don't understand is how you could do so much for the refugees during the fall of Damir and ignore those suffering now."

"Sybil took care of the refugees, not me. I provided the visas when they arrived. I will do the same for those aboard ship."

"If they make it."

"As President, I have to focus on the bigger picture--ending the entire slave trade along the Great Lakes."

Peter jumped to his feet and raised his voice. "So, if it costs five hundred or so African lives, so what?"

"Sit down." Dani's words were sharp— commanding and threatening at the same time.

Peter froze.

"If you want to talk about this, Peter, sit down. Now." Dani tapped her phone for the Secret Service. An agent slid into the room and stayed hidden in the hallway.

Peter flinched.

"Sit."

This time, Peter sat.

Dani sent the agent outside and said, "Peter, you of all people should know every situation has at least three perspectives, all of which may be right for different reasons."

Peter stared at her.

"Where was your outrage when you went to the Vanderhagen Tawandian mines and saw the African workers' conditions? Did you raise their wages? Clean up the human waste? Increase their diet? Create better housing?"

Peter blinked.

Dani said, "Or did you simply do what you were sent there to do—find the diamond thieves. Where were your priorities in Africa?"

"I followed Uncle James's orders. I know now I was wrong."

"Too little, too late."

Peter said, "I thought I didn't have the power."

Dani laughed. "Really. What about your power to seduce those who stand in the way of cartel-orchestrated economic programs? Isn't it you who pulls the strings to clear away any naysayers who stand in the way of cartel progress?"

Peter's hands went to his head. "I've got a headache. I need my pills."

Dani didn't move.

Peter let out a scream. "I need my pills."

The agent ran into the room from the hall.

Sybil appeared from the bedroom hallway holding a pill bottle. "I've got them, Peter." She grabbed a glass of water from the table and slipped into the chair next to him. Handing the pills and the water to Peter, she said, "Here. Take them. You'll be fine."

Dani stood, sent the agent away, and followed him. Before leaving the room, she turned and said, "Peter, no matter how close we are, don't ever forget who you're talking to."

Chapter 47 ▶ Tidal Basin, Washington D.C.

Sunday, 28 April, 1 p.m.
Peter joined Sam and Taxi waiting at the Tidal Basin.
"I'm afraid I have bad news. The President has told
me in no uncertain terms to stay away from the Olivia
Bay and let it dock at its port of destination.
Something's going on and we're not to alert the ship's
crew to any irregularities."

Taxi said, "She is willing, apparently, to sacrifice
African lives to serve her agenda."

Peter said, "Despite the President's words, I get
the sense she is as concerned as we are."

Sam said, "Ah yes. We're talking the bigger
picture."

Peter nodded.

Sam said, "If we had only pirated the Olivia Bay
in the mid-Atlantic, we could have saved even more."

Silence.

Taxi said, "All true, but not our fate. We must
accept our shortcomings and try to do better."

Peter said, "You don't understand. We've been ordered to back off."

Sam said, "There's another problem: logistics. There's a fair bit of travel from the Atlantic, through the St. Lawrence Bay, and the Seaway locks before Ogdensburg, the first U.S. port."

Taxi said, "Are you suggesting we work through Canada, more specifically Newfoundland, so we are not bound by Presidential orders?"

Sam said, "Canada may see the situation in a different light."

Peter said, "Careful. You're treading on a political tightrope."

Taxi said, "Listen, go back to the President and offer this alternative. It will distance her from the decision and still save lives. Once the refugees are safe, we can bring them into our relocation program."

Peter said, "It sounds so simple."

Sam said, "You're right to be skeptical. If the President wants to get involved, she'll have to make the call to Canada. If not, she can step aside and plead ignorance, so she can't be blamed if we fail."

Taxi put his hand on Peter's shoulder. "You can do this. Go once more into the lion's den and make it happen."

Peter said, "Or, we can just not tell her."

Sam said, "Not happening. She's my boss. If we ignore her, we can wind up in federal prison for a long, long time."

Taxi said, "Let's focus on the people whose lives are at stake and create a detailed plan we can show to the President. She has to know we're serious."

Chapter 48 ▶ Gramercy Avenue, New York City

Sunday, 28 April, 4 p.m.

Rachel entered the living room with her jacket on and Chris's draped over her arm. "Chris, I'm going to take Zeus out for a walk. Want to come?"

Zeus ran over to his leash and sat. His tail beat a happy rhythm on the floor.

"Sure. I could use a break."

They walked to the park, spent time at the doggie run, and ordered sundaes at the outdoor café, with an ice cream scoop in a cup for Zeus.

Rachel said, "This is the life."

Chris nodded. "Perfect."

"I've been thinking."

"Uh oh. Rachel, could you think tomorrow?"

"You're kidding, right?"

Chris laughed. "Okay. Shoot."

"It's about us having children."

"It'll happen when it happens."

"Well, it's not happening and I'm thinking invitro or adoption."

Chris didn't answer.

"How can you be silent? You must have been considering one of them."

"Not really. We've only been married for six months. Kids take up a lot of time, physical and emotional. I'm enjoying the quiet of us."

Rachel flushed.

Chris said, "What's going on?"

"I've been off birth control since a couple of months before the wedding. I wanted to surprise you. I wanted the baby to be my gift to you, to us."

"I'm surprised you made such a decision all by yourself."

"I thought you wanted kids. I've seen you with your family. You love being in the middles of your siblings, nieces, and nephews."

"It's easy to be joyful in the spirit of family two or three times a year. But every day, I don't think so."

Rachel's eyes teared. She reached out and touched his hand. "I've been a mess thinking I've failed you somehow. When all this time, you weren't even thinking of having children."

He put his hand over hers. "Is that what all this vacation talk has been about?"

"Yes."

"Do you want a child?"

"I'm not sure. At first, when I expected to be pregnant right away, I was excited. When it didn't happen, I wasn't sure. Today, I don't think it's a good time. We're both so busy, we hardly have time for each other."

"Come on." He stood and pulled Rachel to her feet. He wrapped his arms around her and whispered in her ear, "This discussion bears further analysis. Do you agree?"

She lifted her chin and kissed him. "Now?"

"You bet."

Chris paid the bill and they returned to their apartment building. As they approached, his phone went into emergency mode, issuing an irritating pulsing sound accompanied by a flashing red screen.

Nikolai met them at the door. "The tech guys on 2nd floor need you ASAP."

Chris glanced at Rachel. She said, "Go. I'll be upstairs when you've got it sorted."

He ran to the stairs.

Rachel looked at Nikolai. "Did this just happen?"

"Yes."

"I'm sure Chris will take care of it in no time."

Nicolai said, "There is also some news for you." He handed her a bunch messages written on yellow sticky notes. "Your publisher and your agent have left 'call me' messages."

Rachel took the information and looked at her phone. "I didn't get them because I turned my phone off. Thanks, Nikolai. I'll call them back as soon as I'm upstairs."

The calls turned out to be more than just a hello. Details had to be worked out. A slew of preorders had slammed the publisher as a result of her article on railroad towns.

More calls. One to her publicist and one to her web designer to help track requests. After the last call, Rachel stretched and looked at the time—four o'clock. How did it get so late so fast?

She left her office, walked down the stairs, and. went to the living room. She expected Chris to be either working or stretched out on the couch. He was nowhere to be found.

She pulled out her phone and texted him. "Feeding Zeus and lying down for a nap. We'll walk him and eat when you get done. Xoxo."

Rachel opened her eyes when she heard the apartment door open and close. "Chris?"

"I'm home. I walked Zeus and brought food."

"What time is it?"

"Eight. It took longer than I expected."

She went to the kitchen area and slid onto a bar stool while Chris unpacked the meal. "Tough night?"

Looking into her eyes, he said, "The core of ICU was attacked with the intention of bringing it down. This has been the worst night of my career."

Rachel saw the devastation in his rounded shoulders, unruly hair, and darkened circles under his eyes. She ran to him and held him. He hugged her back, resting his head on her shoulder. They didn't move until he said, "Come on. I've got to eat something."

They ate dinner without much conversation.

Once the food revived him, Chris said, "I've been working full out since we got back. Octavius must have put his whole team on a multi-pronged coordinated attack on ICU's system."

"Octavius did this? Are you sure? Did they get in?"

"I'm sure. They penetrated our primary defense which triggered the emergency alarm system. In effect, they played Whack-A-Mole with us. Every time we figured out a fix, another problem popped up. The randomness of location and module made it a harrowing experience which I hope we never have to deal with again."

"Is it fixed?"

"For now. We stopped it before it could destroy any of our security installations and beefed up our defenses."

"You beat Octavius again."

"I did, except this time it's not gamesmanship, it's war. He means to destroy me and take ICU. Do I sell or fight?"

Rachel said, "Not even a question."

"If I fight, it will take all my energy for a while and the baby-making will have to be put on hold. If I sell, baby-making will have my complete attention."

"Don't you dare put this on me."

Chris laughed. "I'd like to. You've always wanted to be a part of my business life. Now's as good a time as any."

Rachel stared at him. Seconds ticked by before she said, "I can't tell if you're teasing me or not. If you're serious, I say fight the bastard."

"Good. I agree. Although, I'm surprised. What's got your hackles up?"

Rachel didn't answer. Instead, she got up, retrieved her open laptop from the bedroom, and returned to Chris's side. "Listen to this." She read aloud. "Ms. Allen uses a very privileged perspective to denigrate a corporate philosophy designed to relieve workers' concerns for housing, food, and education." She scrolled down. "Mining towns brought together workers from outlying areas and formed cohesive supportive communities. Disparaging remarks by author Allen dismisses the positive aspects of strong family bonds."

Chris said, "Let me see."

She handed him her computer.

After scanning the remaining remarks, he said, "You also received some high praise. However, I agree there were a disproportionate number of negative reviews."

Rachel said, "Octavius has sent his trolls to dismiss me."

"It's more than that. He wants to crush us."

"He's not being very subtle."

Chris stood and said, "You write another article. I'm going down to my tech team to do a little hacking of our own." At the door, he turned, "Since Octavius wants a war, we'll give him one he won't forget."

Chapter 49 ▶ White House, Washington D.C.

Wednesday, 1 May, 9 a.m.
On her way to the Oval Office, Dani stopped at Isabel's desk. "Is the EEA announcement ready?"

Isabel said, "Yes," and handed her the folder.

Dani took it and read the document. "You and Terence did a great job. Make this an Executive Order ready for this afternoon. Also, ask Cecil to meet with me at nine-thirty."

Isabel picked up her phone.

Dani said, "Wait. First, have the kitchen send up a pot of coffee and a continental breakfast." Without waiting for a reply, Dani strode into her office.

<~<~|~>~>

In the White House residence, Sybil and Peter sat at the breakfast table.

Peter said, "I can't stay here anymore."

Sybil said, "Don't be so sensitive. You've had a disagreement with Dani. You're both human."

"It's not that."

"Then what?"

"Dani was right. I went to Tawanda to follow orders, not fix anything. I did see the horrendous conditions. No simple action on my part had any chance of changing anything without disrupting the whole economic reality. As a result, I'm partly responsible for the destruction of Tawanda."

"Peter, stop beating yourself up."

"Easy to say, Mom. Still, no matter how I look at it, I'm as guilty of blind obedience as the Nazis convicted at Nuremberg."

"It was your first job for my brother. You wanted to impress him. End of discussion. You didn't have the time, resources, or authority to do anything else."

"Ignorant and complicit."

Sybil said, "You don't have the time or luxury for recriminations. We have other things on our plate."

Peter said, "Go ahead. Tell me."

"I've been working on the cartel formulas and there are big problems. We need to rethink our portfolio positions because, by my calculations, their value is over-inflated."

"Impossible. The cartel's always beats the stock market percentages by a lot."

"Peter, listen to me. The increasing differential between the haves and have-nots is distorting the data."

"Come on. Don't you think Octavius is aware?"

Sylvia said, "I don't know him well enough. His past performance is no longer a predictor of future fortunes. What I do know is if I factor in consumer spending for equivalent income data, our stock value drops almost sixty percent."

Peter shook his head and said, "Impossible."

"We don't see it, because Octavius must be calculating on some Gross National Product variation."

Peter pulled out his phone.

Sybil said, "What are you doing?"

"Calling Octavius. Have him check out your findings."

Sybil got to her feet and grabbed the phone out of his hands. "Are you doubting me?"

"No, just double checking."

"Don't ask him. Check it out for yourself."

"Mom, you're being ridiculous."

Sylvia sat. "Why do you think Dani rejected your efforts to rescue the slave ship?"

Peter's eyes widened. "How do you know about that?"

"I overheard your conversation. So, tell me why."

Peter said, "To protect Octavius and the cartel. The ship is bound for his port in Chicago."

"Really? You think Dani would sacrifice hundreds of people so Octavius, the cartel, and our family could make a profit? Do you see her as aiding and abetting human trafficking?"

Perspiration bubbles dotted Peter's hairline and upper lip. "I..."

Sybil said, "Don't defy her and don't call Octavius. Your time is better spent saving our investment portfolios."

"Wait, Mom. Our family is involved. If the cartel members know about this, how come I didn't?" Peter pushed his chair away from the table and stood, sat, and stood again. He raised his voice. "What's going on? Did I miss some indoctrination ceremony? What?"

Sybil said, "Peter, sit down."

Peter stomped away from the table and returned. "I know I'm new at this but I'm voting on issues I don't even know about. I'm putting lives at risk without my knowledge."

"Peter."

He finger-combed his hair and then grabbed it. At the top of his voice he said, "I'm a fucking moron. A tool. A go-for." He slammed his hands on the table, sat down, and whimpered as he said, "I represent holdings as vast as the other members and yet I don't fucking know anything. They must regard me as a complete idiot."

Sybil put her arms around him. Comforting him, trying to be as calming as she could, she said, "I don't know everything either. Also, I can be shortsighted. I should never have brought this up. I forgot you're in recovery and I've overwhelmed you." She gave Peter his phone and stood. "Come with me. We can do this."

Chapter 50 ▶ Tavius Global, Chicago, Il

Wednesday, 1 May, 3:30 p.m.
Octavius stood before the huge office window and stared at Lake Michigan's tidal waves. He had just learned his orders were being carried out—Terence Mitchell was as good as dead. The President would listen to him now.

Next, the Gregory hit. He went to his desk, lower right-hand drawer, and pulled out one of several phones. He pulled up the only saved phone number and called. At the connection, he said, "Are you in New York?"

The Ninja said, "Yes."

Octavius said, "Do it."

He returned the phone to the drawer, closed it, and pressed the intercom. "Send in my executive team. I want to see the announcement presentation."

He received an instantaneous response, as if they were waiting outside the door. The men filed in and sat at the conference table. The marketing vice president revealed the large presentation screen and hooked it up to his computer. "I'm ready, sir."

"Go ahead. Make me want to buy this package whether I need it or not."

Marketing gulped. "We begin with the Tavius Global Enterprises logo. This fades to background as we highlight our premise. Tavius Global Enterprises is committed to providing our employees with a safe, self-contained, and sustainable environment to addresses all aspects of our workers' needs."

Octavius said, "This does not excite me. In fact, it's boring. Where's the excitement? Brilliance? Revolutionary idea? If I don't look like the great innovator I am, I'll find a better team."

Marketing said, "We can definitely do better, sir. Clearly, we were focused on translating your ideas into a formal outline."

"Forget formal. I want impact." He took a few steps away from the table, stopped, and did a one-eighty. "Something like, 'Meet your employees' needs and exceed profit goals.'" He repeated his actions. "Tavius Global has pioneered a total sustainable worker-centered, family-friendly environment." He stared at each man at the table. "Get it?"

They all nodded.

He looked at Marketing. "Show me the pictures."

"Yes, sir." At the end of the slide show, Marketing read the last screen. "Comprehensive Employee Priority Systems distributed exclusively by Tavius International Enterprises, including design, construction, and software for security and administrative systems." He looked to his boss.

Octavius slapped his hand on the table. "Not even close. I want people clamoring for this product. I want to see a waiting list as long as Michigan

Avenue. Give me an ending like, 'Be the corporate revolution,' or 'Profit from worker reliability,' or 'Change today and profit tomorrow.' Something, anything, that makes every CEO pick up the phone and call me."

All the men said, "Yes, sir."

Octavius said, "Bring me results tomorrow morning at nine or I'll have a new team in place by noon."

After the team left, he contemplated a new world where President Dani Mitchell listened to him and took orders without pushback. The attack on Terence Mitchell would take care of that. The attack on the Gregory duo would not only make it possible for ICU to become his but also owning the original source code would make him a fortune. He smiled involuntarily. An exceptional day for him and Tavius Global.

Chapter 51 ▶ White House, Washington D.C.

Wednesday, 1 May, 3:30 p.m.
In the Oval Office, Dani sat in the high-back wing chair sipping tea. She did not change her position when the Vice President arrived. He positioned himself in front of Dani and said, "Good morning, Madam President."

"Cecil, thank you for coming. It's been a few days since we last spoke."

"Yes. I'm so sorry I disappointed you regarding the environment coalition."

"I'm sympathetic," Dani said. "Everybody wants to be known as an advocate without committing to real meaningful and measurable change."

Cecil said, "I agree."

"Good, because I'd like you to invite as many recognized activists as you can find in the next few hours to the Oval Office for the Emergency Environment Act Executive Order signing today at four. Include Terence, who wrote most of it, and the twins."

"An Executive Order t-t-today?" Cecil said in an uncharacteristic stutter, "C-C-Can't you give m-m-me another c-c-couple of weeks to bring people to the t-t-table?"

"No."

"P-P-Please. We rushed our last effort. We didn't give people enough time to prepare their strategies."

"You mean Mr. Octavius, don't you?"

Cecil nodded.

Dani said, "He's had years, as have the others, and produced negligible results."

Cecil said, "I understand. Activists today for a signing at four."

"Thank you, Cecil."

The Vice President left like a man on a mission.

Not five minutes later, Dani felt her phone vibrate and answered. "Octavius."

"Cecil has told me you're going to put the EEA through despite my objections."

Dani said, "You're not the one on the hook for disaster prevention, clean-up, or restoration. I am."

"I represent companies all over the world, which will implode under stricter guidelines. Our stockholder dividends will destroy our economic future, second only to the loss of jobs and abandoned communities."

"Octavius, your leadership could minimize the damage. Yet, you've refused and encouraged others not to step forward. As a result, this country is now years behind our carbon footprint goals while contributing more pollution than any other country on earth, including China."

"Two more weeks would change nothing."

"That's what you said last year."

"It has taken longer to build the model and work out the challenges than I expected. Unpredictability has plagued the project from the moment we went live."

"This country can't wait. I must make my commitment and get the funding. In two weeks, or whenever you're ready, you will probably be the first international company to support and enact the EEA across the board."

Octavius said, "Perhaps, but second to you."

Dani said, "Yes."

The call ended at three-twelve.

Isabel announced Yosef.

He knocked, entered, and said, "We may have a problem. The informant aboard the Olivia Bay has reported rough seas have slowed their progress in general and now they are in a storm southwest of Newfoundland."

Dani said, "Canadian waters?"

Yosef nodded and said, "The captain has electronically registered the Olivia Bay for its passage down the seaway and designated the cargo as freight remaining on board. The registration listed Tavius Global Enterprises as the destination and purchaser. The official cargo is goods for manufacturing and printing, shipping in cargo containers sitting on the main deck."

"Do you know how many people are being trafficked?"

"Three holds of one-hundred people each. There is a food and waste exchange three times a day. It is the only time the holds are opened."

Dani said, "When is the ETA at Ogdensburg?"

"May 3rd, and Chicago, May 10th."

"Thank you, Yosef. Keep me in the loop."

Yosef said, "Ma'am. If the Olivia Bay gets battered and goes down, a couple of Canadian Coast Guard Cutters will not have time to get there. If by some miracle they make it, they won't be able to save all those people below deck because they won't know they exist until it is too late."

"Clarify."

Yosef said, "Get them out now. You already have proof of port of call because the Olivia Bay has registered it. If we catch them unawares, we may be able to confiscate any and all paperwork."

Dani said, "As much as I would love to see Octavius's face when the ship docks at his facility, I can go with this new plan. In fact, I'll give you a team and back-up."

Dani pulled out her phone, scanned her contacts, and call the Secretary of Defense. "I need a confidential favor. Please order a ship from the 2nd Fleet to prepare for a possible three-hundred-person rescue exercise off the coast of Newfoundland A.S.A.P."

The Secretary of Defense said, "You're talking Canadian waters. Shall I call their Coast Guard?"

The President said, "Not at this time, as this is only an exercise. However, I suggest having contact and assistance protocols in place. Should there be an S.O.S., I want to be sure we have the ability to assist immediately."

"Understood."

Dani ended the call and said, "Yosef, keep me informed."

As he left, Isabel walked in and said, "Cecil informed me there will be twenty people here at three-forty-five. I suggest you go take a breather so we can arrange everyone in here and you can make an entrance."

"Good idea. Have you heard from Terence?"

Isabel said, "Why would he call me?"

Dani said, "Not necessarily. He might not have been able to get through to me. I'll give him a call while I freshen up. He worked on this, and I'd like him to be here."

"I understand."

Dani left the Oval Office for the residence and called Terence. His phone rang and went to voice mail. She called the twins. Ivan answered and she said, "Where are you?"

Ivan said, "Just got home. Getting ready for the signing."

"Is Isaac with you?"

"Uh-huh."

"Your dad?"

"We haven't seen him. Where are you?"

Dani put her phone away and said, "Right behind you."

Ivan turned and smiled.

Dani said, "I'll be ready in two minutes. See you downstairs."

As she walked into her room, she called Terence again. Still no answer. Something's off. She didn't call him often, but when she did, he always answered. Always.

He'd see she'd called and call her back any minute, so Dani refreshed her makeup, tidied stray hairs, and tucked in her blouse. She smoothed down her jacket, straightened her neckline, and checked her shoes. One final look in the mirror and she froze.

Head of Security Wesley Warren stood at her bedroom door. "I'm sorry, ma'am."

Dani spun to face him. "What happened?"

"Your husband's been in a car accident and hurt pretty bad."

"How bad?"

"He's being evaluated."

Dani stiffened. "Anyone else hurt?"

"The two agents in the car with him."

"Do we know who? Or even why?"

Wesley said, "I'll have answers for you as soon as we evaluate the CCTV footage and process the scene."

She said, "Where are the boys?"

"Downstairs. I passed them on my way but didn't say anything."

Dani said, "Give me a minute."

Wesley left the room and closed the door.

Dani sensed this was no accident. She had defied Octavius. *He timed his revenge to warn me not to go forward with enacting the EEA. If he thinks he can control the President, he's got another thing coming. One show of weakness and he'll win. I will get through the next hour and do my job and I won't fall apart. Octavius be damned.*

She joined Wesley. "Do you think those who caused the accident meant to kill Terence?"

Wesley said, "The vehicle was battered by three others, like they knew their target and the armored car Terrence rode in." He pulled out his phone and showed her pictures taken at the accident scene. "What do you think?"

Dani looked at the mangled mess in the middle of an intersection. "I'd say yes."

"I agree."

Dani said, "Let's go with it. Lock down the hospital and secure Terence. Have the doctors report he's in critical condition and keep him isolated."

"Ma'am?"

"I don't want the man who engineered this to go unpunished."

"We will get him no matter what."

"No, Wesley. You won't. I will."

As they walked to the Oval Office, Wesley made the call.

When he finished, she said, "Good. Here's my plan. I'll do the EEA signing in Terence's name and returned to the residence immediately. Gather my family. Notify Bruce. Put an agent with the boys and have them wait for me outside the presentation. We'll go in together, if they can. If not, take them back. Tell them we'll go to the hospital later."

Once the boys came into view, she knew they didn't know. They were hanging out, leaning against the wall. She approached them. "Something terrible has happened. Your father has been in a terrible a car crash."

She opened her arms for a family hug. They didn't respond. They slid down the wall, sat on their heels, and held their heads. Dani leaned over, touched their shoulders, and said, "I have to do this signing to honor your dad. You can join me or not. I'll go directly to the residence when it's done."

The boys didn't respond.

She turned her head toward Wes and said, "Take care of them. I'll be done in fifteen," and walked into the Oval Office.

Fifteen minutes later, Dani left the Oval Office.

Wesley approached. "I have the video."

Dani watched. "He never even saw it coming."

Wes said, "No. No one did."

As she made her way to the residence, Dani pulled out her phone. Her first call went to Cecil. "I know you alerted Octavius. You should also know Terence suffered traumatic injuries in a horrific car crash minutes before the EEA signing. I want you to know I do not consider it a coincidence." She ended the call before he could respond.

She made another call. "Beth, how soon can you be on-site at Tavius Global to carry out the tax inquiry?"

Beth said, "Why? What changed?"

"Terence was in a car crash. He's in critical condition. I'm sure Octavius ordered it."

"Do you want me to investigate?"

"No, my Head of Security is in charge."

"What do you need me to do?"

Dani said, "I want you to nail that bastard for tax fraud and human trafficking plus whatever else you can find. How fast can you do that?"

Beth said, "I'm on it. We can be on-site within three days."

Dani said, "Do it." She put the phone away and walked into the living room to face her anxious family, Isabel, Peter, Bruce, and Yosef.

Sybil stepped up to embrace her. "I'm so sorry."

Dani said, "Where are the boys?"

"In their room."

Sybil stepped away so Peter could take her place. "I'm..."

Before he could finish his thought, Dani said, "Do it."

"What?"

"Intercept the Olivia Bay while it's still in the Atlantic Ocean, release its human cargo, and get complete copies of its paperwork. Keep me out of it. This is strictly a rescue mission. If the ship hasn't radioed an S.O.S. before you get there, you send it."

"Now?"

"Yes, because I believe Tavius Global is behind Terence's accident."

Peter took a step back. "Are you sure?"

"Does it matter? I thought your interests lie in saving people's lives."

Peter stiffened and gave her a salute. "I'm on it."

Dani said, "Good. Go with Yosef. He has a man on board the Olivia Bay. Take Sam and Taxi. Call me when it's done."

She nodded to Yosef and watched the men leave the room. With the pressure off, Dani collapsed into the closest chair. By habit, she looked over at the bar, expecting Terence, smiling, to have her drink ready. His absence hit her hard even though he was a shit, abandoning her for another, living a lie without explanation. Yet, over time, he'd become a good friend and remained a good dad.

Ivan and Isaac appeared with reddened eyes and tear-stained cheeks.

Dani held out her arms, "Everything's going to be okay. Your dad's going to be okay. I promise." This time, the twins ran into her embrace.

Chapter 52 ▶ Gramercy Avenue, New York City

Wednesday, 1 May, 1:30 p.m.
Rachel sat in the living area with Zeus curled up at her feet and the TV on. As she edited her second essay on human rights, she waited for Dani's announcement on the Emergency Environmental Act. She looked at the time and texted Chris, *Dani's on in 30.*

She smiled at his thumbs-up emoji and went back to editing until her peripheral vision caught the TV monitor flickering. She looked up and put the sound on.

A reporter said, "...ABC News, and I'm here at the scene of a devastating car crash which has sent Terence Mitchell, President Dani Mitchell's husband, and two Secret Service agents to the hospital. Police reports indicate a large black truck and two cars struck Mr. Mitchell's car. The scene is blocked off and investigators, both local and federal, are on the scene." She stopped talking and looked to her right, nodded, and returned to her audience. "I am told Mr. Terence Mitchell, President Dani Mitchell's husband, is in critical condition and route to the hospital."

Rachel picked up her phone and called Chris. "Terence was in a car crash."

He said, "When do you want to leave for D.C.?"

She said, "It's close to rush hour. It's going to depend on when we can get out of here."

"You're right. I'll make the arrangements and let you know. Give me an hour or so. My team is just finishing up a key phase of our current project."

"Okay. See you soon."

Rachel turned the sound off and returned to her revision. Something on the screen made her look. Dani spoke from the Oval Office.

"First, I'd like to thank all our guests who are climate and environmental activists. Your work – science, activism, and reporting – proves the case for this Environmental Emergency Bill." The camera zoomed in. "I had hoped the EEA would be an act of Congress. Unfortunately, major U.S. companies and majority stockholders would not come to the table, citing a conflict of interest. They erroneously do not see their job extending to stakeholders.

"However, as your elected President, it is the exact definition of my job. I am committing funds and expertise to minimize the impact of a changing environment on millions of Americans.

"Another activist, Terence Mitchell, spent long hours crafting this EEA. He would have been here had fate

not intervened. Therefore, I
sign this EEA executive order
in his honor."

Rachel watched. In contrast to Dani's
Presidential composure, tears welled in her eyes.
When the broadcast ended, she texted, "*Dani, I'm so
sorry. We'll pray for Terence's recovery and be on our way
to D.C. as soon as possible. Rachel.*"

Zeus whined.

Rachel petted him. "It's okay, Pup. I'm okay."

He stared into Rachel's eyes and got to his feet—
his gaze unwavering. "Whuff."

She said, "What?"

Zeus wagged his tail.

"Are you hungry?"

Zeus backed up and jumped around in a circle,
his tail wagging like an unhinged rudder.

"Okay. Okay. Your ability to tell time still baffles
me."

Zeus barked twice.

Rachel laughed and stood. "Let's go."
Once she'd filled his dish, Zeus dove into his food.
Chris called.
She put him on speaker.
He said, "Be prepared for a long jail sentence. The
team's copied the Tavius Global Chicago server and
tucked it away."
"I can't believe you're saying you did something
illegal?"
"Not me, but maybe."
Rachel said, "Good. When he gets crazier, and he
will, we've got something to bargain with."
Chris said, "I'll be right up to walk Zeus with you."
"I'll be ready.
"

Chapter 53 ▶ Gramercy Avenue, New York City

Wednesday, 1 May, 4:15 p.m.
The Ninja closed the phone without saying a word. Perched on top of a building facing the Gregory apartment's rear windows, the assassin knew Plan D was not optimal. Preferable would be to get inside the apartment itself and plant an explosive with an electronic detonator. Then, from several blocks away, push the button and leave town.

The Ninja looked around. This position was too exposed, but other options were unavailable. After researching the apartment plans, it was obvious the couple lived in a fortress with electronic surveillance and all kinds of access keys. Even if the man at the front desk could be distracted, gaining access to the stairs, much less the elevator, would have been time-consuming. Once inside, getting out would have a whole other set of risks, one of them being the damn dog.

Crouching behind the low wall surrounding the roof, the Ninja opened the case and removed the two pieces of an RPG-7 anti-tank rocket launcher. After putting them together, the Ninja attached the rocket, which had been modified to reduce the charge. The Gregorys were the target—no one else had to get hurt.

The Ninja sighted the apartment. Although the woman and dog were present, they had to wait for the man to appear. At that moment, with exacting precision, they'd fire, and the missile would obliterate all of them.

<~<~|~>~>

Nikolai sat at his desk, the security monitors facing him. He had a cup of coffee and a slice of warm banana bread in front of him. He enjoyed this late afternoon repast because he never left Gramercy Avenue until after rush hour.

As he ate, he watched the monitors. He knew the daily patterns of life in and around the building like his own name. Cameras showed the street in front, the area in the back, the interior stairs, and elevators of all three contiguous apartment buildings. He scanned the images with such exaggerated confidence, he almost missed the anomaly. Something or someone was on the roof of a building facing the back of 215 Gramercy.

He sat up, put the coffee down, and zoomed in. It looked like a ball with an antenna.

"That can't be right." He sharpened the image. "A person with gun. A person with a rocket launcher aimed right at this building."

Nikolai called the police. Next, he tried to reach Chris and Rachel. Neither answered. He unlocked the undercounter drawer and grabbed his gun. The 9mm Browning HP stirred memories of when he had been forced to serve, kill, and ravage people, towns, and fields in the Bosnian-Serbia war. Still, it felt at home in his hand. He ran for the stairs, keys jangling. There were windows at each landing. He could shoot from the top window. If he couldn't take out the shooter, maybe he could deflect the missile.

He tried Chris again. This time, Chris answered.

Nikolai, breathing hard, said, "You huh, huh, have to get huh, huh, Rachel and Zeus huh, huh, out of the apartment, huh, huh, now. Gun."

Chris flew up the stairs before the call ended. He and Nikolai reached the top at the same time.

Nikolai smashed the window as Chris barged through the door to get to Rachel.

With two hands holding his gun, he sighted the target. Peripherally, he saw police enter the rooftop, but he didn't let them distract him from his mission— taking the missile out.

He knew it a fool's errand when he saw it, but he had to try. In a fraction of a second, Nikolai had to gauge the missile's speed and trajectory. He had to get ahead of it by enough time to allow him to pull the trigger for the bullet to intercept the ordinance. He couldn't do the math, so he let instinct and experience take over.

Under his breath he said, "Zero chance. One-hundred percent effort."

The police rushed the shooter. Too late. He took the shot.

The missile took off, emitting a tracer when the wings emerged.

Nikolai focused, calculated, tracked, and fired.

Chapter 54 ▶ Gramercy Avenue, New York City

Wednesday, 1 May, 4:30 p.m.
Rachel left the phone on the counter, expecting to be back as soon as she changed her clothes. Zeus, her ever present shadow followed her. She was almost ready when she heard the door bang open, and Chris scream out her name. As she turned, she heard an explosion, smelled fireworks, and felt her body lifted off the floor.

<~<~|~>~>

The blast threw Nikolai against the wall. The door to Chris's apartment hung on one hinge.

Jack, from J&J Security on the ground floor, raced up the stairs. "What happened?"

Nikolai nodded to Chris and Rachel's apartment. "A missile exploded just outside the apartment."

"You okay?"

Nikolai said, "Fine."

Jack extended his hand to help Nikolai stand and said, "Chris and Rachel?"

Nikolai pointed and followed Jack into the apartment.

"Jesus," Jack said. "There's glass everywhere mixed in with everything not nailed down."

Nikolai called out, "Chris! Rachel! Are you okay? Anybody hurt?"

Groans. A whine. Sirens outside.

The men worked to clear a path to the bedroom.

"Are you guys crazy?"

Without turning his head, Nikolai said, "I've got to get to the bedroom."

A fireman grabbed Nikolai and said, "Get out of here and let us do our job."

Nikolai said, "We're looking for two people and a dog."

The fire company captain walked in, looked at Nikolai, and pointed to the door. "Out. Now. We'll take it from here."

Jack called out. "I've found Chris. I need help."

The captain used his communication device. "I need EMTs up here now."

Nikolai ignored the order and moved forward to see Chris stretched out on the bed and unconscious. He looked around the room. "Rachel?"

Groan.

EMTs and another fireman appeared.

Nikolai pointed to the closet. "She's in there."

"Okay, sir. Step out of the way. Bill, over here. Help me with this."

A third fireman appeared. Two unblocked the closet and found Rachel—alive.

The captain signaled for another EMT team.

Nikolai called out, "Zeus! Zeus! Where are you boy?"

The whine came from the bathroom. Zeus lay wounded, blood seeping from a cut in his side.

Nikolai said, "EMT, over here!" as he tried to stem the blood flow.

A fireman said, "For the dog?"

Nikolai growled. "Do we fight it out or do you get someone?"

The fireman made the call.

Nikolai, eyes tearing uncontrollably, stayed with Zeus until help arrived.

With Zeus on his way to the hospital, Nicolai collapsed. The captain called for another stretcher. He knelt down next to Nikolai and said, "Come on. You've had a rough time. Let me walk you downstairs. We've got to let my team make sure all fires are out and the building is safe."

Nikolai nodded. He allowed himself to be led to an ambulance. "Wait, I don't need to go to the hospital. I'm fine."

The captain stepped aside and the EMT said, "A few scratches and a small gash. I can take care of that here if it's okay with you."

Nikolai nodded.

When the EMT finished, the captain walked over and put his hand on Nikolai's shoulder. "Had the missile exploded inside, instead of outside, a lot of people would have died. Word has it you're the sniper who nailed that sucker."

Nikolai looked at him for the first time.

The captain said, "Damn nice shot."

Chapter 55 ▶ White House, Washington D.C.

Wednesday, 1 May, 5:30 p.m.

Dani, the twins, and Sybil sat at the dining table. No one ate. No one said anything.

Dani said, "Come on. We must eat something. There's still so much to get through."

Isaac grabbed half a sandwich, put it on his plate, and removed the top piece of bread. He peeled the tomato slices off the egg salad and added a slice of cheese. He sighed. "I miss Chris and Rachel being here."

Ivan said, "Yeah. They must have heard."

Sybil said, "I'll call." She held the phone to her ear while she waited for Rachel's cheerful voice. "She's not picking up."

Isaac said, "I'll call Chris. His phone is always on." A minute later, he said, "No answer."

Ivan said, "I'll call the tech team, they'll know."

Dani's phone rang before he could make the call. Beth. Dani said, "Tell me."

"Rachel, Chris, and Zeus are in the hospital. Nikolai called us. Their apartment was bombed."

Dani said, "How are they doing?"

Beth said, "All are in emergency care. I don't know anything yet. Waiting for an update from Nikolai or Helene. I'll let you know as soon as I know."

Dani said, "Text me Helene's and Nikolai's phone numbers anyway."

"Will do," Beth said. "We've asked for all site reports and images. We'll know more after we review them, and the fire department has finished its assessment."

Dani said, "Any ideas who's behind it?"

Beth said, "Your guess is as good as mine. The police had the shooter in custody. Before they could interrogate, the shooter died by hara-kiri. Even though the police thought they did a thorough search, they found a ninja staff sword in the body. Apparently, it had enough flexibility to be hidden in a waistband. And get this. It breaks the skin like the stiletto wound Rachel suffered. I think they're planning to distribute the shooter's face and see if anything turns up."

Dani said, "At least Rachel and Chris don't have to worry anymore."

"Eric and I will make sure this is handled. We'll send a team to Gramercy Ave while we finalize plans for Chicago."

Dani said, "What's your ETA?"

"How does Friday sound?"

"Good." Dani put down the phone and said, "I just realized you can be sad and mad at the same time."

Sybil said, "You bet you can. The only is cure is pie."

Dani stared at her for ten seconds and said, "A la mode."

Isaac jumped out of his chair. "Ivan, cut the pie. I'll get the ice cream."

After dessert, Dani called Terence and put her phone on speaker. "Hi."

"Dani, this is Bruce. Terence is a little groggy, so I'm going to put the phone on speaker and hold it so he can hear."

Dani said, "Terence, Isaac, Ivan, and Sybil are here with me. How are you doing?"

"Okay. Good pain medication."

Dani said, "Concentrate on healing."

"I'll be fine."

Isaac and Ivan said, "Love you, Dad."

"Love you too."

Dani said, "Good night. Talk to you tomorrow."

Isaac said, "When we visited him earlier, he didn't make too much sense. How bad is it really?"

Dani said, "He got pretty banged up. He's in critical care because I want him away from the press for a few days."

Ivan said, "You're gonna catch the guys who did this, right?"

Dani nodded. "Absolutely."

Isaac said, "Isn't it strange? You've been so adamant about us not driving because we could get hurt or targeted, and it turns out Dad, who wasn't even driving, was the one who got hurt."

Dani smiled. "I guess there's the lesson. Try as we can, we can't control everything." She looked at the twins. "Still, being who I am, I'm still going to try. So, the "no driving" rule is still in effect."

Sybil said, "Boys, our job right now is to act responsibly and not talk about your father to the press or social media or to anyone outside this circle. Do I make myself clear?"

Dani put her arms around Ivan's and Isaac's shoulders. "She's right. I've got plans in place to make sure the people who attacked your father are put away for good. For the plans to work, you have to help with your silence."

The twins replied in unison. "We promise. Don't worry."

Dani didn't get her update on Rachel and Chris until the next morning when her phone rang at eight. The ID said, *Rachel.* Dani said, "Hi, I'm so glad you're okay."

"Madam President, this is Helene Allen, Rachel's mother."

"Helene, I'm so glad you called. Please tell me how Rachel and Chris are doing."

"Right now, they are both resting after surgery. They were very lucky," Helene paused. Dani could hear her trying to control her anguish. "Zeus, too. Thank God."

Dani said, "I know what you mean. I don't know what Rachel would do without him."

Helene cleared her throat. "The blast tossed them around like paper dolls. Rachel flew into the closet. Chris hit the stone wall behind the bed." She sniffed, trying to control the liquid running from her eyes and nose. "Their bodies were pelted with debris."

Dani said, "I'm so sorry, Helene."

"The doctor said they'd both recover but he couldn't commit to what extent." More sobs. "We'll know more when they wake up."

Dani said, "Is there anything I can do?"

"Pray."

Chapter 56 ▶ New York City, NY

Wednesday, 1 May, 10 p.m.

Rachel heard someone calling her name. Even though it sounded muffled, near and far at the same time, it was a familiar voice. A hand holding hers. No, not holding, more like massaging.

"Rachel. Honey. It's Mom. Come on. Wake up."

"Maybe you shouldn't push her. She'll wake up when she's ready."

"Harry, the doctor said the sooner the better."

Rachel smiled. Her parents were here. Why? Why were they here? Did she call them? She tried to open her eyes.

Helene said, "Look. Her eyelids are fluttering." She leaned over Rachel's body and, with a moistened cotton ball, wiped Rachel's unbandaged eye.

Rachel felt the coolness and, with a little more effort, opened her eye to see the relieved faces of her parents.

Helene said, "Welcome back. You've just come out of surgery. The doctor said you did well."

Rachel said, "Where am I?"

"Hospital," Harry said. "You've been in an accident and got banged up pretty good."

Helene said, "Don't let the bandages scare you. They'll be off in no time. Right now, what you need is rest."

Rachel looked around the room. "Where's Chris?"

Helene said, "He's still in surgery. We're getting periodic updates and the doctors are sure he's going to make it."

Tears rolled down Rachel's cheek.

Helene wiped them. "Now, now. This is a private room. They'll bring him here when he's out of recovery. Don't worry. This is all temporary. You, Chris, and Zeus are going to be fine."

Rachel managed a thin smile before slipping into a deep sleep.

Chapter 57 ▶ Newfoundland, Canada

Thursday, 2 May, 7 a.m.

Peter, Sam, Taxi, and Yosef took a puddle jumper from Nova Scotia to St. John's, Newfoundland. Winds whipped the small plane through the rain with belly lurching drops and pressure headaches.

Although the pilot apologized several times, the men waved him off. They were focused on the radio call broadcasted over the plane's loudspeaker. In between the crackles, static, and smashing waves, they heard the desperate call from the distressed ship.

"This is the Olivia Bay. S.O.S. This is the Olivia Bay. S.O.S. The crew has abandoned the ship. We've got approximately two-hundred-fifty people on board, most below deck in cargo holds. I'm in the wheelhouse and trying to hold a course west. I've got two other passengers helping, but I'm not sure we're doing much good."

The connection ended. Yosef pulled out a notepad, flipped through to the last page and dialed the number.

"Coast Guard, St. John's station, Information Officer."

Sam grabbed the phone. "Officer, I'm Sam Reynolds with the U.S. State Department on a special mission ordered by President Mitchell. We're here to help evacuate the Olivia Bay."

"Yes, sir. We've already dispatched rescue."

"Are you aware it's over two-hundred-fifty people?"

"I... I..."

Sam said, "Never mind. I think there's an aircraft carrier coming to assist. I do not have confirmation or location. I'm coming in..." He looked up, and the pilot handed him a slip of paper. He read it out loud. "On your runway one. We're four men and want to transfer to a rescue boat. We have dive gear but can use as many air tanks as you've got. Can you make that happen?"

"I'll be ready, sir."

"Good man. ETA one-minute forty."

Taxi pulled out a handkerchief and wiped his brow. "Do you guys realize the landing could've gone either way?"

Yosef said, "I had no doubt we'd make it." He looked at Taxi. "Okay, there were two minutes I choose not to relive. We're safe because we're supposed to get to that rescue."

A jeep met them on the tarmac and took off to the St. John's Harbour waterfront, stopping next to a large commercial fishing boat.

Peter looked around frantically. "Isn't there a faster boat available?"

The captain, standing by the gangplank, said, "You'll not find a faster boat in the harbor. The last

Coast Guard boat left ten minutes ago. We'll be right behind them."

Sam gave Peter a double pat on the back. "Don't worry. Stay focused."

The men and their gear boarded the Maryjane, felt the engine rev up, and the boat left the dock. After putting on their diving suits and life jackets, they went to the enclosed observation deck.

Yosef said, "The water seems calm enough. I wonder if the Olivia Bay is floundering due to structural damage."

Peter, eyes forward, said, "We'll know soon enough."

Sam, with a map in his hand, said, "We're in The Narrows. The Atlantic is dead ahead."

The loudspeaker crackled. The captain said, "The coast guard is approaching the ship. It's listing. Five to fifteen-foot waves with gusty winds. People are on deck clinging to railings, ropes, and debris. Others are in the water, some flailing their arms while others seem lifeless."

On the bow with his companions, Peter's hands gripped the railing as he leaned into the wind water spray. He said, "Come on. Come on. Faster. Faster."

Taxi said, "Hang on. We'll be there."

In an instant the water changed—the Maryjane hit the turbulent North Atlantic Ocean. She rode the waves like an Olympic champ. Peter saw the bow cut through the dark green water, churning it, the air bubbles creating a dark to light spectrum topped with white foam. Other times, he had been fascinated by the action of a boat on water. Today, all he wanted to see were people to rescue.

Minutes passed like hours.

Through their binoculars, Peter and Sam scanned the ocean. Crew members did the same on the port and starboard. The air quality changed. Fuel and engine emissions told the men they were approaching the wounded vessel. Shouts and fingers pointed to the horizon—the Olivia Bay. Finally, they were in the rescue zone.

Peter searched the water for victims. He nudged Sam. "There's someone." He pointed to the lifeless body riding the turbulence. "I'm going in."

Taxi said, "I don't think so. Your head is still bandaged from the fall."

"The wetsuit head gear will keep it dry. I'm fine and I'm strong."

"Peter, my friend, listen to me."

"Leave me alone. I'm doing this. Period."

Taxi looked at Sam. Sam shrugged and got Peter ready. With a tug on Peter's lifeline, he made sure the air tank was ready to go. "Okay. Be careful."

Peter adjusted his face mask, tightened his life-preserver.

Taxi said, "I'll work the ropes and pull people on board, including you, Peter, you are in trouble. I will not wait for permission."

Peter gave him a thumbs-up.

Sam said, "Yosef, you coordinate deck operations with the captain."

Yosef saluted. "Aye, aye, sir. You and Peter can be the heroes." He spun on his heels and left for the pilot house.

Sam looked and turned to Yosef while waving his arms. The fishing boat slowed close to the body. Peter jumped overboard.

Peter felt wave after wave wash over him. If not for the air tank and wet suit, he knew he'd be a goner. What should have been a quick retrieve took forever. The rough ocean and driving rain seemed to thwart his every effort. Peter never gave up.

As soon as Peter had the body in his grip, Taxi, assisted by other crew, pulled Peter back to the boat. When Peter had hold of the ladder, Taxi lowered a rescue stretcher. Peter looped one foot around the ladder while he maneuvered the body into the stretcher. He signaled and the crew hoisted it up.

On deck, Peter watched as Sam did CPR. No response. The crew, with great care, wrapped the body and put it in ice storage below.

The Maryjane continued toward the crippled Olivia Bay.

Sam saw another body and waved to Peter and the captain. The boat got close, and Peter did a quick retrieval. This time, on deck, the CPR worked.

<~<~|~>~>

Taxi took the shivering man below deck and wrapped him in a woolen blanket. He laid the man on a cushioned bench, partially sitting with legs out straight. Dark eyes, on a field of reddened white, stared at him.

Smiling, Taxi walked to the cabin's mess to prepare hot tea. He returned to the man and offered him a cup of warmth. From within his cocoon, the man exposed a thin arm with outstretched fingers. Taking the cup, the man nodded his appreciation.

Taxi watched for a few minutes, giving the man a chance to feel human again. He asked, "Do you speak English?"

The man nodded.

"My name is Taxi. Can you tell me what happened? Were you crew, passenger, or..." Taxi hesitated. "Or cargo."

"Cargo."

Taxi said, "I am so sorry. You are safe now."

The man nodded, put down the cup, clutched at the blanket, and closed his eyes.

Taxi got up and laid the man down on the bench. He adjusted the guard rails and went topside.

A large wave washed over the boat as they entered the official rescue zone. The Canadian Coast Guard and the crew from the Nimitz-class aircraft carrier USS Dwight D. Eisenhower (CVN 69) of the 2nd fleet were hard at work trying to rescue people before the Olivia Bay sunk to the ocean floor.

Noise filled the air. Boat engines, screams, and crews shouting orders. Under it all, the hollow echoes of Olivia Bay's cavernous holds as the waves beat against her hull. She listed toward the sea of rescuers. With each wave, she belched more people overboard. They were met with shouts, horn blasts, roaring engines, and open arms. The entire rescue could be characterized as organized chaos with each boat and ship knowing where it needed to be and what it had to do.

Yosef, now on deck, helped with medical needs while Taxi worked tirelessly with the ropes and stretcher. Sam, in the water at the base of the ladder, worked the stretcher. Peter swam like a man possessed. He never stopped or rested until the search and rescue ended.

Back aboard the Maryjane, Peter still didn't quit. He turned on the fog light and grabbed the binoculars.

Taxi tried to take them away.

Peter gave him a hard elbow and said, "No. I have to make sure no one is left."

Taxi said, "Do not obsess, my friend. The coast guard and the U.S. destroyer are doing the final search. We have to go back." He put his arm around his friend. "You know we can never save them all."

Peter froze.

Sam came up from behind, wrapped Peter in a blanket, and released the binoculars to Taxi. He led Peter inside and forced him to sit. Only then did Peter collapse, sleeping the entire trip back to shore.

In the end, seventy-three people survived, including Yosef's contact, the man who worked the radio. One hundred eighty-seven died or were lost at sea.

The newspapers were all over the story. Reporters seemed to multiply faster than fruit flies. The Telegram's evening edition gave the rescue top billing. Pages were filled with stories of bravery and eye-witness accounts. The radio operator attributed the disaster to a roped cluster of partially submerged shipping containers which ripped a hole in the hull. The Olivia Bay's captain never saw them until he hit them. After sending out the S.O.S. he and the crew abandoned ship. They had not yet been apprehended.

At nine o'clock in the evening, Peter, Sam, Taxi, and Yosef sat around a table in the far corner of a local bar and gulped down two rounds of beer and nursed the third.

Peter said, "They were ahead of us all the way."

Yosef said, "Who?"

"The traffickers."

"They knew what they were doing. I'm sure it had happened before."

Sam said, "As soon as they got into trouble, they made the call to abandon ship. Even with all this press, they may still get away."

Peter said, "Fuckers."

Taxi said, "Unbelievable. Every electronic and paper trail destroyed."

Yosef said, "Don't give up. We know where they were going. We'll get them dead to rights—just not today."

Peter finished his beer. "I needed it to be today."

Taxi said, "I don't think I will ever get what I saw today out of my head or the anger out of my heart. Every one of those people, dead or alive, is family. Their pain, my pain."

Peter cradled his head in his hands, eyes covered. "Oh man."

Taxi put his arm around Peter's shoulders. "You could not have done more than you did."

Sam said, "Remember, don't tell your mom. I've a feeling she'd kill us for not tying you up in the wheelhouse."

Peter said, "My executive functions are not all back. I'm not responsible for my impulsive decisions. You guys are safe."

Sam said, "I'm not taking bets she'd agree."

Peter looked up. "Taxi, in Tawanda, the sink hole swallowed the encampment in one gulp. No one had a chance to scream or cry out. The earth opened to receive thousands of refugees and collapsed on top of them. The silence. No survivors. A horrifying moment seared into my memory."

Taxi said, "I remember."

Peter said, "This was different. We had to watch the struggle, hear the screams, and smell the degradation. We bore witness. We were so damned helpless."

Sam said, "We did, you did, the best we could."

Yosef said, "If you hadn't pressured the President, we wouldn't have had naval support and forty more could've died. You made a huge difference."

Peter took a long gulp of beer. "Not enough."

Taxi said, "The fight against the nature of man and natural forces is timeless."

Yosef said, "And endless. We can never do enough."

Sam looked at Yosef and said, "You knew about this?"

Yosef sipped his beer before he spoke. "My sources informed me, and I let the President know immediately."

Taxi said, "Does that mean you have intel regarding the human trafficking out of Tripoli?"

"Not personally."

"But accessible."

"In a sense."

Peter slapped his hand on the table. "Enough with the word games. If we wanted to pursue putting a significant dent in human trafficking, we would not be without resources. Is that true?

Sam and Yosef exchanged looks.

Peter said, "Guess it's a yes."

Taxi said, "When?"

Peter smiled. "I got no other place to be."

Sam said, "Wrong. We have to get to the Tavius Global port just north of Chicago before Tavius Global people delete all the information about the Olivia Bay delivery from their server. Once we're done, you've got to go home and take a well-deserved, necessary rest so you can properly heal."

Yosef said, "You go. I want to stay here, talk to survivors, and record their stories. I'll get the information to nail the traffickers."

Taxi said, "I'll stay with Yosef."

Sam stood. "Come on, Peter. We'll take the 'copter."

Taxi saluted. "See you on the flip side."

Chapter 58 ▶ Tavius Global, Chicago, Il

Friday, 3 May, 8 a.m.
In a synchronized action, FBI, Treasury Agents, DHS, and Coast Guard, with the National Guard on high alert, surrounded the Chicago Tavius Global Enterprises compound, while police monitored access roads within a two-mile radius.

Two IRS officials entered the compound. Security escorted them to Octavius's office. "We have a warrant for an onsite and documents inspection to be carried out immediately."

Octavius sat behind his desk. "I'm sure there's a mistake."

"No mistake."

Octavius said, "I'm calling my lawyer."

"Our agents will be confiscating documentation and two will be stationed outside your door. Here's the card of our FBI contact who is now on site. Call Agent Neilson if you have any questions."

<~<~|~>~>

Once alone, Octavius picked up the phone and called the President of the United States. "Dani, what's going on? Didn't I tell you no federal interference?"

Dani said, "I'm in a meeting, may I call you back?"

"No. You must do something now. The warrant, which my lawyers are reviewing, is an infringement on my rights. I want you to get the IRS out of here now."

"Please hold. I'll be right back."

Octavius yelled into his phone, "Don't..." and heard dead air. He drummed his fingers on the desktop as he waited and vowed she'd never serve another term.

Dani returned. "Hi, Octavius. Sorry for the wait. I had to reschedule."

"Don't ever put me on hold again."

Dani ignored his outburst. "You called about something. Tell me?"

Octavius said, "As I mentioned, I have the IRS in my waiting room with warrants. Get them out of here."

"I can't. My hands are tied on this one."

Octavius pounded the desk with his free hand. "I told you last week."

"You mentioned an FBI warrant as I remember. I did stop the investigation. The IRS, though, is something new. Do you want me to look into it? Find out why they've got a warrant?"

"I want you to order them out of my office and off my compound."

"Octavius, I would if I could. They've already got a warrant which means any action must go through the Justice System. You must have your

lawyers working on it by now. I expect that's your
only option at this point."

"Don't you dare abandon me, Dani. I put you in
office and I can take you out."

"Where were you when I needed your support
for the environmental initiative?"

"The timing was bad. I'm on a tight schedule
preparing to announce breakthroughs in industrial
management and environmental management."

Dani sighed. "I thought you prided yourself on
the big picture. It couldn't have possibly hurt to
support my national and global initiatives."

Octavius said, "If you had waited like I told you
to, I would have been able to announce the "how" to
make your vision a reality."

Dani said, "Nothing is preventing you from
sharing your vision."

"I've got every federal operative in the world
outside my door. How do you expect me to do both?
Get them out of here."

"Hold on," Dani said. "Isabel just gave me this
morning's briefing. Apparently, the IRS is looking
into a simple tax matter."

Octavius said, "You are playing with forces
beyond your control. Forces running deeper into the
fabric of the global economy than you can imagine.
Back off, Dani. You and your family stand to lose
privilege, power, and financial stability."

"Really? Sybil has been reviewing the data and
programs you've been using to control the cartel.
She's found your metrics sorely out of sync with the
actual, real world, real people statistics. In other
words, the cartel is operating in a bubble liable to
burst any day now, washing away billions of dollars."

"Sybil knows nothing."

"I suspect she knows a lot, and you, alone, plan to profit handsomely when you choose to reveal the discrepancy."

Octavius said, "End this investigation now!"

Dani said, "No."

<~<~|~>~>

Beth and Eric waited outside the massive gates in a black SUV for the IRS agents to give them the okay to enter the Tavius Global Enterprises site to prove or disprove the assertions found in the tax returns.

Within fifteen minutes, the gates opened into the Tavius Global complex. Agents rushed to take control of their assigned areas, keeping in constant communication with the command center van parked at the Welcome Center and behind the black SUV.

Beth and Eric got out and stood in the plaza, phones in hand, on call to help facilitate the elimination of any resistance. They watched employees carry on their normal activities as the raid proceeded in the administration building, next to the Welcome Center, and the manufacturing and shipping center at the North end.

Information billboard-sized screens dotted Main Street, which ran the whole length of the complex, and kept workers updated with schedules, deadlines, and general information. Without warning, they went dark. Seconds later, Octavius, seated at his desk with his hands folded on the desktop appeared on the monitor. The Tavius Global Enterprises logo flanked by the American flag loomed behind him.

Beth elbowed Eric. "If he's going for the Supreme Ruler vibe, he nailed it."

Eric smiled and used his phone. "Control, tape the presentation."

Beth called Dani. "Octavius is making a presentation. Is it local or a national ad?"

Dani said, "National. I'm watching it."

Octavius, the presenter, backed by the Tavius Global logo, spoke in a professional and sincere voice.

"The corporate sector has long been criticized for its partiality to shareholders while ignoring stakeholders. I wrestled with the conflict between profitability and public responsibility until I developed, designed, and implemented a model to addresses both.

"It is a small city, community, and workplace where everyone has equal and free access to a balanced and crime-free life with clean air, potable water, housing, food, jobs, education, transportation, and healthcare. By taking the time to build an infrastructure designed to mitigate the effects of the climate crisis, our model provides our population with a stress-free utopian life.

"Tavius Global Enterprises has built two such complexes and is breaking ground for three more. In addition, we are making our model, complete with plans and software, available to others who want to make a difference.

"Watch the following presentation. Amidst the pollution, flooding, fires, droughts, and pandemics, corporate sector companies will now be the tools of change, responsive and responsible, havens of security and happiness, and the saviors of our future."

Eric said, "C'mon. We've got to expose this prison for what it is before people start banging the walls to drink the poisoned Kool-Aid."

Beth said, "On it. I'll take the admin building and make sure we get all the data we need from the computers and the server."

Eric said, "Good. I'm off to the North end."

They each took off.

Inside the administration building, Beth worked to make sure all employee records, personal, job related, and financial were intact, readable, and collected. She had to get all of them to be able to determine the missing Winnie Santiago's charge of corporate homicide, as well as tax evasion based on falsifying employment numbers.

<~<~|~>~>

Eric took his time driving to the North end. His eyes darted from people to buildings to the pristine environment to the light traffic. Most people walked. Still, there were plenty of skateboards, bikes, and electric golf-carts and bus vans. No one appeared to be in a rush to get anywhere, yet they all appeared to be going somewhere. The other thing he noticed was the quiet. No dogs barking. No loud conversations. No confrontations. No laughter. No energy.

He shivered. He pulled to the side, took out his phone, texted to himself. *The complex feels perfect and horrifying at the same time. It is full of living beings but not full of life. Hard to explain and weird to experience. Will have to come back and check it out.*

He returned to his mission and arrived at the manufacturing center. He saw the main plant on his left, shipping and receiving in front of him, and the Tavius Global Port on his right. Above the complex, the beautiful Spring Day almost hid a distant narrow band of dark clouds. He pulled out his phone and checked the weather. *Clear Skies.* He looked up at the sky and thought, *not for long.* He called Beth.

Beth said, "Where are you?"

"Manufacturing. Agents have unlocked the gates."

"I'm done here. Everything I need is in the truck. Backup systems have been turned on."

Eric said, "Send it out, now. There's a dark sky on the horizon. It could get messy here."

"Okay. Will do. See you in five."

"I'll be at the dock. Something's going on."

Beth said, "Roger that."

Eric smiled. He still loved hearing her voice. "Back to business." He drove to the building called Tavius Global Enterprises Port Authority. He showed his FBI badge to the guard and entered the building. He walked through a cargo area toward a crowd of people at the far end. He stopped as two men walked in his direction, dragging a man between them.

Eric said, "Sam. Peter. Who's your friend?"

"I want to know, too," Beth said, stepping off the golf cart.

Sam said, "This guy is the U.S. Customs Agent assigned to this port and complicit in a human trafficking coverup."

The rumpled accused said, "Allegedly complicit."

Sam looked at him and said, "Don't you worry. We'll prove it."

Peter said, "A ship called the Olivia Bay went down off the coast of Newfoundland, Canada. We just found out the crew has been apprehended and held in Newfoundland. Only seventy-three people out of more than two hundred-fifty survived the disaster. We have to look at the paperwork here to link everyone on the Olivia Bay with Tavius Global, which we suspect is a major player in the slave trade."

Beth waved her hand. Five agents appeared. Two took the customs agent and three continued on to commandeer the intake station. "They'll get control. You two," she said, looking at Peter and Sam, "go into the office with an agent and find the paperwork you're looking for, as well as any other similar deliveries."

Eric said, "Keep in touch." He turned to Beth. "Let's take the cart and get a look at the factory."

An agent met them at the factory door and said, "I've got updates for you."

Eric said, "Go."

"As soon as Tavius Global managers knew we were here, they evacuated the workers as well as themselves. However, our people were in place and corralled them."

Beth said, "How many?"

"We had ten coach busses ready to go and had to order four more. So, the estimate is seven hundred, give or take. All appeared to be well taken care of. Healthy looking. Same clothes as the above ground workers, only faded. Probably hand-me-downs."

Eric said, "Have you been through the factory and living quarters?"

"Nothing unusual in the factory and work areas. Your basic sweatshop set up. Living areas resemble submarine quarters. Not spacious, but adequate."

A wind horn blasted. Storm warning announcements blasted from loudspeakers. Two large SUVs pulled up. A window lowered. The driver said, "Get in. We don't have much time."

Beyond the vehicles, Beth saw Peter, Sam, and the agents herding three restrained employees between their ranks. They reached the first vehicle and got in.

Sam rolled down his window. "We're taking these guys in and processing the data. We'll meet you at the administration building next to the Welcome Center."

Beth waved as they sped away. She turned toward the manufacturing building. "Wait. I want to see for myself."

Eric said, "Later. We've got to go now."

Beth got in and Eric slid in beside her. Wind slammed the car door shut and rain poured from the sky. The SUV surged forward.

Eric took Beth's hand. He wanted to talk to her, but the storm's roar made it impossible. He mouthed, *are you okay.* She nodded. He couldn't see out through the side windows because they were fogged. He leaned forward to see what the driver saw. The windshield wipers were on full speed. Visibility – zero, except for a series of moving lights. He turned to Beth. "Look. We're in the midst of a runway landing to safety."

They made it to the Administration building, exited the SUV to the sound of whipping rain slickers, and followed agents inside, up two flights of stairs, and into the compound's windowless control room.

Peter and Sam said, "Welcome," in unison.

<~<~|~>~>

Beth managed a thin smile as her eyes took in the storm on the multiple monitors connected to the closed-circuit television cameras. She could see the entire compound as the damaging rain, wind, and thunderstorms plowed through.

Eric said, "We're in a derecho."

Beth said, "A what?"

The engineer clarified. "A line of intense, widespread, and fast-moving windstorms and occasional thunderstorms moving across a great distance with damaging winds and occasionally tornados. A derecho comes in quickly and creates a path of devastation faster than almost any other weather system. We're talking trees, buildings, and anything else not anchored, including livestock and wildlife. The derecho is recognizable by the horizontal rain, the short duration, and extreme damage, more than any other weather system."

Eric said, "This is not going to be good."

Beth looked at the monitors. "How come we can see? Inside the car, visibility was zero."

The Tavius Global control engineer said, "The cameras are protected, and images are filtered depending on conditions."

Beth said, pointing her finger at a monitor, "The wind is picking up everything not nailed down and tearing apart everything else. The debris is smashing into everything. It's not going to be pretty when this is over."

Eric pointed to the monitor focused on the indestructible transparent steel water control barrier Octavius had engineered to offset the rising Lake Michigan and any storm surges. "The barrier sensors are determining water levels to prevent flooding."

Beth said, "I'm no engineer, but it doesn't look very effective."

The control engineer said, "It's confused because the torrents of rain plus runoff have filled the shore side with more water than the lake side and it's not equalizing as quickly as normal. I'm going to control it manually."

Beth said, "Wait. It looks like it's equalizing on its own."

All eyes returned to the monitors.

Eric said, "What's that?"

A tornado formed over Lake Michigan. The swirling winds sucked the water into the air above and created a whirlpool below, turning the shoreline into a long stretch of beach.

Beth said, "This can't be good. The barrier looks unsteady."

The control engineer said, "The shifting pressure on the steel barrier is affecting its moorings."

Eric said, "You're right. There's movement."

Lights started to flash in the control center.

Beth said, "Look. There's beach on both sides. Now the entire wall is exposed."

The control engineer said, "When I was stationed in Southeast Asia, tsunamis behaved this way. You know, sucking the shore dry and sending water back in twelve-to-twenty-foot-high waves."

Eric said, "Will the barrier hold?

The control engineer said, "Without water, the barrier is dropping to ground level."

Beth pointed at the monitor. "Look. The giant wave. It's coming."

The control engineer became supercharged as he tried to override the sensors and get the barrier to rise. He couldn't do it.

They watched as the huge wave of water, released by the diminished tornado winds, surged to shore. Without the barrier, the entire compound took the hit. The barrier sensor responded. The wall rose. It stopped the incoming water and trapped the flooding inside the compound, overwhelming the sewers and waste plant.

<~<~|~>~>

Octavius watched the storm in his office. His mind filled with the power of nature, the magnificence of Lake Michigan, and the angry skies, erasing the hate he felt towards Dani. He spoke to the storm. "We are all powerful. Nothing can withstand the force of our nature."

He watched the tornado form. He saw himself holding the genie's lamp, polishing it with his jacket sleeve, and releasing an inhuman force. He held his arms aloft. "Show me your power and I'll show you mine."

The tornado grew higher. Its winds grew stronger. It sucked up the water and turned toward him.

Octavius laughed the laugh of gods, confident behind his window of transparent steel. Something made him look at the barrier, his finest piece of engineering. It was destined to make him king of the world. Except, he couldn't find it. The beach extended beyond the barrier. The barrier, sensing no water pressure, had disappeared into its casing.

He said aloud, "No worries. I can fix that." He returned his gaze to the stormy lake and angry tornado. "If this is a test, I will pass with flying colors. I, and I alone," he pounded his chest, "will save the world from the ravages of climate change and make a fortune doing it."

He laughed when he saw the tornado hiccup and discharge three javelin shaped objects on a path directly toward him. "So, you want to play chicken, eh? Don't. I'll win."

Octavius never flinched because he *knew* technology would save him. He *knew* the window would withstand the force of the attack and render the missiles harmless. Just as he *knew* he was the right man, at the right time, with the right solution.

He *knew* he was safe.
He was wrong.

Chapter 59 ▶ White House, Washington D.C.

Saturday, 4 May, 11 a.m.
Dani had visitors in the Oval Office—Beth, Eric, Peter, and Sam. She said, "Where are Taxi and Yosef?"

Sam said, "They are in Canada helping to process the Olivia Bay survivors."

Peter said, "From Canada, they're going to Libya, specifically Tripoli, to help break up the human trafficking rings operating freely in that region. Sam and I plan to join them."

Dani turned to Isabel. "Get in touch with Yosef. I want to talk with him after this meeting." She returned her gaze to Peter and Sam. "Tell me about the rescue."

She listened to their account. When they were done, Dani said, "Thank you for all you did. Sam, let's talk later to see if we can come up with a way to modify our customs procedures to ensure human cargo does not slip under the radar."

Sam said, "We'll make notes."

"Excellent. Do it now. Afterwards, Peter, come upstairs for lunch. We have to talk."

After Peter and Sam left, Dani said, "Tell me everything."

Beth and Eric recounted their experience at Tavius Global Chicago.

Beth said, "While we were in the control center, we watched the tornado snake across Lake Michigan, debris being tossed like a shotput. At one point, we felt the building shake."

Eric said, "We were in the middle of a derecho."

Beth said. "As soon as we could, we went to the director's office to make sure Octavius was safe. We never expected to see the window in pieces and Octavius dead."

Dani said, "His pride wouldn't permit him to take cover." She paused. "What about the people and the compound?"

Eric said, "The compound is full of broken glass, wood, and junk. Some trees are down. Most of them were young enough to bend, although they lost lots of leaves. Any vehicles, bikes, and skateboards not stowed were bashed about by the wind and water. They all need to be replaced."

Dani said, "What about the people?"

Beth said, "Above ground, people gathered in the center of buildings or in the Welcome Center Mall. All survived. Below ground, specifically in the manufacturing area, people fled though underground tunnels as soon as they heard the Feds were coming."

Eric said, "Yeah, but we were waiting for them. They are being housed until they can be processed and resettled."

Beth said, "What's going to happen to Tavius Global with Octavius gone?"

Dani said, "I'm not sure. There is a board and I'm sure he had already picked a successor."

Beth said, "Madam President, if we're done for now, Eric and I want to head to New York and see Rachel and Chris."

Dani said, "I've talked with Rachel. She's okay. Mostly fractures. The clothes closet took most of the blast. Chris is not as good. The blast threw him across the room and slammed him against a brick wall. Aside from some broken bones and a neck injury, he appeared okay. However, his mobility, vision, and speech were affected. He appears to be getting a little bit better every day and will enter serious rehab as soon as they think he's ready."

Eric said, "Which if I know Chris, is sooner rather than later. He's not going to be happy until he's one-hundred percent back."

Beth said, "Zeus?"

Dani said, "He made it through surgery and is now back home with Rachel."

"They'll be fine. It's all good news."

Dani said, "I hope you're right." She stood up. "Have a safe trip and give them my best."

At the door, Beth turned. "Gilbert Abrams and his people are going through the Tavius Global documents. When we have answers, I'll let you know."

Dani nodded. She picked up her phone and called Sybil. "Are you in the family quarters?"

Sybil said, "Yes."

"Is Peter with you?"

"Yes. He's in the living room with Sam."

"I need to talk to you two alone. Be up in forty-five minutes for lunch."

"Okay. We'll be here."

Dani made another call. "Wesley, you can give the doctors the okay to report Terence's progress to the press. Find out when he's good to come home to the White House and let me know."

Dani, Sybil, and Peter sat down to lunch. The twins had ordered subs and went with the Secret Service to pick up their dad.

Dani said, "It's good to sit here with you. It has been a very hectic week."

Peter said, "That's the biggest understatement I've ever heard."

Sybil said, "More important, what are we going to do without Octavius?"

Dani said, "I want to talk to you about our future."

Peter said, "We're listening."

Dani said, "Octavius has been the cartel's de facto chair by force of his personality and financial investment in many member holdings. Under his leadership, the group has done pretty well."

Sybil said, "It could have done much better except for his manipulating the data and calling for decisions without including stakeholder fallout."

Peter said, "So, not such a good job."

Dani said, "The question is, what do we do going forward?" She looked at Sybil and Peter. "Which of you wants to remain as the Vanderhagen face in the cartel circle?"

Peter said, "I hated waiting around for weekly half hour meetings, wading through all the data, and the administrative work of running the Vanderhagen portfolios and businesses. I'd rather be active instead of chair-bound—if Mom agrees."

Dani said, "Sybil, how do you feel? You already run the PRAISE Foundation. Do you have enough time and energy?"

Sybil said, "I'm going to have to think about it. It's been interesting stepping in for Peter, but long term is a different matter."

Dani said, "Maybe this will change your mind." She got up, walked into the living room, and retrieved three manilla envelopes from her briefcase. Returning to the table, she gave one to Sybil and one to Peter, sat down, and opened hers.

Peter looked through the papers and said, with a smile, "You're giving us your executive doodles?"

Dani laughed. "I know it looks that way, but they're serious doodles. We have to talk about this before going forward because PRAISE, Vanderhagen Holdings, and even the cartel could be a huge force for change."

Sybil said, "What are you talking about?"

Dani said, "I've been getting interest in the Tavius Global model compound."

Peter said, "Isn't that an issue for Tavius Global?"

Sybil said, "I agree. What does this have to do with us?"

Dani said, "Octavius's company town was a dressed-up prison. Workers felt safe, with access to all basic needs and healthcare, but no one could leave or express individuality. The cashless pay concept left workers wholly dependent because they were never able to acquire equity."

Peter said, "Octavius preyed on the vulnerable, exploited the needy, and trafficked the destitute. I'm not seeing any upside here."

Dani said, "Tavius Global took it too far. However, I have worked with the Tawandian immigrants and relocated them in areas like Kryller, Missouri, where they expanded the communities, created jobs, and proved diversity works."

Sybil said, "So, a similar concept without walls."

Dani said, "Yes. Government housing, startup money, and equipment, as well as healthcare and support as needed."

Peter said, "I know. Taxi told me how you also stopped a potential race riot."

Dani put up her hands. "I admit there have been problems, but we've addressed them as we learned about them. However, the point I'm making is that these "new" communities are working and can be replicated."

Sybil said, "It doesn't sound like anything we need to get involved with."

Dani said, "Except the real lesson learned from Tavius Global Chicago is that climate change fosters extreme weather which is destroying our coasts, rivers and their tributaries, and our flatlands. Octavius thought he had the technological answers to protect his investment. Yet, today, the Chicago compound is a ghost town. It can be rebuilt, but it is likely to suffer again and again."

Peter shuffled through his packet and held up a map. "Is this related?"

Dani nodded. "The scientific data shows which parts of the country will be least likely to deal with natural disasters, such as fire, heat, drought, flooding, and massive storm systems. I circled the areas climate migrants would naturally target for resettlement."

Sybil said, "Sparsely populated. No major cities. In fact, they're in the middle of nowhere."

Dani said, "Bingo." She leaned in. "We, the government, will partner with private and humanitarian interests to create working communities with affordable, low-cost housing, human services, and universal telecommuting included in the infrastructure."

Sybil hit the table with the flat of her hand. "I'll do it. I haven't heard anything this exciting in years."

Peter sat up straight and his eyes lit up. "I get it. That's where our interest in hemp coincides with new industrial initiatives—both are necessary and green. In fact, with Octavius gone, I'll see what land I can buy while his company may not be paying attention."

Dani said, "Before you do, I'd like to propose we get a few more people on board. Right now, Vanderhagen Holdings is family owned and managed. We need a board of advisors to help us cover our bases and keep us mindful of our stakeholders."

Sybil said, "I'm not opposed. Especially since you are, while President, divested of all interest in our operations."

Dani said, "I'd like to suggest Chris for his technical background, and Rachel for her human rights advocacy; Ivan and Isaac, as they are the next generation of inheritors; and Taxi for his world view of the human crisis."

Peter said, "I'd also like to include Sam. He's done and seen it all. His position in the State Department will be a conflict, though."

Sybil said, "Yes. Talk to him. Let him make his own choice."

Dani said, "Also, in time, Beth Neilson and Eric Jerrod. A good start is with people we trust. Going forward, others may prove to be important to our mission and we can include them at our discretion."

Sybil stood up and said, "This reassessment meeting of our agenda going forward is adjourned." She looked at Peter, "Stay on top of the landholdings and let me know when you plan to leave for Libya." She turned to Dani. "And you, Madam President, make damned sure you get re-elected."

Chapter 60 ▶ Gramercy Avenue, New York City

Friday, 21 June, 11 a.m.
Nikolai sat at the reception desk in the lobby of 215 Gramercy Avenue. Things were pretty much back to normal after a hectic six weeks of repairs, upgrades, and shopping. He took it as a personal mission to make sure Chris and Rachel's apartment was totally restored and in order when they were ready to move back in.

He remembered his conversation with Rachel days after the explosion.

She said, "I'll be back in two days. Don't rush with our reconstruction. My mom's going to stay with me in number 4 at 213 Gramercy. J&J security will oversee our hospital visits with Chris."

Nikolai said, "Chris will not return soon?"

"No. He's going to have to stay at the hospital a little longer. Could be as much as a month. He needs the ongoing therapy."

"Do not worry about anything here. I am in control. I have the okay from the police and fire department to start the remodel. I am planning to make it look like nothing happened."

"You have the original plans?"

"Of course. I never throw anything out."

"Please send me a copy. I may want to tweak them a bit."

"I will make copy and bring them to you when I visit later today."

Nikolai stood when a woman walked in accompanied by an alert fawn Great Dane wearing a "SERVICE DOG" harness.

He walked around the desk to greet them. "Who have we here?"

The woman said, "I'm Kathy from the Park Rescue where Mr. and Mrs. Gregory adopted Zeus."

Nikolai said, "A great dog."

She said, "I was devastated to read about the bombing. I hope they're doing well."

Nikolai said, "They are."

She said, "I've done a bit of snooping and worked with our shelter's trainer. We think we've got the perfect dog for Mr. Gregory to help with his recovery."

Nikolai looked at the Great Dane and petted him on the head. "Who is this guy?"

"This is Rufus. He's trained as a balance support dog. This will be his first real job. I think he will get along nicely with Zeus."

Nikolai smiled. "I guess we need to find out." He pulled out his phone and called Chris. "You've got visitors."

Chris said, "Not now."

Nikolai said, "Trust me. You want to meet them."

Chris said, "Okay. They've got five minutes."

<~<~|~>~>

Rachel, in her bathrobe, entered the living area, Zeus by her side. "Who called?"

"Nikolai. He says we have visitors we must meet."

"I hope another reporter hasn't plied him with baklava."

Chris laughed. "I guess we'll find out."

"If it's true, this time I want a cut of the bribe."

Chris rolled his wheelchair away from the desk and grabbed his two canes.

Rachel said, "What are you doing?"

He said, "I have to practice, or I'll never get better."

She watched, tense, ready to help. He locked the chair wheels and scooted to the edge. Pressing on the wheelchair arms, he got the leverage and raised his body to a standing position. Once vertical, he put a cane in each hand and walked with effort.

She relaxed. "You're doing much better."

Chris said, "Better isn't independent. I'm determined to fully recover."

Rachel walked over and hugged him. "You will. We'll get through this."

He said, "Are you planning to get dressed?"

She gave him a kiss. "Right now."

Zeus growled and barked. He ran to the door and started sniffing the bottom.

Rachel walked over to grab his collar when she heard the knock. She ordered Zeus to sit and opened the door.

Chris saw them first.

"What! No way! Nikolai. You're out of your mind."

Chris pivoted one-hundred-eighty degrees and walked back to the wheelchair accompanied by a Great Dane.

Zeus rose to his feet.

Rachel said, "Stay."

They both watched as Chris sat down and Rufus licked his face.

Chris put his hand up to shield his face but wound up embracing the dog's neck. "Good boy. Good boy." He looked at Rachel. "We can't, right?"

She turned to look at Nikolai. "What's the dog doing here?"

Nikolai said, "Ask Kathy. She's from..."

Rachel glanced at the woman. "I remember you. You worked with me to get Zeus trained."

Kathy smiled. "Yes. When I became aware of Chris's recovery issues, I found Rufus. He's a dog specifically trained to help people with balance issues."

Chris said, "He's a horse, not a dog."

Rachel giggled. "You'd look funny using a French Bulldog for balance."

Kathy said, "He's a young dog, loves walks, and lying on the couch."

Chris grunted as Rufus gave his cheek another lick. "Looks like I'm out-voted on this."

Zeus barked.

Rachel said, "Okay, you can say hello." She walked over with Zeus, petting him the whole time. Without any fuss, the sniffing greetings commenced, and tail wagging ensued.

Rachel kissed the Great Dane on the head. "Good boy, Rufus."

Nikolai said, "We're going to leave this love fest. I'll make sure you have what you need in the next couple of hours."

Kathy said, "You have my phone number. Call me if you have any questions. I'll come back in a couple of days to complete the adoption registration and give you an hour of training. In the meantime, I'll leave Rufus's harness and my card. Go to my website for an introduction to balance support."

Rachel looked up and smiled. "Thank you."

After the door closed, Chris said, "Two dogs are going to be a big change for us."

Rachel said, "No more late mornings."

He said, "And walks two to three times a day."

She said, "Maybe even a bigger bed."

"No way. Dogs will definitely sleep on the floor. I'm not letting them get between us. That's sacred territory."

"Definitely. Besides, it's reserved."

Chris said, "For us."

Rachel said, "For the baby."

"What baby?"

Chapter 61 ▶ October 3rd U.S. News

Front page: 60% Popular Vote Elects Dani Vanderhagen Mitchell U.S. President

<~<~|~>~>

Back Page 8, below the fold: Lucy Kilmer Guilty-- Gets Life

The End

A Note from the Author

I hope you enjoyed reading ISOLATION as much as
I enjoyed writing it.

If you did, please consider leaving an unbiased review
on Amazon or the site where you are a verified
purchaser.

PREVIEW of EXECUTION.
Working title of Book 5,
CHAPTER 1

In the dining room at precisely 7 a.m., Dr. Samuel John Drekerson, Junior, sat at the table, looking through the windows at the calm waters of Lake George, in northern New York State.

A believer in climate change, JD bought this property less than three years ago as his safe place. It boasted a sparsely populated area, situated high above sea level, and continuous access to drinking water, clean air, and food production—while the rest of the country struggled. His primary mission focused on staying alive in order to ensure life, as he knew it, on earth. His goal focused on reducing the world population down to a manageable level.

His breakfast had been the same for years. Two eggs over easy on white rice, a cup of strong coffee, and a wedge of sharp cheddar cheese. He ate with intention, savoring each bite. With only a half a cup of coffee left, he opened his e-pad.

He skimmed the electronic versions of five newspapers, diving deeper into the text if he sought more information.

He finished both his coffee and the updates at the same time. The wall clock behind him chimed eight times. JD stood, left the dishes for the housekeeper. Before going to work in his basement lab, he went into the living room, sat at his grand piano, and did his scales.

Attacking each note as if he were playing a grand march in a packed recital hall. His body moved in waves as his head nodded and his hands flew up and down the keyboard. He focused on nothing else until he finished. With limbered fingers, he went downstairs.

Twenty years ago
Wuhan Tianhe International Airport

The twenty-five-year-old man, dressed in jeans, striped shirt, and all-weather zippered sport jacket, did not resemble the heir to drug and chemical fortune. He had flown commercial much to his father's disdain. As he walked down the stairs from the plane to the tarmac, he could see a contingent of Chinese men nervously scanning the passengers. By raising his hand, he put them at ease, and they ran to meet him.

The spokesperson for the group bowed and said, "We welcome you, Dr. Samuel John Drekerson, Junior, to the Wuhan affiliate laboratory of Drekerson Drug & Chemical. We are at your service for anything you might need."

Junior bowed in return and said, "Please call me JD. I am excited to work alongside your research virologists. Thank you for approving my request."

More bowing. His luggage appeared. A woman stepped forward and escorted him into one of three limousines. The procession took off for the twenty-minute ride to DD&C Labs. Inside the walled, gated, and guarded perimeter, the complex looked like a wealthy estate, a stark contrast to the heavily populated industrialized city surrounding it.

The first building was the guest and executive residence.

"Mr. JD, this is where you will be staying. Your company reserved a suite for you, and your luggage is waiting there. In the morning, your guide will meet you for a tour of the facility and show you to the lab in which you will be working."

JD smiled and bowed his head. "Thank you." Minutes later he collapsed on the bed. Two hours later he woke up starving. After a meal in the dining room, he went into the bar, ordered a beer, and found a comfortable chair on the balcony overlooking a spectacular garden.

"Another newcomer," the woman said. "My name is Aaliyah. May I join you?"

He turned his head and said, "JD. Of course. It looks like we're the only two awake."

She said, "Is this your first time in Wuhan?"

"Yes."

"Why are you here?"

JD shifted in his chair to face her. "I'm an environmentalist and virologist. This lab focuses on pandemic strains of viruses. I want to know more about their specific constructs and behaviors." He paused. "And you?"

"I'm also interested in pandemics. Ebola has hit Africa hard. Their health systems have contained it but not eradicated it. I, too, want to learn more about fighting health issues like this. It is a terrible way to die which I would like to learn how to prevent."

JD smiled. "What are the chances that two humanitarians happen to meet on a deserted balcony in China?"

Aaliyah laughed. "This is not Casablanca, although it is nice to know I might have a drinking buddy to end the intensive research and study days."

JD said, "Count on it."

"How long are you planning to stay?"

"A month. You?"

"The same, except I've been here two weeks."

JD said, "I'm already sad you're leaving so soon."

Aaliyah shook her head. "Those lines don't work on me, soldier."

He smiled. "Good to know."

She got up. "Perhaps we'll talk more tomorrow."

He watched her go and returned his gaze to the garden.

JD knew he didn't qualify as an Esquire model. Too tall. Too gangly. Too nerdy. His dating experience bordered on non-existent. He never had time. Always working. Studying. Planning. Trying to do the impossible by changing his father's intractable stand against the demands of climate change. Still, his life goal centered on figuring out a path forward to win over the naysayers, protect global resources, and ensure the wellbeing of as many people as possible.

He also had to hang on to his wealth and power to effect change. It was a tall order. JD knew it. He'd be ready.

For the next two weeks, JD worked long days and relaxed with Aaliyah. Depending on their schedules, they sometimes met for dinner and a drink afterwards. Most often, it was only for a drink.

Aaliyah claimed her chair on the balcony. "Did you realize it's been two weeks?"

JD said, "It feels like either a day or two years. The intensity is exhausting."

"I know exactly how you feel."

"It's good, right? We're trailblazing solutions. Someday, we'll be recognized as heroes."

Aaliyah said, "If we're successful."

JD said, "Not an option. We have to be."

She nodded and stood. "I am tired, but I couldn't go to bed without talking to you. I'll be leaving first thing tomorrow."

JD rose out of his chair. "I'm going to miss our talks."

Aaliyah pulled out a card. "Here's my information. If, on your journey, my expertise can help, please contact me."

JD took out his wallet and extracted his business card. "Here. I'll trade you. Do the same. Maybe our paths crossed here for a reason."

"Maybe." Aaliyah offered her hand. "Good-bye."

JD grasped it. "It's been a pleasure."

An awkward silence settled around the too-long handshake before their hands dropped. He watched as she walked away and wondered if he should have done more, said more, offered more. He put his wallet away and pulled out his phone. Seated, he called the front desk and arranged for Aaliyah to have first class service to the airport, an upgrade to first class seating, and a driver when she landed.

JD put down the phone and told himself it was the best he could do. Then, he ordered another beer and watched the sky darken.

At the beginning of his last week in Wuhan, JD saw his first SARS-CoV-2 coronavirus with its spike protein surface. He found it in a dead bat. As soon as the lab realized what they were dealing with, they placed the virus in its own storage unit, instituted protocols, and restricted access to prevent contamination.

JD worked in the isolation unit. He took careful notes, made his own diagrams, and experimented on developing mutations. When it was time to return home to the States, JD copied all his notes and stole virus samples, all of which he smuggled out of the lab. He left his original work and the cloud address of his lab work with the lab supervisor. They knew everything he knew on a scientific level. The only thing JD kept to himself were his growing theories about pandemics.

End of EXECUTION, Book 5, Chapter #1

EXECUTION will be available Summer of 2022. For more information, check out http://carolbluestein.com/

In Closing ▶ ABOUT THE AUTHOR

C.L. Bluestein lives in Slingerlands, New York. Her ideas for projects are fueled by absurdity and puzzles—i.e., how, why, and how come things work—whether it is functional or mental, psychological or physical, political, or just plain interesting. More about the author at: http://carolbluestein.com/
　She is a freelance writer, a member of the International Women's Writing Guild (IWWG), https://iwwg..org/, and a writer for The Good Men Project, https://goodmenproject.com/

Seduction Series:
#1 SEDUCTION – Love, Loss, Leverage, Murder
#2 PERCEPTION – Love, Loss, Leverage, Murder
#3 ISOLATION – Love, Loss, Leverage, Murder
#4 DECEPTION – Love, Loss, Leverage, Murder

Her **You Want Me To Do What?** is available now. Walk in the sandals of our ancestors through this engaging interactive contemporary scripted Story of the Exodus/Passover for Jewish and Interfaith Families. Targeted but not limited to tweens.
"You Want Me to Do What" is the most innovative addition to the Passover literature I've seen. This is not just another pretty Haggadah....these interactive mini-dramas will make ANY Seder using any Haggadah come alive for all ages." Cantor Charles Bergman, Los Angeles, CA
Free download at http://carolbluestein.com/

Twitter: @clbauthor
FB: Carol Bluestein
Web: http://carolbluestein.com/